The Divine, Book 7

M.R.FORBES

Published by Quirky Algorithms

Seattle, Washington

This novel is a work of fiction and a product of the author's imagination.
Any resemblance to actual persons or events is purely coincidental.

Copyright © 2016 by M.R. Forbes

All rights reserved.

Extinction

1

I shuddered a little bit as I came out of the timewalk, taking a few stumbling steps and putting my hand up to the nearest wall for balance. Alyx fell onto her hands and knees, her voice a sick whimper as she leaned down and vomited.

"Geez," Obi said. "I told you to get here, man. I wasn't expecting the Star Trek."

I looked over at him. It had been a while since I'd seen Obi. He looked good. Probably better than I did.

"Sarah," I said. "What happened."

"Landon," Alyx said, recovering more quickly than I was. "I smell gore."

"You don't know the half of it," Obi said. He stepped toward her, putting out his hand. "Obi-Wan Sampson. You are?"

"Alyx," she replied, taking his hand and using it to lift herself up.

"Angel or demon?"

"Demon."

"Yeah. I should have guessed that."

She was wearing a pair of tights and a baggy sweater. It was a lot more conservative than her earlier choices.

"Based on what?" I asked.

"The first thing she did was smell the blood. I'll get you up to speed this one time because you look like you just crawled back from Hell."

"That was a few days ago."

"I believe you. Take a look around if you want, Landon. This place is nothing but death, thanks to Sarah and her new boyfriend."

"You said Adam was here. Give me the whole story."

"You want the long version or the summary?"

"Use your judgment."

"Okay, so you know I've been here for the last few months, helping Sarah and Brian deal with the changelings. It's been pretty rewarding, to tell you the truth. Or at least it was. A few days ago, Sarah comes to me and asks me if I ever have nightmares. I tell her that of course I do. Everyone does. Although, mine have gotten worse since I've known you."

I glared at him.

"Yeah, well, she tells me about how she used to have nightmares, back before you got stuck in the Box. Back before she helped save your life. She tells me about how you used to be able to visit her there, to fight for her in her dreams. Then she tells me the nightmares are returning. She doesn't know why, but they are, and she doesn't have you to to help her fight them now."

"She never told me any of this," I said.

"She also told me she felt like a burden to you. A needy pyschopath who can't handle her own crap. She didn't want to tell you any of that. She said, 'we're friends, right?' And I said 'Yeah, of course we are.' And so she described the dreams. Landon, man, they gave me my own set of nightmares."

"What did she see?"

"This," he said, motioning to the room ahead of us. I hadn't paid any attention to it in my dizziness. I did now.

The floor was littered with changelings. They were all dead. They were all covered in blood. Their insides looked to have been torn out by a serrated knife.

Or a pair of serrated wings.

Extinction

"Only worse than this," he said. "Much, much worse. She said it was inevitable. That it had been bound to happen the moment Gervais touched Josette. A union like that was never meant to be. She was an abomination, and she had a role to play."

"That's bullshit," I said.

"That's what I thought, too. Trying to shift the blame and not take responsibility? That isn't the Sarah I know."

"And that's where Adam comes in," I said. "She always had a thing for him."

"Maybe once upon a time when he was a blonde pretty-boy. I got a peek at him, Landon. I don't know what you did, but he's lost it. His chest is covered in scars, and they look self-inflicted. His eyes are deep red. Everything about him oozes evil."

"Hate is the root of real evil," I said. "He hates me for killing his archangel girlfriend."

"You killed an archangel?"

I could feel the judgement from him. "They were creating a weapon that would turn the balance. I didn't have a choice. God didn't agree with what they were doing either. That's why he fell. Of course, Adam blames me for that, too."

Obi stared at me, trying to accept my reasoning. He shook his head. "Whatever, man. It isn't about that right now. The point is, he isn't just a fallen angel. He's a certifiable monster, and somehow he managed to get Sarah under his thumb."

"Is it a coincidence that you survived when nobody else did?" I asked.

The comment perked Alyx up, and she moved a little closer to Obi.

"I don't know, man. Sarah had me dead to rights. She could have killed me. I was coming up from the gym downstairs when I came on her and Adam doing their thing with the changelings. He pointed at me, she came over and grabbed me. We looked at one another. She didn't seem scared or remorseful for what she was doing, but when she stabbed me with those wings of hers she didn't go very deep. Just enough to ruin my shirt. Then she tossed me aside like a bag of garbage."

"So she let you live?"

"Pretty much."

"The last time, she was at war with herself. The good side against the bad side. I helped the good side win. In that sense, she was right. She'll always be a bit of both, like me. The evil side was always going to come back, but I thought she was strong enough to handle it. I guess not."

"Not when Adam was involved, I guess."

"Any idea where they went, or what their goals are?"

"Armageddon," Obi said. "Not for humans, though. For Divine. She wants to kill them all."

2

Kill all of the Divine.
I let the idea of it roll around in my head a little bit.
Kill all of the Divine.

My first instinct was that it didn't seem like such a bad idea. The Divine were the reason that humankind was under threat in the first place. It was their war that caught people in the middle, causing mass destruction, the killing of innocents, and feeding a whole lot of strife into the world.

Then the logical side of me caught up. That was a one-sided argument. The Divine weren't bad. Demons were bad. The servants of God fed the hungry, clothed the naked, healed the sick. If the Demons weren't around, they would be caretakers for the meek of humanity until the End of Days.

That was the problem there. The End of Days. The Rapture. When God would take up all those who believed in Him and leave the rest of us for demon food. If Heaven were willing to maintain the status quo concerning believers and non-believers, I would happily be out of a job.

But they weren't. I had seen firsthand how their millennia of war had changed the nature of the relationship between Heaven and Earth. The Angels I knew were doing their best to skirt the rules to win; fallout be damned.

Adam was the poster-boy for that.

Look where it had gotten him.

And now Sarah was caught up in the storm. The one human on Earth who might be able to help him achieve such a lofty goal. But she had spared Obi, which meant the evil side of her hadn't won over completely, at least not yet. It meant there was hope that I could stop him, stop her, stop this, before it got completely out of control.

It was a new wrinkle in the war between good and evil. A war I had remade myself to fight and was already worn out on once more. I had been in self-imposed exile for two years after the Beast was destroyed. I stayed out of the affairs of Divine and mortals alike, using the time to lick my wounds and reflect. That reflection had seemed so clear at the time, but now it was muddy and faded.

What had I accomplished since my return? The balance had remained intact while I was gone. Hell, it almost seemed like it had been on autopilot without me.

Now?

Abaddon had been set free, and he had killed hundreds on his march to Central Park, an event the media had portrayed as a terrorist attack using a yet-to-be-identified poison gas. I had killed an archangel, and caused an angel I had once considered an ally to fall. I had taken one student under my wing, and quickly got her killed, and she wasn't the only ally of mine that had wound up dead. I had also been duped by Gervais not once, but twice.

And while nearly all of this was going on, all I had been able to think about was the Great Were standing beside me, of throwing her onto a bed, tearing off her clothes, and giving in to my darkest side.

I had been so close to doing it. I would have done it if Obi hadn't called. Maybe I loved her. Did it matter? Gervais was out there in control of a Fist of God, with Rebecca's spirit trapped inside. Sarah had been falling under the influence, and she had been afraid to talk to me. I was the Diuscrucis, a perfect balance of good and evil. But did I have to be? Did I even want to be?

Extinction

Ever since I had come back, the war between Heaven and Hell had only escalated. Ever since I had come back, things had only grown more and more out of control.

Was it coincidence? Maybe. Randolph Hearst was working to get his teeth into Abaddon almost since the day I returned. Satan had been the one to send Gervais back, in part to punish him, and in part to punish me. Where would the former archfiend be without me to play the foil?

The first time we met, Dante told me the universe would always find a way to even the score. Was my presence causing the escalation, or was it holding everything in check? Which came first, the Divine or the Diuscrucis?

I didn't know. I wasn't sure if I would ever know. The only thing I had confidence in was that I had failed Sarah in a big way, and now it was my responsibility to set things right. Whether it was for the sake of the balance, for my own sake, or for Sarah's was about as clear as my reflection.

"Landon, you okay, man?" Obi said, snapping me out of my inner monolog.

"Not really," I replied.

It wasn't just Adam and Sarah I was worried about, though that alone was more than enough. She was stronger than me in a lot of ways, even with the Beast-mode I had taken. If her evil side attacked me unhindered, she would probably win. And, the longer it took me to get to her, the more in control that part of her would become.

On top of that, there was no way in Hell that Gervais wasn't going to try to take advantage of this situation. Adam was strong, but Gervais with the Fist and the help of that traitorous asshole Zifah was a different level entirely. If his worm-tongue managed to convince Sarah to change sides again, it was going to be more than the Divine who were in trouble.

It was going to be everyone, and everything.

I locked eyes with Obi. He knew if I said I wasn't okay that he should probably be worried, and I could see a hint of that in the creases on his forehead. He held my gaze, though, not letting me see him sweat.

"We need to know where they went," I said. "We need to know right now."

3

Of course, needing something and getting it are never the same thing.

It didn't matter how badly I wanted to know where Adam had taken Sarah; I didn't have the power to locate every Divine on the planet instantly. As far as I knew, nobody did.

I did the only other thing I could do. I sent Alyx to watch television in hopes of catching a report on strange occurrences like terrorist poison gas and put Obi on scouring the Internet for news of the same.

That process worked well enough for most demons, but I had a feeling it wasn't going to be so easy with Adam. He had worked with me. He knew how I operated. If he didn't want me to find him, and I had a feeling he didn't just yet, he would know to stay quiet until he was ready for the confrontation.

My goal was to confront him before that.

"Alichino," I said when the demon picked up.

"Who is this?" he replied.

"Landon," I said. He would have a better memory of me than most, now that he was living in Espanto's former compound with us.

"Oh. Landon. Yeah, I should have guessed. Wait a minute, why are you calling me? Last I remember you were here. How long ago was that?"

"Since you saw me? About thirty minutes. I'm not there anymore. I'm in France."

He cackled. "The City of Love. Good call, Casanova. Although I don't think Alyx needs you to wine and dine her first."

I clenched my teeth, my earlier thoughts still fresh. I had let my lust get the better of me. I deserved better, and so did Alyx, even if she didn't know it.

"I'm at Sarah's place," I said. "We've got a problem."

"Gervais?"

"No. Adam."

"The angel?"

"The fallen angel."

"Right. What kind of problem."

I described the situation to him. When I finished, he whistled.

"Damn, Landon. I don't know how I'm supposed to help you with this. I'm having enough trouble getting a bead on Gervais and the Fist."

"Drop that for now. Gervais will turn up wherever Sarah is now that her evil side is in charge. I'd bet my life on it. I need to know where Adam is hiding."

"Yeah, sure, I'll do my best."

"Are you writing this down?"

"Yeah, of course. What do I look like to you?"

"You don't have a way to contact Dante, do you?"

"I don't have a red phone or a big red button if that's what you're asking. I can pass a message along, but it could be a day or two before he gets it."

I considered whether or not I wanted to bring him into this. He had advocated killing Sarah all of those years ago. He was going to blame me for whatever happened.

He also knew more about diuscrucis than anyone. I needed him.

"Do it," I said.

"Okie Dokie. Will do." He paused for a moment. "Hey, Landon?"

"What?"

"How bad is this?"

Extinction

"Humans and Divine are both going to die. I'm sure of that. How many depends on us."

"That's not an answer."

I ended the call. I didn't answer him because I didn't have an answer. If I were comparing this to the Beast, this probably wasn't as bad as that.

Then again, maybe it was worse.

I made my way from the worse scene of carnage up to Sarah's bedroom. It was her private space, and as a result had avoided the chaos and bloodshed. Alyx was sitting cross-legged on the bed when I entered. I paused for a moment, looking around. The walls were pink, the carpet thick and white. The bed was four-posted wood, elegant and youthful. I felt another twinge of guilt.

The television was on across from Alyx. She didn't look my way when I came in. Her eyes were glued to the broadcast.

"Do you speak French?" I asked.

"Wi," she replied. "All of the major human languages. Espanto made me learn them because he didn't want to." She made a disgusted face.

"What did you find?"

"Nothing related, I don't think. Two people were shot near the Arc."

"Who shot them?"

"They don't know."

"Probably a demon, but not the one we're looking for."

"Yes."

I stared at her for a moment, tempted to have a talk with her about what I was feeling right then and there. Looking at her made it harder. She was an addiction, and she wasn't even trying.

"Have you checked the other outlets?" I asked.

"They're all reporting on this."

I expected Adam to lay low. That didn't mean I liked it.

I felt the other words bubbling up from my chest toward my lips. Did I have to say them now, as if that were more important? If I didn't say them now, would I be able to say them later?

"Alyx, I want to talk to you about something."

She looked at me. "You feel guilty about what we almost did."

I stopped mid-thought. "Yeah. How did you know?"

"I can smell your moods."

"You can?"

"Yes. You wear your heart on your sleeve, Landon. It doesn't only display in body language, but in your scent, too." She smiled.

"I just don't want to mess things up, and I don't just mean with you and me. I'm pretty sure I love you. I don't want to treat you like a plaything, even if you want to play, too. I also don't want the world to fall apart because I'm too distracted. If I had been more accessible, Sarah might have talked to me."

"And she might not have."

"Allie-"

"I understand. I do. I want to be with you, Landon. Part of that is conscious desire, part of that is written in what Satan made when he put us on Earth. I can't change that."

"I'm sorry."

"Don't be. I can't change it, but I can control it if it is making your life harder."

"In a lot of ways, it isn't."

"But in a few ways, it is?"

"You're hard to resist, even against my better judgment." I hesitated. "Yes."

"Back in the airport, you asked me to set aside my instincts to help you. I've tried to do that. I've tried to be good when all I have ever come from or known is evil, and I've done that for you." She stood up and walked over to me, putting her face close to mine. "I can do this for you, also. I will not push or entice or tease. When you are ready, you can come to me. I will always be willing."

Then she kissed me. Not on the lips. She seemed to know what that would do to me. Her mouth brushed my cheek.

"Now, let us find your sister."

4

We didn't head straight to Obi. I figured he would find me if or when he found something, and there wasn't that much I could do in the meantime. Adam and Sarah were on the lam, and they wouldn't pop up again until they were ready to cause trouble. Maybe Dante could get me some useful information, but that required that he knew I was looking for him. However Alichino planned to contact him, I hoped the response would be quick.

In the meantime, Alyx and I set about cleaning up the mess. I won't lie and say it was an easy job. It wasn't. Every one of the victims had a family once, before the Beast's power had infected them and turned them into a sort of false Divine. Every one of them had come here looking for a new life with people who were going through the same thing as they were. Outcast from society. Lost and alone.

Sarah had been doing something similar the first time I had met her. Caring for the Awake, the people who could see the Divine. That community had crumbled in almost the same fashion as this one, though the fault that time was squarely Gervais'. I could imagine how Sarah might feel to repeat the history. It would only lend to her belief that the death and destruction were destiny and not the work of evil.

And Adam was evil. There was no question to that. He hadn't fallen because of me. He had fallen because his soul was turning dark. Everything else was a coincidence. Did God or Archangel Michael know what he and the other archangel had been doing together? I doubted that was allowed in the Kingdom of Heaven. In any case, his true color had shown through.

Black.

Alyx was a tremendous help in removing the bodies. She wasn't at all squeamish around blood and gore, and she set about picking up the corpses with a workmanlike attitude, shifting to her Great Were form and lifting three or four at a time. Their blood spilled onto her, matting her fur and leaving her looking as if she was coming in from a battlefield. She didn't comment on it, only taking a few minutes to vanish to Sarah's shower once her part of the work was done.

In the past, she might have paraded herself naked in front of me after, on her way to grab some new clothes. She did nothing of the sort, dressing in private in a pair of Sarah's jeans and a thick sweater. It was conservative to the point that it was still sexy.

At least she was trying.

I used my power to pull the blood together, cleaning it all from the floors and walls and compacting it into a small blob. Then I pushed it out the window and into the woods at the edge of the mansion's grounds, next to where Alyx had placed the bodies. We stood over them for a few minutes in silent reverence before returning inside.

Obi was waiting at the front door as we entered. He had his laptop in his hand, holding it open a crack, so the screen stayed on.

"That was a nice thing you did," he said.

"What was?" I asked.

"Praying for them."

"I didn't say a prayer," I said.

"You paid your respects. You don't need to say anything. It's still a prayer."

"I said a prayer," Alyx said, surprising me. "Not out loud."

Obi smiled. "See. I'm glad you found someone smarter than you. Not that it's much of an achievement."

Alyx giggled. Even I cracked a smile. I had missed Obi.

"Did you find anything?" I asked.

He nodded. "It might be nothing, but considering we're already at nothing, it can't hurt to check it out. It's a couple of days old. I didn't know I would need to look for it, or I would have noticed it earlier." He held up the laptop and opened the screen. I recognized SamChan immediately. The post was a jumble of letters.

"It's a polyalphabetic cipher," Obi said. "The kind Angels like to use."

"Angels use SamChan?"

"Not directly. The Touched do. That's how they communicate."

"And you think this is related to Adam why? He's a bad guy now."

"The text is subtle, but this is an anti-establishment propaganda piece. It's calling for recruits to speak out about unjust practices."

"Unjust practices? In Heaven?"

"Yeah, right? That's why it caught my eye. There's a downside."

"What is it?"

"It's in Italy."

"Let me guess. Near the Vatican?"

"Right on."

I turned to Alyx. "Do you?"

"Si," she replied.

"You can't bring her, man. They'll sniff her out from a mile away."

"Then she'll wait a mile and a half for us. She can cover that ground in about three minutes."

"Damn. What kind of demon are you, anyway?"

"Great Were," Alyx said.

"No way."

"Way," I replied.

"I thought you were done with those things after Ulnyx."

"She's a special case," I said, putting my arm around her shoulders.

Obi looked at us for a few seconds, his left eyebrow going up. "Oh. I see how it is." He looked over at Alyx again. "You said a prayer?"

"Landon's been telling me that being born evil doesn't mean living evil," she replied. "That I can choose for myself."

"Mephistopheles changed," I reminded him.

"Okay. I hear you. So you'll wait in reserve nearby. It's cool. That means it's you and me up close to the action, Landon."

"I was expecting as much. You're sure you won't be recognized?"

"The call was for the Touched. I'm not exactly Touched, but you know I lean good. I don't think I'll stand out in that crowd. You, on the other hand?"

"I won't stand out at all."

"Can you teleport us to Italy?"

I shook my head. "No. It wears me out to move like that, and if I do again now, I won't have anything left to deal with Adam if he shows up at the party."

"We only have a few hours."

"There's a benefit to knowing demons."

Obi made a face. "Damn. I hate moving through rifts."

"I've got some contacts in the area," I said. "Alyx, did you know Lylyx?"

"No."

"Really? She was Ulnyx's mate. She took control of their pack when he left. She helped me fight the Beast. Well, the whole pack helped me fight the Beast. There weren't many of them left, but the ones that made it out are staying out of sight out in the countryside near Rouen."

"They won't have the power to create a rift," Alyx said.

"No, but they'll know the fiend who does."

"All right," Obi said. "Enough chit-chat. You have a plan, let's get moving."

"It isn't much of a plan," I said.

"When is it ever?" he replied. "You've always done okay making it up as you go."

"Sarah's gone," I said, feeling the pain of it in my soul. It was going to be my fault if she went full-evil. "I wouldn't call that okay."

He didn't try to console me, or convince me I was wrong. I had always admired that about him.

"All the more reason to hurry," he said.

5

The chateau Sarah had been living in had belonged to Gervais before she had taken residence there. I had never been in favor of her decision to make it her home base after everything that had happened in that location, but she was of a mind that she could convert all of that evil energy into something good. When she had opened her home to the changelings and started getting more serious with the only one of them that had become an angel instead of a demon, I had started to believe that she could succeed in that goal.

Now Brian was buried out in the back with the others, and my initial fears had been realized. Normally, I preferred being right about things and having my distorted worldview confirmed.

Not this time.

Being Gervais' former estate, there was a large collection of expensive cars being stored in the garage beside the main chateau. I had taken a Ferrari from there once, picking almost at random from the group. I grew up in the city and didn't care that much about cars. Obi was a different story. He pointed each one out to me as we walked the aisles, running down stats that were meaningless in my ears. Torque, horsepower, camshafts, turbo.

Extinction

Whatever.

I knew he was talking because he was nervous. He felt responsible for Sarah, the same way I did if not more. He had been here with her. Maybe he should have seen the signs? How could he, when he didn't know what to look for? I didn't blame him, but I knew he would be blaming himself, and there was no way to talk him out of that.

"We'll take that one," I said, pointing at an SUV in the corner. "It looks a lot more comfortable than these racecars."

"The Bentayga," Obi said, smiling. "Good choice. It's the newest car in the fleet." He paused.

"What?" I said.

"Brian bought that car for Sarah. Did you know it's the only one here that didn't belong to Gervais?"

"Cars don't have auras. Did she ever drive it?"

"Once. She was like you." He mimicked her. "Car? What's the point? Obi, I've got wings." He returned to his own posture. "Half of which are razor sharp. Anyway, Brian thought she'd like to have a car that didn't belong to her old man."

We reached the car. I circled to the passenger side, while Alyx moved immediately to the back.

"I guess that means I'm driving?" Obi said.

"If we hit any trouble on the way, Alyx and I will need our brains free to take care of it."

"I can't argue that." He opened the driver's side and got behind the wheel, hitting the starter and getting the engine going. It had a nice sound to it. "And trouble does seem to follow wherever you go."

"Everybody wants a piece of the diuscrucis," I said. "We mainly have to worry about angels. They'll be able to track Alyx. The good news is that they don't usually want to get involved with her. Too much risk."

Obi looked into the rear view, checking Alyx out again. "Hard to imagine," he said.

She responded by partially changing, her tiny hand elongating out into a massive claw.

"That makes it a little easier."

He got us moving, the door to the garage opening as we neared it, and closing after we were through. I felt a sense of sadness to leave the place behind again. Every time I had ever visited, it had been for the wrong reasons. I should have stopped by more often.

We were on the road for thirty minutes before anyone spoke. My mind spent the time cycling through every decision I had made since that day in the museum, when I had approached a pretty girl to ask her not to touch the ancient artifacts on display, and she had responded by blowing me to the afterlife. Every decision had so many possibilities, so many outcomes. What would have happened if I had done anything differently?

What would have happened if I had never taken up Dante's mantle at all?

That was where I wound up stuck. What if I had never become the diuscrucis? Charis would have been forced to fight the Beast on her own. True, but would the Beast have ever gotten free in the first place? I had found Sarah, which had wound up leading Gervais back to her, which had led the Beast to her. I had given Rebecca an opening to steal the Holy Grail, which in turn had gotten her involved.

Was the world better off without me?

I had my chance after the Beast was gone. I could have joined Charis in the universe, but I didn't. I chose to stay because I thought it wouldn't be. That I was standing in the center, holding both good and evil aside so humanity could simply be. Was that truth or arrogance?

"So, Landon," Obi said, breaking me out of my head. "You said you were in Hell a few days ago? What was that like?"

I blinked a few times to bring myself back to reality. I looked out the window. We were on a small road in the middle of a green landscape. It felt good to be out in the open. I breathed in deep, taking in the moment. A moment was all the universe would spare me.

"I thought I could do it," I said, not answering his question. "I thought I could recruit people to help me keep the balance. I was wrong."

"You recruited me," he said.

"And you're still alive because you distanced yourself before it was too late. My sole recruit? She's dead. Killed by Gervais. I'm worried the same thing is going to happen to you."

"You're worried?" He laughed. "It's my ass, my decision."

"That's what Rose said."

"You can't control everything, man. You want people to have free will; then you have to deal."

"I know. But I feel like everything is spiraling out of control. Gervais is here, Obi. He's on Earth, and he's gaining power. Even once I stop Sarah, I still have to deal with him."

"You've handled worse."

"I've gotten lucky. That luck is going to run out sooner or later."

"You think it's luck? I don't, man. I think you've got help."

"Dante? He can only do so much."

"No, not Dante."

I considered for a moment. "You mean God?"

He shrugged. It wasn't a neutral shrug.

"That doesn't make any sense."

He shrugged again, glancing over at me. "He can't get involved directly, right?"

"That's a pretty big leap."

"Leap of faith," he said. "Yup."

I was silent for a minute. I didn't have the energy to try to wrap my head around that one right now.

Obi looked into the rear view mirror again. "So," he said, shifting the conversation once more. "How did you two meet?"

6

Alyx and I had gotten Obi up to speed on current events by the time we reached the countryside outside of Rouen. He had listened attentively, throwing in his comments at the right times, and sucking some of the weight out of the story. His part in my war had cost him pretty dearly, but time had helped heal some of those wounds, and he had managed to return to his old self, to the generally positive attitude that had made him such a good friend. It was something I desperately needed, and he seemed to know it.

We pulled off to the side of the road. Alyx climbed from the back as soon as we stopped, taking a few steps away from the strong scent of the car's interior leather and putting her face into the air. She turned with the breeze, her small nose twitching as she sought the scent of other weres.

"That way," she said, pointing off toward a hill in the distance. "Ten miles or so."

"Hold on," Obi said from the car. "Let me check the GPS."

Alyx glanced at me. I smiled, looking back at Obi. "We'll meet you there," I said.

"What?"

Alyx shifted, her body growing and changing, morphing impossibly

Extinction

from a five and a quarter foot woman to a fifteen-foot monster. I didn't hesitate to climb onto her back, grabbing some of the hair at her neck to stay rooted.

"You've got to be kidding me," Obi said, shaking his head at the sight.

"See if you can find a road that leads out that way. If not, we'll find you. Alyx has your scent."

"Do I have a choice?"

"Does it look like you have a choice?"

He produced a pad from his pocket, scribbling a note on it so he wouldn't forget about me. "See you there, I guess," he said, waving.

I waved back as Alyx lurched forward. It took her a few strides for her gait to even out, but when it did it was the best mode of ground transportation around. She flew across the landscape, the grass below her a blur as she pounded across the landscape. She loved to run, and I could feel her excitement as she did, along with the joy she got from the freedom. Was she feeling the same joy in being free of Espanto and free to make her own choices? I hoped so.

We covered the distance within ten minutes, the open ground giving her a chance to hit full speed. She slowed when we reached a small picket fence lined with chicken wire. A large herd of goats was behind it, and their heads all perked up at once at her approach, as they began baying to one another in fear.

The noise drew the attention of their keeper, a slight Asian man in a simple cotton shirt and jeans. He had been resting in the flatbed of his pickup, and he sat up and stared at us only moments after Alyx returned to her human form.

"Where did you come from?" he asked, his eyes narrowing as he tried to figure out how we had gotten so close without being noticed.

I looked over at Alyx. Weres didn't like the sun much more than vampires did, although they could survive in it.

She shook her head. This one wasn't a were. A fiend, maybe a turned? Not a threat, for sure.

"We're looking for someone," I said. "Multiple someones, actually. Do you know if this farm belongs to them?"

He looked at us suspiciously. His eyes stopped on Alyx. "It might."

"Do you know me?" Alyx said.

"There's something familiar about you," he replied. "You remind me of Onyx."

"Is Onyx in charge?" I asked.

"Yeah. She won't like it if I let you onto the property, though. Not without her permission."

"Can you call her? I'm sure she'll talk to me."

He hesitated. "What is this about?"

"I'm trying to get to Italy in a hurry," I said.

"Have you tried the airport?"

"Faster than that."

His expression turned more suspicious.

"And why would Onyx help you with that?" he asked. "We're not looking for trouble, or to draw attention. We don't want to get involved."

"Like it or not, you're involved," I said.

He heaved a resigned sigh and jumped down from the truck. He was even shorter on the ground. He walked toward me, putting his hand out as he did. It started to burn with hellfire. Hard to control hellfire that was usually only found in the hands of serious demons. Who was this guy?

"I don't like it," he said. "Not at all. And we don't want to be involved. I don't know who you are or who you serve, but I think you should go."

"I can't," I said. "I really need to get to Italy, and there's only one way that's fast enough to suit. We don't have to fight. Just call Onyx for me, and I'll take care of it. I'm sure she'll want to help."

"Last warning," he said, raising his hand.

I was running out of patience. So was Alyx.

"Landon," she said.

"Go ahead," I said to the fiend. "Give it your best shot."

He smiled, thinking I underestimated him. And maybe I had a little. The hellfire burst from his entire hand, not just his fingers, a stream of heat that I could feel from across the distance.

I didn't fight back. I let it wash over me, accepting it. It didn't burn. It didn't destroy. It fell apart as it hit me, my power negating it, turning it into

Extinction

pure energy that would return to the universe.

"What?" he said when he saw it had no effect. "That's not possible."

"Surprise," I said. Alyx tapped me on the shoulder and pointed back the way we had come. I turned and saw the Bentley off in the distance, heading our way along a narrow dirt road. "My name is Landon."

His head tilted to the side. "The diuscrucis?"

I nodded.

He smiled. "Why didn't you say so in the first place? That car with you?"

I nodded again.

"Come on. We better get to the house ahead of it. I'm Francois, and you are?"

"Alyx."

He put his finger up and then leaned in a little closer. "My vision isn't what it used to be. You're one of them, aren't you? Do you know Onyx?"

"I'm not sure," Alyx said.

"What do you mean?" I asked.

"I was taken when I was a pup," she said. "But I had a sister named Onyx."

7

We met Obi in the driveway of the cottage where the werewolf pack was living. It was a relatively small building, at least one hundred years old, though it was kept in impeccable condition. A brick face, a thatched roof, and thick shades were all that could be seen from the outside. There was a minivan sitting in the driveway already, and it almost made me crack a smile to think of a van full of weres driving into Rouen for groceries.

It turned out that Francois was a fiend of no small power, a secret gem of a demon who had decided he preferred the company of Onyx to the trappings of power that so many of his like-kind were enamored with. In a weird turn of events, he had accepted her as his master, even though his control of hellfire proved he could have easily claimed that control for himself. He wasn't like other fiends, and he said that Onyx wasn't like other weres, either. She didn't eat human flesh or blood except to stay alive, and that blood was typically stolen from hospitals or purchased on the black market from others who had stolen it from hospitals.

Why?

Because Ulynx had dedicated the Delta Pack to the Diuscrucis, and the Diuscrucis wasn't in favor of it. Onyx and her followers were all that was left of the Great Were's once powerful pack.

That was my fault, too.

"This looks like something right out of Little Red Riding Hood," Obi said as he climbed out of the Bentley. "How many big bad wolves do we have?"

"Eight," I said, quoting Francois. "All that's left of Ulnyx's original pack."

"How many did there used to be?"

"Four hundred," Alyx said. "At least when I was with them."

We still weren't sure if this Onyx was Alyx's sister. The name was common enough among weres that it wasn't guaranteed. I could tell by the look on her face that she was eager to find out.

"Obi-Wan Sampson," Obi said, holding out his hand to Francois.

"Francois," the fiend replied, not taking the hand. "No offense, but my touch is caustic to humans." He turned his hands over, showing off the demonic runes tattooed into them.

"Yeah, no problem," Obi replied.

Francois led us up a few steps to the front door, knocking three times, pausing, and then knocking six times. He waited a few more seconds before opening the door.

"Onyx, my love, we have visitors," he announced.

It was dark inside the home, but the smell of the weres was unmistakeable, even to me. I immediately heard motion upstairs, following the sound to the corner of the house and down.

She appeared in front of us a moment later. She wasn't a spitting image of Alyx, but she was close. Similar height, similar build, similar facial features. Her mouth dropped open when she saw the Great Were.

"Alyx?" she whispered in a soft growl. "Is that you?"

Alyx's face changed as well, a smile spreading across it. "Onyx?"

"It is you," Onyx said, rushing toward her. The two sisters embraced, whining to one another as they hugged.

"I thought you were dead," Alyx said.

"I thought the same of you. Who? How?"

Alyx separated herself from her sister. "I want you to meet Landon

Hamilton. The Diuscrucis."

Onyx turned to me and then fell to her knees. "My Lord," she said, bowing her head.

Alyx looked at me with pride. I was embarrassed.

"Please, you don't have to kneel to me."

"You are the leader of the pack," she said. "It is my honor."

I had gotten a similar reception from Alyx when we met. All because Ulnyx had tried to steal my body after I destroyed him the first time.

"Man, I wish a woman would do that for me sometime," Obi said.

"Shut up," I replied. "Please, get up."

She listened this time, getting back to her feet.

"What are you doing here in France?" she asked, returning her attention to Alyx. "Where have you been all of this time?"

"A prisoner," Alyx said. "Landon set me free."

"Truly?"

"Yes. Whatever you have heard, the Diuscrucis is more powerful than that."

"I have heard that you have been to Hell," Onyx said.

"You heard that already?" I replied. "How?"

"We are here to hide from the war, Diuscrucis," she said. "How can we if we don't keep tabs on it?"

"Hide? I don't understand."

"There are so few of us left and only one male to mate with. Ulysyx. He is almost beyond breeding age, and so far has delivered only one pup. If we are dragged into the fight, we will be extinct before long."

"Then I'm sorry to say; I'm here because I need your help."

"You need us to fight?" she asked, her face falling. "I will do as you command, but the pack-"

"Not to fight," I interrupted. I could see the relief. "I need to get to Italy within the next four hours."

"You need a rift?" Francois said.

"Yes. Can you make one?"

"No. I can power it, but I don't have the materials to build it."

"I thought you just needed some rocks?" Obi said.

Extinction

"Riftstones are more than rocks. They must have a minimum sulfurous component, or they can't make the proper connection. Stones like that are not easy to come by on the French countryside."

"We need a rift," I said. "I was hoping you would know where we could find one, and a demon to power it."

"As Francois said, he can power it," Onyx said. She put her hand on his shoulder. "You will need to go into Rouen with them. Talk with Gerard."

"Gerard?" Francois said. "I-"

"Do not talk back to me," Onyx growled, baring her human teeth at the fiend. The message was received.

"Yes, Master," Francois said. "I will take them to Gerard."

"Who is Gerard?" I asked.

"A fiend," Francois replied. "One of many who have wished to recover the area in the aftermath of Gervais' demise. He has a rift you can use."

"We'll leave immediately," Onyx said. "Let me alert the others." She opened her mouth, emitting out a series of shrill barks.

"You're coming with us?" Alyx asked, pleased.

"Of course," Onyx replied. "I haven't seen you in ages, sister. I still remember the night you were taken. So many of us were killed that night." She lost some of her enthusiasm to the memory. "It still wounds me to think about. But you're here, now. I never thought it would come to pass. If you have business with the Diuscrucis, you will be leaving again. I want to know you once more before you go."

"Me, too," Alyx said. "I never believed I would see anyone from my pack again, let alone my direct family. I'm thankful to God for the opportunity."

"God?" Onyx said, confused "What does He have to do with it?"

"Everything," Alyx said, leaving me as surprised as her sister was.

It was one thing to say a prayer for the deceased, another to openly embrace His name. It was a new development and had come out of nowhere. Barely three hours had passed since we had nearly spent the afternoon having passionate, lustful sex. Did she regret her actions as much as I regretted mine? Was that why she had been so willing to accept my decision, or would she have come to the same conclusion regardless?

It didn't matter. It was where she was right now. It was to be expected that once she embraced her freedom, she would begin testing it.

I was proud of her for that, even if I didn't completely agree with her assessment. I had been upset with my moral compromise, not because of the judgment of an absent father.

Onyx responded with laughter. "I don't know where you got that idea, sister. We are creatures of Satan. God cares nothing for us or our kind."

"I don't believe that," Alyx said. "Landon says we are free to choose our own path. We don't have to be evil."

"No, but we do need to partake of human blood to survive. Does God agree with that?"

Alyx was silent.

"Believe me, sister; he doesn't," Onyx said. "That is why we must beware of the angels in Rouen. They have hunted us before, and they will continue to hunt us until the end of days. That is the way of things."

"Things can change," Alyx said softly. "Right, Landon? I don't have to hate the angels."

She was looking to me for affirmation. For comfort. For all of the things she was, experienced with the world wasn't one of them.

"It's something you have to live with," I said. "But remember that the angels don't always know the will of God. Keep in mind where we're headed and why. They seem to be speaking for God less and less these days."

"Man, I don't know what this war is coming to if a Great Were becomes more devout than the Heavenly Host themselves," Obi said.

Or a fiend serves a were who doesn't eat human flesh. Or a spirit is trapped in a magic suit of armor.

End of days?

It sure was starting to feel like it.

8

Obi drove the five of us into the city. I had never been to Rouen before, and I was amazed by how the place maintained a middle-ages feel despite the passage of time and some of the modern conveniences that came with it. I remarked on it to Onyx, who only scoffed.

"The Cathedral is visible everywhere, which means the angels can see us wherever we try to hide."

What would the angels think of a car containing a fiend of Francois' power and a Great Were? I knew they wouldn't leave well enough alone if we lingered too long.

"Bring us to Gerard and we'll be out of here before they can figure out why we came," I said.

"Gladly," Onyx replied.

She had spoken only briefly with Alyx on the trip, and the warmth of their reunion had quickly turned cold in response to her sister's sudden faith. I couldn't really blame her. God was a tough pill for some people to swallow, let alone a demon, and I was pretty sure she blamed me for Alyx's attitude. My guess was that she was only helping me now because of an obligation to what she believed I was, not because she wanted to.

"Stop the car over there," Onyx said, pointing to one of the few spaces within the city that would accommodate a car the size of the Bentley. "There are no motor vehicles allowed on the streets where Gerard's shop lies."

Obi followed her instruction, pulling over to the side. We piled out of the car, and all of us save the former Marine looked to the sky as we did. I didn't see any angels, and by Onyx's reaction, I knew she didn't either.

"Let's hurry," she said. "We have a clean break."

She led us down a narrow street, then another narrow street, and through to a third. All of the buildings looked the same here; tightly packed and old. There were small storefronts at the ground level, selling everything from food to hats to musical instruments.

"Gerard owns a butcher shop three blocks that way," Onyx said, stopping suddenly. "Francois will take you the rest of the way."

"You aren't coming?" Alyx asked.

She seemed somewhat oblivious to her sister's disinterest. Maybe that was just how their kind was? I had never seen them interact as families before, but I had relived some of Ulnyx's memories. It hadn't seemed that way to me then.

"I need to return home. Good hunting to you, sister."

She turned to leave. As she did, I noticed the streets were empty.

Damn.

I scanned the sky in search of angels. When I didn't see any, I looked to Alyx. She shook her head.

"I don't smell anything," she said.

I gathered my power, preparing for Onyx or Francois to turn on us. What other option was there? Except they didn't. They were as confused as I was.

"What the hell?" Obi said.

Seconds passed while we waited for something to happen. I had never experienced anything like it before. The people left, the Divine came. The fighting started. It seemed almost comical when you thought about it too much, but that was how it was supposed to work.

It came from nowhere, literally materializing in front of us.

"Shit," I said.

Extinction

The Fist of God pointed its right hand at Francois. Scripture-laced bolts fired from its wrists, the proximity sending them straight through the fiend's chest and out the other side. He fell over in a burst of sulfur and blood.

"No," Onyx said, changing as she did.

Alyx changed as well, while Obi grabbed a small knife from his left boot. It looked ridiculous next to the two weres, especially next to Alyx, but it was all he had.

The Fist vanished.

"Oh, come on," I said, reaching out with my power and wrapping it around us. "Where are you?" I shouted.

I waited for Gervais to answer. He didn't. The Fist re-appeared when it butted up against my shield. This time, Zifah was seated on its shoulder.

"Nice trick, isn't it, Landon?" he said.

Onyx charged the armor. It disappeared again, and she pounced on empty air.

"An invisible knight?" Obi said. "Man, I thought things couldn't get any weirder."

"You have no idea," I replied.

The Fist appeared behind Onyx; the other wrist pointed at the were's back.

"Landon," Alyx said.

The bolts fired. I threw my power at them, catching them before they could strike her, turning them back on the Fist. It turned to the side, letting them bounce off harmlessly.

Alex pounced, her claws reaching for the demon. The Fist vanished again, appearing a moment later on the other side of the street. Alex wrapped herself around nothing, sliding on the street, spinning around and growling.

"Really, Landon," Zifah said. "Save your energy. I didn't come here to fight."

"Then what did you come here for?" I asked. "You used me."

"I'm a demon. Using people is what demons do." He cackled. "Gervais sent me here to warn you to stay away from Sarah. He's taking care of things, and you need to stay out of the way."

"Taking care of things?"

Onyx had recovered from her pounce, and she charged again, coming hard and swiping at the Fist. It raised its arm, catching the blow and deflecting it with ease. Its other arm swung around, hitting the were in the gut and sending her through a nearby store window.

Zifah laughed at the outcome. "I know what you're thinking. Gervais wants Sarah's power. That's it exactly. When he finds her, he's going to take it."

"That's his daughter," I said. Not that it mattered to the demon. Josette was his sister, and that hadn't been enough to stop him.

"Yeah. That's what I said, but you know Gervais. Anyway, he wanted me to show off the Fist of Gervais to you, so you would know you can't win, and you should leave well enough alone. I messed up a couple of times, went to the wrong place, killed a couple of demons I probably shouldn't have." He laughed again. "You stand out like a sore thumb as long as you have Alyx with you." He looked at her. "Hey, sexy."

Alyx ignored him, keeping her eyes focused on the Fist. If Gervais wasn't attacking me outright, it meant he wanted or needed something from me. Even if it was just the opportunity to gloat.

What else was new?

"Rebecca, are you in there?" I said. "Can you hear me?"

The Fist didn't react. Zifah was amused.

"She can't hear you. She's barely even there."

I knew they needed some way to control the armor. Considering Zifah was sitting on the thing's shoulder, I was willing to bet he was doing it somehow.

"I'm surprised Gervais trusts you with his toy," I said.

"Why wouldn't he? We have a deal."

"A deal between demons?"

"Normally I would agree, but it goes like this: Gervais gets Earth, I get Hell. It works for me."

"What about Heaven?"

"Heaven gets destroyed."

"Then Hell comes to Earth, and you get nothing."

"I know the leftovers won't be much, but I'm small. I don't need much. I just want to see the look on my father's face when Gervais tears his head off."

"So you're good with being number two?" I asked.

"It's more than I ever got before."

"Maybe we can work something out?"

"A counteroffer?"

"Yeah."

"Like what?"

I thought about it for a few seconds. There was nothing I could offer him that trumped control of Hell, and Gervais knew it. That's why he trusted him with the Fist.

"I didn't think so," Zifah said. "No hard feelings, Landon, really. I like you. But I have to do what I have to do, you know?"

"Yeah," I replied. "So do I."

The smile vanished. "What does that mean?"

I reached out with my power, grabbing the knife from Obi's hand and flinging it toward the demon. It moved faster than any human-thrown object could. It almost moved fast enough.

Zifah screeched and climbed behind the armor, narrowly avoiding the blade. The Fist vanished again.

It didn't return.

"Was that smart?" Obi asked.

"Probably not, but I think he made the point he wanted to make."

As long as I was with Alyx, I could be tracked. I already knew that. More importantly, I had barely held my own against the Fists before, and now it seemed that Rebecca's power had given it the ability not only to disappear but to teleport as well.

Fantastic.

Gervais didn't need anything from me. He was gloating. Rubbing it in my face. He had tricked me, killed Rose, and won himself a prize I couldn't compete against, and in his arrogant assery he wanted to make sure I knew it. His hate for me ran that deep.

Son of a bitch.

Onyx climbed from the storefront, rushing over to the pile of ashes that were all that remained of Francois. She leaned over them and howled.

A shopkeeper appeared a moment later, followed by a few more mortals. They saw Onyx as a human, leaning over nothing and crying. They ignored her, returning to their business as if nothing had happened. All except the owner of the store that had been damaged, who pulled out his cellphone to report the vandalism.

Alyx approached Onyx, leaning down beside her and putting her arm around her shoulders. "I'm sorry," she said.

Onyx glared at her for a second and then leaned into her, accepting the consolation. I bypassed them, walking over to where the bolts had fallen and picking them up.

"Gervais is going to be pissed at Zifah for losing these," I said, showing them to Obi.

He examined them. "Man, how did they get the scripture printed so small?"

"A laser etching machine and a computer program. It's all out of operation, which means these are irreplaceable."

He nodded. "I have an idea for this. Maybe when we have a few hours we can do a little engineering."

"Whatever you're thinking, I'm game."

Alyx helped Onyx to her feet. She looked at me, meeting my eyes. She didn't need me to speak to know what I was going to say.

"I'll take her back," she said, saving me from having to demean her and order her to stay.

I would have if that's what it took. I needed to get to Sarah before Gervais did, and now that I knew what I was up against, I knew I couldn't do that with her so close. Her aura was too powerful, and right now I needed to be inconspicuous.

"I'll find you when this is over," I said.

She stepped toward me, and I wrapped her in my arms.

"You know I want to come with you," she said. "It's against every instinct I have to let you go without me."

Extinction

"Believe me; I want you to come. It's too much of a risk to Sarah."

"It is easy to be selfish," she said. "I don't want to be. This isn't easy."

"I'll be okay. I survived the Beast. I survived Hell. I always find a way."

"You better."

She leaned up, and I kissed her. Not like it was the last time. Not like it would be very long before I kissed her again. I had to believe that, even if I wasn't feeling it. Things were spinning further out of control, faster and faster with every minute. I didn't know if I could reign it in.

I didn't know if I could win this time.

She smiled her cute, deadly smile and returned to Onyx, taking her by the arm and leading her away. I watched them go until they turned the corner and then turned to Obi.

"Okay," I said. "Now I'm mad."

9

I didn't have that much time to be mad before the angels showed up.

I wasn't surprised when they entered the small avenue, one from each connecting street. There was no way they had missed the Fist, and there was no doubt they would be interested in it. I hadn't vanished from their radar, which meant one had been perched somewhere during the fight, watching events unfold.

Of course, they had also waited for Alyx to leave before closing in.

"It's just one thing to another with you, man," Obi said as the angels approached.

I fought to quell my general frustration. Taking it out on them wasn't going to accomplish anything, and would probably make things worse. If I was calm, maybe I could even get them to help me out.

"Who speaks for you?" I asked before they had even reached us.

"I do," one of them replied.

He was off my left shoulder, a dark-haired man in a sport coat and slacks. He wasn't wearing a blade, which meant he could summon it. Experienced. That was good. The newer angels tended to be more eager to push for a fight.

I shifted to face him more directly. "Landon," I said, holding out my hand.

He took it readily. That was a surprise.

"Alfred," he said. He looked over at the broken store window. "We saw the battle."

"It wasn't much of a battle."

"Anything that keeps the Diuscrucis in a stalemate is an immediate concern to us."

The rest of the angels arrived. There were six in all. They gathered around, not threatening, but making it clear they didn't want us to take off without saying goodbye.

"It's a pretty big concern to me, too. Jane didn't fill you in?"

"She did," Alfred said. "We have been watching out for the Fist, and for you. We didn't expect it to display that level of power."

"Neither did I."

"Gervais has caused problems in this area in the past. For years the Cathedral was home to only two or three angels at a time, because he would see us killed if we tried to gather in numbers. We attempted to rally against him one time. He and his followers slaughtered nearly a dozen of us that day."

Alfred said it like he had been there. He probably had.

"I take it you knew Josette?" I asked.

He nodded. "I was her mentor during her first assignment. She was a beautiful angel. So pure of heart and strong of spirit. Her fall was unfortunate. Her return to Heaven glorious."

That one caught me off-guard.

"Return to Heaven?" I asked. Her soul had been trapped inside me, and it had taken the work of a djinn to set it free. I had always assumed it had gone to the universe, like Charis or Abaddon.

Alfred smiled. "Yes. You didn't know? When you freed her, the Lord gathered her once more into His arms and gave her a choice. She chose to return to His Kingdom as an acolyte, to spend her eternity in prayerful meditation."

"I didn't know. Is she happy?"

"As happy as all of His children in Heaven are, yes, I believe so.

Acolytes are not permitted to leave the boundaries of their convents, nor speak beyond prayer. I have seen her, though. She looks content."

I was happy to hear the news. It was almost enough to wash away some of my anger.

"The Fist is a problem," I said. "And one that's going to get a lot worse in a hurry. Are you familiar with Adam?"

"The First {what was it called again?}? He is fallen."

"Yeah, and he's taking his evil roadshow a little too far. He's convinced Sarah to join him."

"Sarah? The true diuscrucis?"

"That's the one. Gervais has set his sights on her before. He's got her targeted again. And Adam is using her already. He plans to destroy all of the Divine."

"All?" one of the other angels said. "That isn't possible."

Alfred raised his eyebrow toward the seraph. That was all it took to put him back in line.

"Dark days are coming to the world, Diuscrucis," he said. "The archangels have sensed it. When you defeated Adam, you set something in motion that may be too big to stop. Machinations centuries in the making."

"I stopped the Beast," I said. "I can stop this."

I said it. That didn't mean I completely believed it.

"It may be beyond even your ability to stop. We believed Sarah was on the path to good. Brian was such a positive influence on her. If she has turned, the world will burn. That is how it is written. That is how it will pass."

"I don't believe that destiny is immutable," I said. "God gives everyone free will. That means anything can change at any time. Where do the archangels stand in this fight?"

"You know they can't get involved directly. They have tasked us with finding a way to stop Gervais before he can use the Fist to gain control over the demon hordes."

"Do you have any leads on that?"

"The Fist is covered in protective scripture. It is a perfect agent of Heaven."

"Or a perfect agent for a demon who wants to gain control of other demons."

"Yes. And now with what we have seen? My confidence is not high."

"We need to stop it, too," Obi said. "Even if we save Sarah, we can't have Gervais running wild with that thing."

"Yes, I understand," Alfred replied, looking at me. "It seems were are on the same side once more."

"Does that mean you'll stop plotting to destroy me for a few weeks?"

He smiled. "That is not my decision to make. What is your next move, Diuscrucis?"

"We're trying to find Sarah. We have a lead on where Adam might be taking her, or at least where there might be someone who knows something. We need to get to Italy in the next few hours. To be honest, we were on our way to see a demon named Gerard about his rift."

"Gerard? That fiend can't help you. The rift is an artifact from when Gervais controlled this area. He hasn't the power to operate it."

"Gervais went right after Francois," Obi said. "Coincidence?"

"Not a chance," I replied. "Maybe our lead isn't as tenuous as we thought. If Gervais is trying to keep me away, he must suspect that I can still get through to Sarah before he can."

And if Zifah retreated without trying to kill me it was because the diminutive demon wasn't convinced he could. The Fist was powerful, but it couldn't act on its own. It needed someone to control it. Zifah had power in his own right, but he wasn't Abaddon.

And I had destroyed Abaddon.

"I need to return to the Cathedral and speak to my superior,' Alfred said. "Please, Landon. Allow us to escort you to the airport."

"Airport?" Obi said. "We'll never make it to Italy in time."

"On my honor, you will," Alfred replied.

I didn't need to think about it too much. Angels were nothing if not good for their word. If Alfred said he was going to help, and that he would get us to Italy in time, I believed him.

"Lead the way," I said.

10

Alfred didn't disappoint.

He was waiting for us when we arrived at the nearest airfield, a smaller airport that mainly serviced privately owned aircraft, the majority of them being two or four seaters. He brought us to a separate hangar, and revealed a sparkling Gulfstream to us, already warming up as we climbed the steps into it.

As he told it, the jet belonged to a nearby vineyard whose owner donated a large portion of the wine they produced to the Church each year, along with a sizeable financial donation and the offer to use his private jet whenever it was available. While angels themselves had no use for something that could fly, the Archbishop had taken advantage of the offer on more than one occasion, which is why they knew the plane was available. A quick phone call had gotten the wheels in motion, and thirty minutes later we were on our way.

"I've been ordered to stay with you through this," Alfred said as the plane tilted, rising quickly into the air.

I leaned back in my soft, white leather seat, glancing out the window as Rouen shrank beneath us and the plane backed back toward Italy. The flight would take close to three hours, which wasn't going to leave us a ton of time once we arrived in Rome. Still, it was way more comfortable than going through a rift, or dealing with another demon.

"Can we expect any other help?" I asked.

"Not immediately." He paused, and I could tell there was something he wanted to say but didn't.

"Angels keeping secrets?" I asked.

Alfred looked away. I glanced at Obi.

"What aren't you saying?" Obi asked Alfred.

The angel still didn't look at us. I had him figured out from the moment we met. He had been Josette's mentor, which meant he was one of the good ones. He wouldn't be able to lie in good conscience, and withholding information was as good as lying.

He held out for a few minutes until the jet had leveled off at twenty thousand feet. Obi and I waited patiently, exchanging knowing looks.

"Okay, fine," he said, turning around. "There has been some dissent in Heaven since Adam was cast down."

"Dissent?"

"He was trying to do the will of God. That's what the others believe. They think it's unfair that he was punished for that."

"He was cheating," I said. "Bending the rules about as far as they could go."

"But not breaking them," Alfred said. "That is the contention. Some of the others say the rules are a guideline, not hard and fast. More of them say the rules are outdated and don't align with the needs of the seraphim to fight a modern war against the demons."

"Seriously?" I said. "The laws the angels follow weren't just written thousands of years ago and left open to interpretation. The archangels are still around."

Alfred bit his lip and shook his head. "Some of the archangels are agreeing with them. They're going back on their original beliefs in what the Lord intended when He made His laws. They say that they would not be able to contemplate such alterations unless it was part of His grand design. Some of them even say that because you exist, it is proof of the need to change."

"Because I exist?"

"You're a child of God, Landon."

"I'm a diuscrucis. A cross between an angel and a demon. Half good. Half evil."

"And still a child of God, as all things are. Even the demons, indirectly. Do you think you would exist if He didn't wish it?"

I opened my mouth to speak, but nothing came out. I had never thought about it that way before.

Alfred smiled at the response. "Something for you to think about. My point is that Heaven is fractured somewhat, with the angels breaking into opposite camps. Those that believe Adam was in the right, and those that believe he sealed his own fate with his actions."

"But wouldn't questioning his fall be questioning the will of God more directly than the belief that Adam was simply following orders?" Obi asked. "I mean, if God made him fall, it was because he deserved it."

"Unless you are a seraph who believes the decision was unjust. Or a mistake."

"How does an angel believe that God is fallible?"

"A good question, my friend. It is another layer of darkness on the future. The last angel who questioned God's perfection was Lucifer."

"And he started a war in Heaven," I said.

"Yes."

We were all silent for a minute while the weight of that sank in.

"So the others don't know you're here," I said.

"No. We don't know who might be at this meeting. Either the angels or their Touched. If word got out that we were helping you, it would compromise your anonymity, and your mission."

"But if we get into trouble?" Obi asked.

"Two of my flock are following the plane. They will be waiting, prepared to lend aid. It is not as much as I would hope to provide, but it is all we can risk right now."

"It will be enough," I said. "So, Alfred, how long have you been part of the fight?"

"I was a soldier in the First Crusade, in 1096," he replied. "I was killed during the siege of Jerusalem."

I didn't know much about the Crusades. I did know that 1096 was a long, long time ago.

"I spent two hundred years in Heaven. At first, I refused to answer the call. I was weary of war. Of fighting. One day, I was in the Garden, sitting in a field of flowers and praying. A young girl approached me. She was seven or eight years old, with long brown hair and such an innocent, innocent face. I asked her where she had come from, and if she was lost.

""I'm not lost," she replied. "I came from Rouen, in France. I was killed by a monster."

"Rouen was my birth city. "A monster?" I asked her.

""Yes. It was like a person, but with fangs and claws. It bit me. It hurt, and also felt good. Then my poppa came into the room with a sword. He stabbed the monster, and it screamed and left. He held me and cried and told me he was sorry, but he had to save my soul. Then he stabbed me, too, and here I am."

"She was bitten by a vampire. That was when I realized that what they had called a Crusade was misguided faith. This was the real Crusade. The real war. I would be selfish to allow children like her to die while I sat in the Garden and did nothing. I have been here since."

"So you've fought Gervais before?" I said.

"Many times. He is the worst abomination that has ever walked this Earth, save Abaddon. Perhaps he is worse still, as he always manages to find his way back."

"What about Adam?"

"I know of him, but my role has always been as a guardian. Our paths have rarely crossed."

"I have a feeling our paths are going to cross soon."

"Yes."

"If there are other angels willing to join him, you may have to kill them."

"I cannot. Not before they fall."

"They won't fall until they act out in evil," I said.

"Yes."

"That might be a problem, don't you think?"

"It is not up to me to judge their hearts, Landon. If I die for my faith in them, then I die."

"Even if the whole world is the cost of that decision?"

He nodded. "That is the way of faith."

I couldn't help but smile. I could feel his influence on Josette. Or maybe her influence on him.

"That's fine for you," I said. "Just so we're clear, I can't afford to wait that long."

Alfred's face turned to stone. "I don't like it, but I do understand. My orders are to help you. I will not get in your way."

11

"You're sure you won't be outed as a conservative?" I asked.

Alfred finished buttoning his coat. It was a crisp night, the wind blowing sharply and scattering trash and dust across the streets.

"I'm not that well known outside of Rouen, despite my service time," he replied. "I've always kept a low profile, and hardly ever leave the city."

"Did you volunteer to come with us then?" Obi asked. "Or you just happened to be in the right place at the right time?"

"I was the most senior angel available. I have left the Cathedral before, just not often."

We were somewhere in Italy. Somewhere near the Vatican. I wasn't completely sure where. The plane had landed, a car had met us, and we were driven into the area through lightly trafficked streets. Then the car had stopped, let us out, and drove away, leaving us to our own devices.

It was fine with me. I was thankful we had made it and hopeful that we could put a swift end to this whole thing.

As if that had ever happened.

It was two in the morning. There were few people on the streets, and those that were seemed to be heading in the same general direction toward something I couldn't yet see.

It was obvious we were in the right place by the auras that surrounded them. Every one of them was painted good, a blue halo surrounding them. They converged in numbers that surprised me, at least a dozen walking the street ahead of us.

I probably shouldn't have been as startled as I was. We were in Rome after all, only a mile or two from the Holy See, where the good guys were dense enough that there were no demons to be found anywhere nearby. It was for the best that I had left Alyx behind. She would have stuck out more than a sore thumb. She would have been a shining beacon of evil in an otherwise crystal sea, a beacon that would have attracted way too much of the wrong kind of attention.

We crossed the next few blocks, slowly winding up mingled with the others. A teenage girl in a long black dress walked beside me, clutching a rosary to her chest and staring down at the ground. She looked over at Alfred, staring at the angel. He made the sign of the cross, which seemed to satisfy her. She smiled, changed directions, and moved further away.

Two blocks later, we reached our destination. The gathering turned out to be located in another church, which Alfred immediately identified as the Basilica Papale di Santa Maria Maggiore. It wasn't St. Peter's, but it was no slouch. A large, open plaza led up a number of steps into the building itself, which was being lit in the late hour by hundreds of candles. As we reached the entrance, a Touched servant greeted us and passed us candles of our own.

"Welcome," she said. "Welcome to the Mass for Change."

"Mass?" Obi whispered as we each took a candle and entered the basilica proper.

"This is unexpected," Alfred said. "Masses are held to gather the attention of the Holy Spirit. I would have thought the opposition would be hesitant to do so."

"Unless they're trying to make a statement," I suggested. "The mass is to ask for change."

"That is true."

We moved into the nave. Many of the seats were already taken, the candles creating an ambient light that unified all of the holders. Looking back over my shoulder, I could see the crowd would be standing room only.

"We should spread out a little," I said. "I'll take a spot near the door."

"Yeah, good idea," Obi said. "I see a spot closer to the altar. I'll scope things out from there."

"There are angels gathered in the transept," Alfred said. "I will go speak with them and see if I can get any further information. It could be that we aren't the only ones here to observe and report rather than participate."

"If either of you gets in trouble, raise your candle," I said.

"Will do," Obi replied, breaking away and heading up toward the front.

Alfred broke to the right, while I crossed a row of chairs to the left before returning to the rear of the building. I positioned myself next to a column near the exit, crossed my arms, and settled in to wait.

Twenty minutes had passed when the doors to the basilica were slowly pulled closed, the last of the incoming Touched squeezing in behind them. I was amazed at the sheer volume of Heaven's servants in the room. There had to be close to a thousand, if not more, and judging by the languages I heard being spoken, many had come from other parts of the world to attend.

It was a quite a showing for a gathering that Obi had called propaganda. Then again, I couldn't expect him to be unbiased. It was clear he preferred the old way of thinking to the new, especially when his first experience with the new was to watch Sarah murder innocents.

That is if Adam was connected to the event. I wished the link between them was a little more tenuous. That all of these people weren't here to consider doing something God might not approve of.

A bell rang from somewhere within the basilica. It chimed again a few seconds later.

An angel swooped down from the ceiling, landing smoothly in front of the altar.

It wasn't Adam. That much was immediately obvious. The seraph was female, with short blonde hair and a lithe frame.

The gathering had been quiet to begin with. It fell silent at her appearance.

"Brothers and sisters," she said. "Thank you for coming."

Her eyes danced across the crowd. They were bright and blue, and they sparkled as they caught the candlelight. I could see her making eye contact with some of the gathered Touched as she scanned.

Of course, her eyes stopped on me.

It was only for the briefest moment, but it was long enough to leave me wondering if she recognized who I was, or if she had simply recognized that I didn't have an aura. The latter was more likely.

"As you know, we've called each and every one of you here to participate in one of the greatest moments in both human and angelic history. A moment that will forever be remembered across the universe. In a few minutes, Archangel Raguel himself will lead a special Mass to pray for the eyes of the Lord to turn upon us, to take up our voices and hear our words in joyful consideration of our needs."

My ears perked up. Archangel Raguel? I had never heard of them, but judging by the way the crowd gasped, I had a feeling he or she was someone powerful. More importantly, they had come down to the mortal realm to lead the charge. If the demons found out, there might literally be Hell to pay.

"Before that, I wanted to take a moment to reiterate our position. Your brother and mine, the angel Adam, was unjustly cast down from Heaven and made into one of the Fallen, all because he chose to follow the word of the Lord and make every effort to put an end to the Diuscrucis. A responsibility that he was ordered to undertake by Archangel Raguel, after he was given the orders through a vision of Christ himself. We want only for the Lord to hear us, to consider our prayer, and to review His decision to expel Adam from His service.

I hope and pray that He will take our words into His heart. This is about more than the soul of one angel. It is about all of our souls. We dedicate our lives and our eternities to Him. We shouldn't have to fear that He will cast us out when all we seek to do is please Him. Thank you."

She bowed to the assembly, and then spread her wings, lifting into the sky once more. I couldn't see where she landed from my vantage point.

A chant started a moment later. It was deep and rich, in a voice that was beyond anything I had ever heard before. A voice beyond human. I knew it was the Archangel before I saw him. So did everyone else.

The doors swung open nearby. A robed figure stepped through them. I could barely see Raguel's face beneath the cowl, but his lips were moving as he continued his chant. He walked slowly and alone to the front of the gathering, bowing and kissing the altar when he reached it. Then he turned toward us, lowering his hood and revealing a head of short white hair and a wise, chiseled face.

"In the name of the Father, and the Son, and the Holy Spirit," he said, his voice carrying evenly to every part of the basilica. "The Lord be with you."

"And with your spirit," the congregation replied.

"As we begin this mass for change, let us take a moment to offer thanks to our Lord for his kindness and mercy and care. May he see the wisdom in our words, and glory from our hearts."

"Amen."

He began to speak again, a prayer in Latin. I only caught the first few words.

Someone rubbed up against my shoulder. I turned my head in their direction, my eyes suddenly finding themselves trapped against the pale blue of the presiding angel's.

"Welcome, stranger," she said, her smile warm and inviting, as if she meant it. Maybe she did. "Adam told me you might come."

12

"You know who I am?" I asked.

"Not exactly."

That was good. I was starting to feel like my ability to make people forget about me was losing its mojo. Was Adam retaining a vague memory of me, or did Sarah tell him?

"What did Adam tell you, then, exactly?"

"There might be someone in the crowd. Someone different. He suggested that I talk to you, and find out why you were here."

"He's the reason I'm here. I need to meet with him."

"What about?"

"Sarah."

"I don't know who that is."

That didn't surprise me. Adam would have a hard time gaining support if his followers knew what he was really up to.

"It doesn't matter," I said. "Do you really believe God made a mistake? That Adam was treated unfairly?"

"Look up at the altar, friend. Do you know who that is?"

"Archangel Raguel. That's what you said, anyway."

"He is the Archangel of Justice and Vengeance. Two things that so often go together. If he believes Adam has not been treated fairly, then I am inclined to believe it."

"What about Adam? Is he pushing for this?"

"No," she replied. I wasn't expecting that. "He has told Raguel he doesn't want it. He accepts his position."

"I'm not sure I believe that."

"It is as Raguel says. He does not lie."

I looked up at the Archangel again. Adam didn't want this? Nobody could convince me that was true. If his goal was to kill Divine, what better way than to start a war in Heaven? But then, if I was right, what the hell was Raguel's part in this?

"So Adam isn't here?" I asked.

"No."

"Do you know where I can find him?"

"As I said, friend, he isn't involved with this gathering. It is his case that has set the wheels of change in motion, not his direct intervention."

"But he talked to you. He wanted you to talk to me."

"We were friends before his fall. We remain friends now. I spoke to him recently, and he said to me that if a stranger arrives, I was to greet him and treat him as a brother."

That didn't make any sense. I hated when things didn't make any sense.

"Fine," I said. "What should we talk about?"

"When the Mass is over, I would like you to meet the Archangel. We have arranged a separate meeting for the most reverend of our followers. I would like you to attend."

A trap? I almost said it out loud.

"Why me?" I asked. "I'm nobody. Nothing. I don't even have an aura."

"That is how I know you're special," she replied. "Did you know that Jesus Christ had no aura?"

"Almost every image I've ever seen shows him practically glowing."

"His spirit. It was powerful, but it wasn't the same thing. There will never be another like him. You are not like him, but you are different." She had no idea how true both of those statements were. "Please, stay after the

Mass, and I will bring you to the meeting."

"Okay," I said. I had come here for information. If I was being invited to the V.I.P. lounge and a chance to rub elbows with the Archangel who was leading the revolution, I wasn't going to say no.

She smiled, bowed her head to me, and then vanished into the throng. I put my eyes back on Raguel. He was reading from the Bible.

I looked around a little more, at the faces of the assembled. Most of them were Touched, pledged to God and the war against the demons. They followed the Mass with wide eyes and open mouths, in awe of the Archangel. I wasn't in awe of him. Justice and vengeance? I didn't trust him at all.

He finished the readings and moved into the Liturgy of the Eucharist, his servants, including Blue-eyes, helping him prepare the altar. He was leaning over it, preparing to speak when I noticed that there was a candle in the corner that was higher than the others.

At first, I thought maybe it was an accident. That one of the Touched was yawning or stretching. I squinted my eyes to dim the candlelight around me and see across the basilica.

It was Alfred who was holding his candle up. His sword appeared in his other hand as I watched.

I scanned the room, searching for the threat.

Raguel stopped speaking.

The entire atmosphere of the gathering shifted. Devotion followed by fear.

Alfred pointed his sword away from the masses, toward the side of the basilica.

Raguel disappeared in a burst of light.

Something hit the side of the building, sending a shockwave rippling along the floor, the sound of the cracking stone nearly deafening.

The door next to me pushed open. A Touched man stumbled in, his robes covered in blood.

"We're under attack," he managed to say, just before he fell to the ground.

I moved to him, kneeling at his side and looking back out the door.

Extinction

A horde of demons was waiting there. An entire army of every kind of hellspawn I had ever encountered. They hissed and growled, unable to enter the church, but ready for a fight.

Something hit the building again. A fire demon, maybe, trying to collapse it from the outside. The demons didn't need to go in if they forced everybody out.

I looked back that the gathered army of Touched. They were shedding their robes, and revealing themselves to be armed with blessed knives and swords. No matter what happened next, it was going to be bloody.

How had the forces of evil known about this meeting? Had the demons deciphered the coded message on SamChan? I doubted it. There was only one way I could think of.

The building cracked again, and a huge chunk of stone came loose, dropping from the ceiling. I heard screams as the first of the Touched were crushed beneath it, causing a sudden wave of panic to replace the calm defensiveness. They began pushing toward the exit, toward the gathered army that would cut them down easily in their desperation.

I pushed myself past it, moving out into the night at the head of the line. The demons were a thousand strong at least, and as I stood in the center between good and evil, I noticed the solitary figure hanging in the back on a pair of razor sharp wings.

Sarah.

My heart fell, my sense of reason replaced by pure anger. Whether or not she had arranged this, she was participating in it. She was probably here because Adam knew I was here. Because Blue-eyes had told him. He was using her to mock me, the same way Gervais was using the Fist.

And then there was no more time for emotions. The fleeing Touched raced towards the demons, and the demons charged back. I was stuck in the middle of it, which meant I couldn't just stand there and do nothing.

So I didn't.

13

I gathered my power, holding it close as both sides approached, squeezing it within me like a mystical singularity. I could feel the onrush of heat and cool as the demons and the Touched drew ever closer to me. I kept my eyes on Sarah, watching her and trying to meet her gaze. She hovered behind the action, not returning my attention, but not intentionally avoiding it either.

It was as if she just didn't care.

She could have killed Obi, and she hadn't. I knew that had to count for something. At the same time, if Adam knew I was here and summoned an army to challenge me, and sent her to watch, that counted for something, too.

She was somewhere between good and evil right now. What I needed was clarity on that.

The two sides were almost on me. I could almost taste the demons, sulfurous and decayed. I could smell the Touched, their freshly washed hair and their neat, clean clothes. They were both only a few feet away from me.

I released my power, in a sharp line that stretched out from me, reaching across the plaza turned battlefield. It snapped out like a rubber band, and when the armies ran into it, it pulled tighter, slowing the entire approach, forcing the entire charge to fall apart. I wrenched it back toward me, and opponents from both sides were thrown to the ground, knocked over, or pushed back. I couldn't stop a fight like this completely, and there was no point to try. Angels and demons had been battling for centuries; it wasn't my job to make them friends.

I wanted to get to Sarah. I needed to know where her head was at. I started moving forward, certain that Obi could take care of himself, and that Alfred would come to his aid if he couldn't. The first rows of demons were off-balance from my initial outburst, and I moved past them without intercession.

I heard shouting, growling, screaming, yelping. I heard Touched die. I heard demons die. I waded into the thick, the horde a blur of misshapen faces, claws, and leathery skin. Of course, they tried to attack me. I looked like any of the other mortals. I greeted them with hard punches. I pushed them back with my power, I wrapped myself in it and absorbed their strikes. These demons weren't powerful enough to hurt me. I cut through them as a dervish of energy, batting them aside like matchsticks and making a path through the center, my eyes always on Sarah, growing closer to her with each heartbeat.

I was halfway there when she finally noticed me, her eyes landing on mine for the briefest of instants. I thought I saw her brow furrow slightly when they did; her face flashed a look of absolute sadness and guilt. Then she looked away, over me toward the rear. Then she started moving, to my left where a line of Touched were breaking through and flanking the demons.

She drove in at them, grabbing one by the neck, her wings sweeping around and cutting him in half. She dropped from the sky, landing, ducking, spinning and slashing, cutting two more down with those infernal appendages. An angel joined the fray, sword bright with angelic scripture. Her wings wrapped around in front of her as the sword came down, striking against them and skipping harmlessly away. She threw them out, catching him full in the chest and throwing him backward. He caught himself and charged again.

She let him come. A dagger appeared in his hand, slashing toward her as he rushed in. She dropped low again, putting her wings out to the side and throwing herself forward, past the angel. Her wings decapitated him, and he vanished amidst the crowd.

I had never seen her fight like this. I had never seen her act like this. A look had appeared in her eyes, a bloodlust that chilled me to the bone. Whatever had been there a moment ago vanished in the midst of the destruction.

I knew I had to stop it.

I knew I was the only one who could.

I slapped my power out, knocking aside a devil who was getting too close, trying to run me through with his sword. Then I threw the power out behind me, using it to propel me forward, over the crowd and into the sky toward Sarah.

I risked a glance back as I did, finding Obi in the thick with Alfred at his side. The angel was a consummate fighter, a true warrior. Every motion was measured and perfect, every strike, every parry. Obi, on the other hand, was all brute force and emotion, punching a demon in the face and then jabbing a blessed knife into its heart.

I came down a few feet away from her, throwing my power out as I landed to clear the area. Demons and Touched both fell back at the sudden shockwave, before resetting their sights on one another.

"Sarah," I said calmly.

She was twenty feet away, standing on the ground. I recognized the Beatles t-shirt she was wearing. I had given it to her for her birthday a couple of years earlier.

She looked over at me but didn't speak. The fire was still in her eyes. The wanton chaos. It wasn't a good sign.

"Sarah, it's me. It's Landon."

Nothing. No response. No recognition. What the hell had happened to her?

She began walking toward me. No fear, either. No hesitation.

"Sarah, stop," I said. "I don't want to hurt you."

She didn't stop. She didn't slow. Her wings folded in, fluttering ahead of her, each scaled tip like a separate knife, already coated in a layer of blood.

"Damn it, Sarah," I said. "This isn't you. Whatever is happening, I can help."

She kept coming until she was too close. I threw my power out at her. Her wings folded in, blocking her face, and the power washed over them, turned harmlessly aside.

She took three quick steps toward me, her face appearing behind the wings.

"No, brother, you can't," she said, one of them spreading and stabbing toward me.

I had to roll away to get clear of it, and I felt the breeze as it slammed into the ground beside me. I made it back to my feet, then backpedaled just in time to avoid the other wing.

"Yes, I can. You don't have to do this. There's no such thing as destiny."

"I've seen it," she said, coming at me again. "I've seen it all. How it ends. How it must be."

"We can change it. You thought the Beast was going to destroy the world, and we stopped it. We beat him."

"I was wrong. It wasn't the Beast I saw tearing this world apart."

Her wings came at me in a flurry of blows that I could barely see, and barely keep up with. One sliced my shoulder, the other caught my wrist. I pushed myself back, getting a little more distance between us.

"The Divine will destroy it, brother," Sarah said, following me. "Their war will continue until all of it is gone. Until everything is dust. The balance will turn further and faster, beyond anyone's ability to control."

"We won't let it," I said.

"You can't stop it," she replied, a single tear running down her cheek. "You're causing it."

14

Time stopped.

Her words hung in the air between us, a bullet unlike any other, filtering in so slowly and so impressively that it sucked the universe away from me in an instant.

Causing it?

A ton of bricks would have hurt less.

I had given all of myself, all of everything I cared about and loved, to do the job that I was asked to do. To be at the center of the war between good and evil, to fight the good fight, to make sure that humankind was free to decide their own future. I had made more sacrifices than anyone should have to make. I had fallen and gotten back up, drowned and resurfaced, burned and was reborn.

Causing it?

I was doing what I was supposed to do. I had no secret agenda. No ulterior motive. In that sense, I was as good as I could be and proud of that fact. I knew the balance was becoming more difficult to maintain. I knew that the war had been escalating since the Beast had been destroyed.

Or was it since I had returned to it?

Causing it?

Extinction

The Fist of God. Sarah. Adam. Gervais. Now a potential new war brewing in Heaven. I had sensed how things were growing beyond control. I felt the pressure to reign it all in. It was the reason I was there. To stop Adam. To stop her.

But had it all happened because I was here? Because I had taken up the mantle of Champion for Humankind? The balance had always maintained itself before Charis and I arrived on the scene. Was Dante wrong? Had he wanted to keep the status quo, and in his efforts destroyed it?

Which came first?

It wasn't the first time the thoughts had come, but they had been solely prompted by my own uncertainty. Now Sarah was telling me that maybe the downside of my existence was the truth of it. She could see the future. It wasn't always clear. It wasn't always accurate, but she knew it better than anyone else.

Causing it?

What if I was?

I snapped back to reality with every sense heightened. I could smell the demons. I could taste the mortal sweat and blood. I could feel the charge of energy in the air.

Sarah was sweeping toward me, her wings aiming to cut me down. At least now I knew why. She thought she could stop it by killing me and all of the other Divine. Did she know about Gervais? She wouldn't be able to stop the Fist, no matter how strong she had become.

Did that mean that Adam wasn't the bad guy? Or was he using her? Did he convince her that I was the problem? Were her visions even real? He had a hand in creating the Fist; surely he could find a way to fake someone's dreams.

I had no answers. Nothing solid to back any of my decisions. Right now, I knew Sarah wanted to kill me, and whether I was the cause of the discord or not, I couldn't let her. Not while Gervais was still out there. Not until I knew the truth.

I threw my power against her again. Once more, she deflected it with her wings. It slowed her down slightly to defend, and so I pushed again, harder and harder with each blow. It was enough to slow her as I backed away, but not enough to stop her.

I couldn't win this fight. We both knew it. I needed to get out of this. I needed to escape. How?

I could time walk almost anywhere, but that would mean leaving Obi behind. Maybe he could take care of himself, but I wasn't going to do that. There had to be another way.

"Sarah, please," I said, trying to continue the dialog, trying one more time to reason with her.

"I'm sorry, brother," she replied. "It is what must be."

"What if Adam is lying to you?" I asked. "What if he is tricking you with your visions?"

"He isn't," she said.

"How do you know?"

"I've been having them since you defeated the Beast. I've known these days were going to come. I've prayed, Landon. I've prayed that it would change and that I would be wrong."

She changed her tactics, putting her wings out in front of her like a wedge. It was enough to break free of my attacks, to get herself moving toward me unhindered. She came on like a freight train, leading with those impossibly sharp edges.

"He's using you," I said, diving to the side, coming to my feet as she turned, her wings sweeping out toward me.

I smacked one down with my hand. The other caught my side, digging deep and causing me to grunt and fall to my knees. I threw myself back and away as they plunged for the killing blow, narrowly escaping.

"No, brother," she replied, making her final approach. "I'm using him."

I saw her wing rippling toward me. I tried to throw my power at it, but it cut right through. I wanted to duck away from it, but I was too damn slow.

What would happen when I died? I didn't even know. Part of me welcomed the opportunity to find out.

"I do not accept this," I heard Dante say.

Dante?

Extinction

He appeared from thin air, right in front of me. His staff came up, blocking Sarah's wing and pushing it aside. Then he reached back and put his hand on my shoulder.

I felt a soft breeze like a breath tickle my face, and then we were somewhere else.

15

I sat on the grass, my eyes closed. I could hear the faint burbling of a nearby stream, and the whistling of swallows nearby. My side hurt. My arm hurt. My pride hurt.

"Where are we?" I asked, pushing my power throughout my body, using it to begin healing the wounds. I could feel the resistance. These weren't normal cuts.

"New Zealand," Dante replied.

"Not Italy?"

"Too cold."

"You don't feel cold."

"Too close to the slaughter, then. Does it matter, signore?"

"Not as long as you can get me back there. I'll be ready in a minute."

He sighed. "I didn't pull you out of that massacre to let you charge back into it. Did you learn nothing, Landon?"

"Obi is still out there."

"Obi will be fine. He isn't Divine."

"The rest of them are. The Touched."

"And they are going to die, as are every last demon in the army the fallen angel assembled. I'm sorry, Landon. There is no way for either of us to stop it."

I knew he was right. That didn't mean it sat well.

"So you know what's happening?" I asked.

"Si, signore. I was already looking into the rumors when Alichino left a message for me from you. I would have arrived sooner, but I didn't know where to find you. The Mass seemed the most likely place to rendezvous. I'm just glad I made it in time."

"She would have killed me," I said, still not quite believing it. Sarah was the closest thing to family I had. I couldn't comprehend that she would honestly believe that all of this was my fault.

Unless it honestly was.

"She said I'm the reason the war is escalating. That my presence is the cause, not the effect. Is she right?"

Dante looked me in the eye. He didn't speak for a few heartbeats, choosing his words before speaking them.

"It is hard to say," he replied.

"That's not an answer."

"It is very much an answer. The balance is a universal truth, Landon. It isn't under our direct control. It is possible that introducing you to the equation changed the algorithm, yes. But it is also possible that the world would have already burned without you."

"That wouldn't mean I'm not causing it."

"No. But it would mean that your cause is necessary."

It wasn't what I was looking for. Then again, I didn't know what I was looking for. I didn't want to be right or wrong. I just wanted things to smooth out and go my way for once.

"I can't hurt her," I said, changing the subject.

"Landon, I know you are very close to Sarah. I know you don't wish to see her come to harm-"

"No," I said, interrupting. "I mean I can't hurt her. She can deflect my power. Push it aside like it's nothing. If you hadn't stepped in, she would have killed me."

I could still feel the sting on my arm where her wing had cut me. It was healing very slowly.

He rubbed his chin. "I see. Would you have harmed her, if you could?"

"No. But I would have tried to subdue her."

"Subdue?" He shook his head. "I told you she is dangerous, Landon. I warned you that this could happen."

"This isn't like that. She doesn't want to kill humankind. She wants to protect it by destroying the Divine."

"Destroying the Divine is the same as destroying humankind. No matter what the ignorant among the mortals think, they cannot survive without Heaven or Hell. The Divine are as much a part of the fabric of the universe as they are, and as such are required to be."

"What about me?" I asked. "Am I required to be?"

"You're a different story."

"Is that a no?"

He hesitated.

"Is it?" I pushed.

"No, you aren't required to be. Except, you are the only one who can stop her."

"Because of course, I am. How? I just told you I couldn't hurt her."

"You defeated Abaddon, Landon. That was no small feat."

"I stabbed him in the back like a cheap thief," I said. "And Gervais got away with the Fist. Zifah showed up while I was in France. Did you know that?"

"No."

"The Fist is powerful, Dante. Insanely powerful. I don't know if I can destroy that thing either. It's just like Sarah said. The war is getting harder and harder to control. When the wheels finally do come off, everything is going to crash hard."

"You have defeated things more powerful than yourself before. The Beast, for one."

"With help. A lot of help."

"You have help. Obi. Alyx."

"I can't use Alyx. Her aura will lead Gervais right to me."

"Which could be very valuable if utilized correctly."

I was going to say something. I kept my mouth shut. He was thinking

Extinction

way ahead of me. I took a few breaths, staring up at the sky.

"Okay. I'm listening. What do you know?"

"After you defeated Abaddon, I returned to Purgatory to begin doing some research. On Zifah for one, as I had never heard of him before. On Adam for another."

"Why Adam? Did you have a reason to be suspicious?"

"Adam helped create the Fist and is today considered a denizen of Hell, as are Zifah and Gervais. I couldn't rule out that he would help them learn to control the weapon."

I hadn't thought of that, but it made sense. "What did you discover that you decided not to tell me until it was overly important and probably too late?"

He smiled sheepishly. I had hit the nail right on the head.

"I discovered that Sarah had been in communication with him. She was using an old friend of yours to send messages to him."

"Old friend of mine?" I asked.

"The messenger demon. Yuli."

"I didn't think that little cretin was still alive."

"Si, signore. Working for Sarah. Since she was using a messenger, I couldn't determine what the contents of the messages were."

"But she was reaching out to him?" I asked. "Not the other way around?"

"As near as I can tell, that is correct."

So she hadn't been lying when she said she was using him. The idea of her actions being solely her responsibility made me feel sick. She had killed her so-called boyfriend and the changelings because she wanted to do it, not because Adam had put her under some kind of spell.

I sat silently for a minute. I knew the truth, but I didn't want to admit to it. I definitely didn't want to say it. First Josette. Then Charis and Clara. Then Rose and Elyse. Not Sarah, too.

"Landon," Dante said in a way that suggested he knew what I was thinking.

"I have to kill her, don't I?" I said.

"We cannot let her destroy the Divine, and there is no other way to stop her."

"I can reason with her."

"Can you, signore?"

I slammed my fist into the ground. "Damn it," I shouted. I knew I couldn't change her mind on this. It wasn't like when she was fighting her evil side, and I was trying to help her. This was the true culmination of her visions. The real endgame.

It was going to happen unless I ended her life.

"I can't get near her," I said. "My power is useless."

"You took only the smallest fraction of the Beast's power. It was an honorable decision, but also a short-sighted one. Fortunately, you also have one of the most powerful weapons ever made in your possession."

"I do?"

"Uriel's blade."

I had forgotten about the sword that Hearst had trapped Abaddon with, using it to draw out his power and take it for himself.

"The sword is in pieces," I said. It was in Alyx's new home in Mexico, sitting in a shoebox under her bed. "Besides, what would I do with it?"

"First, it doesn't have to remain that way," Dante replied. "Second, do you really need to ask? The blade steals Divine energy. You can use it to increase your power."

"You want me to do the same thing I'm supposed to stop Sarah from doing?"

"As a means to an end, yes. Such increased ability might also give you the upper hand against Gervais and the Fist."

I couldn't deny there was a pretty solid upside, but it wasn't all wine and roses. "Only one person can reforge the sword."

"Si, signore."

"You know what will happen if Uriel comes to Earth. It's bad enough Raguel stopped by to make an appearance."

"Si, signore. I understand the ramifications. That is why Uriel cannot come to the sword. That is why the sword must go to him."

I nodded. "Good idea. There's an angel helping me. One of Josette's mentors. His name is Alfred. He-"

Dante was shaking his head.

"What?" I asked.

"If you turn the weapon over to the seraphim, you will never see it again."

"What if I make them promise to return it?"

"They will not make that promise. Uriel's blade is of unimaginable value to them, and allowing you to use it to gather power? It will never be allowed."

"I can't blame them for that."

"Nor can I. Yet it doesn't change the facts. You must convince Uriel to repair the sword. It is the only chance we have."

"I can't convince him of anything unless..." I paused, the lightbulb finally going on. "You want me to go to Heaven?"

"Si, signore."

"How?"

"You have allies among the angels. Use them."

"You just said the angels would never allow me to do what I need to do."

"You have always been resourceful, signore. I'm sure you will figure something out."

Not that I had a choice. Dante was right. I was too weak to fight Sarah in my current state. If getting Uriel to fix the sword and killing demons with it was the only way to level up, I had to do it.

"Can you send me back now?" I asked. "It seems I have a lot of work to do."

"One moment, signore," Dante said.

He vanished a moment later, returned a few heartbeats after that. Then he reached out toward me again. I extended my hand, touching it to his. A moment later I was standing in Alyx's bedroom. The sheets on the bed were still in disarray from our earlier near-miss. I crouched low, reaching under the bed and pulling out the old shoebox.

"I can't believe you put a priceless relic in that," he said.

"That's the idea," I replied, opening the lid. I lifted the shattered pieces of the blade from it and dropped them into my coat pocket. "You should stick around. I could get used to traveling the world like this."

He smiled. "You know I cannot remain, signore. Though I am pleased to be able to offer you assistance once more."

"I've got the blade. Take me back to Italy."

"Of course, signore. I will remain alert to messages from Alichino, should you require me again. I will also see if I can uncover anything else that might help."

"Thank you," I said.

He replied by smiling and nodding, and then, putting his hand on my shoulder. An instant later I was back outside the basilica.

Dante was gone.

16

Both angels and demons turned to ash when they died.
Touched? They just died.
As I stood in the plaza outside the Basilica, I was surrounded by them.

It was a grisly scene, made all the more real by the line of police cars, fire trucks, and ambulances circling the area, along with the crowds of onlookers who had come to see what happened. How would their minds process this carnage? A meteor strike? More terrorists? They were always a good mental scapegoat for the damage the Divine caused.

The basilica itself looked as though it had been hit by a bomb. The entire eastern wall was collapsed, as was the dome, which couldn't remain upright without the added support. Scorch marks from a fire demon's sword left dark marks on the steps, and dozens of claw marks were etched into the doors. I could see the emergency workers climbing over the rubble, searching for survivors.

The balance was shifting. I could feel it in my gut. Losing a thousand Touched was much, much worse than losing a thousand demons. The only good news was that Sarah had to know that. It meant her next target wouldn't be Heavenly. If she truly wanted to save humankind, she couldn't do it by giving the demons free reign.

Then again, if her father got to her before I did, if he had better luck in convincing her she was on the wrong path, there was no telling what would happen next.

Uriel's sword. That was step one. A weapon that would let me increase my power. That would let any Divine increase their power. I was surprised Gervais hadn't stolen the shards from me. Then again, there was no way he would ever get them put back together.

The thought gave me pause. Was that why Zifah hadn't attacked me with the Fist? If Dante knew the sword could be useful, so would Gervais. I had to assume he was waiting for me to retrieve it, and then he would come for it. It was typical. Maybe a little too predictable. I had to assume it was true. If I managed to convince Uriel to reforge the blade and let me take it back down to Earth, there was no way he wouldn't try to take it.

I scanned the scene, looking for Obi. Dante was convinced my friend would be alive after this. I had confidence in his ability to take out most demons despite the loss of his Divine power, but that fire demon had me worried. He couldn't fight that. The emergency workers looked at me as I started moving toward the basilica, but they didn't try to stop me. As soon as they blinked, as soon as they looked away, they forgot I was even there.

I reached the basilica, climbing over the rubble the same way the first responders were. I didn't call out Obi's name; that would have only drawn more attention my way. I did use my power to subtly push some of the debris aside, to make sure he wasn't under it. I didn't expect him to be. The last I had seen of him, he was outside the building.

I was worried, but not too worried. I moved away from the chaos, heading out past where law enforcement had closed the roads. If Obi had survived, there was only one other place I would find him at this time of night.

The bar was called La Tempesta. The Tempest. I could hear the laughter and talking coming from it when I was still two blocks away. It was tucked back in a small alley, on a cobblestone street that time had forgotten, a passage too narrow for any cars to traverse. The door to it was hanging open, the patrons loitering outside to smoke. They glanced at me as I entered, greeting me with an enthusiastic "Ciao!"

Extinction

The inside was as dim as I expected, and also more crowded. There was a television in the corner, turned off. The reports about the basilica were probably killing the mood, and nobody went to a pub to hear bad news. The benches at the bar were all taken by Italian men and women, some fair, some olive, none as dark as Obi.

I walked through the place, checking the tables. I was about to give up when a bottle cap hit me in the back of the neck.

I turned around. Obi was sitting against the wall, a beer on the table in front of him. He looked tired, a little sweaty, but otherwise no worse for wear.

I went over and sat across from him. He stared at me for a few seconds without speaking.

"I know what you're thinking," I said. "Dante took me. I didn't leave."

He smiled. "I know. I saw him. That's not why I'm staring."

"Then why are you staring?"

"She was going to kill you, man."

"I know. She thinks it's the right thing to do. She said I'm causing the war to escalate, and pretty soon it will be out of control."

"Unless she kills all of the Divine?"

"Exactly."

"You can't stop her."

"I would have if I could. How did you get away?"

He shrugged. "Snuck out when I saw you go poof. The demons didn't want anything to do with me after I cut a few dozen of them down. Not with so many Touched to kill. Sarah didn't see me, or if she did she let me go again."

"Because you're human. Fully human."

"Is that why? I thought she just liked me."

"She does like you. I'm pretty sure she still likes me. What she's doing, she thinks she has to do, or the world is going to end. The problem is if she kills all the Divine, the world is going to end anyway."

"Ain't that a kicker."

I smiled. "A big one."

"So, Dante saved your ass. I figured you'd catch up to me here sooner or later once you saw I wasn't dead. Did he give you anything useful?"

"We'll see. I'm supposed to take the shards of Uriel's sword to Heaven, and ask Archangel Uriel to put it back together for me."

He laughed loudly enough that half the patrons in the pub turned to look at us.

"You're kidding me?" he said.

"I wish I was."

"Man, there is no way that is going to happen."

"Normally, I would agree with you, but the balance is shifting. If the angels don't do something, they might end up screwed."

"Unless they know what Sarah is up to."

"Meaning they'll let her balance things out again?" They would never help me if they knew she was going to. "I don't think they do. Not yet. I have a bad feeling Gervais knows what's going down, though."

"So you need another set of eyes in the back of your head."

"Yeah."

"I'll do my best," he said.

"Thanks. I appreciate you helping me out on this one. Especially considering you aren't the biggest fan of the Divine."

"I'm a bigger fan of the world staying in one piece. I know we've had some rough patches here and there, Landon, but I've always considered us friends. Friends just go through some shit sometimes, that's all."

"Agreed."

He raised his bottle to me, and then took a drink.

"Do you know what happened to Alfred?" I asked.

"He was fighting for a while. He's a total badass, by the way. He teamed up with that angel that opened the Mass, and the two of them took out the fire demon. Sarah got to them, though. I saw Alfred try to save the other seraph, but she did something to him and made him disappear. Sent him back to Heaven or something."

"His superiors told him to help me. I was hoping he could give me a lift to Heaven."

"Maybe he'll show up again. He might be looking for you right now."

"He won't remember me. He might come looking for you."

Extinction

"Good enough, right?"

"I hope so."

"So what do you want to do? Hang out and knock back a few?"

"Don't you need to sleep?"

"Man, I'm too wired to sleep."

"I need to talk to an angel. I imagine Sarah's actions tonight have got them on high alert, and maybe bunkered in. Considering where we are, I know where to find them."

"Not much deduction needed on that one, is there Sherlock?"

"Elementary, Watson. You ready to go?"

He took one last swig to finish the bottle and then stood up. "I am now."

17

The Vatican. The home of the Pope. The home of St. Peter's Basilica. The home base and the largest and most powerful seraphim sanctuary in the mortal realm.

I needed to talk to an angel, and there was no better place to find one.

Of course, these angels weren't friends of mine. Maybe some of them would be lukewarm, but I knew going in that most of them didn't like me, and would have preferred if Sarah's wings had found their way to my heart, or had sliced clean through my neck. Whatever. I didn't have time to worry about that now. My only other seraphim contact was back in New York, and unless Dante showed up right away to teleport me there, or unless I wound up desperate enough to time walk again, I wasn't going to reach her.

No, I had to walk into the lion's den and see if I could make a case. If I failed with the angels, maybe Francis would hear me out?

We climbed the steps to St. Peter's. The square was empty. Silent. We had seen a number of heavily armed guards outside the perimeter, keeping watch for those terrorists. I was sure the angels were watching us make our approach, even if I hadn't tried to look for them. Whenever they showed up, they showed up. I didn't want to make any moves that they took as aggressive. As powerful as I was, I was on the holiest ground on the planet. They could take me if they had the numbers, which was why I had never visited before.

That I was here, now, would send a clear message. It was a huge white flag. An obvious cry for help. I didn't like submitting so easily, but there was nothing else to be done.

We reached the doors to the massive Church. I pushed one of them open with my power, and we moved inside. I was awed by the interior. The scale. The craftsmanship. The hand of God in everything that was created there.

"Hello?" Obi said, his voice echoing in the empty space.

I had expected there would be a guard at least. The place was deserted.

"Echo," he shouted, smiling as it was repeated back to him, the acoustics bouncing his voice around the columns and arches. I looked over at him, and he shrugged. "Just trying to get some attention."

We waited. Nobody came.

"I thought that would work," I said.

"What the heck is going on in here?" Obi replied.

"A thousand Touched died tonight, Diuscrucis," the smooth, low voice said from everywhere, bouncing off the walls without an echo. "A dozen angels as well."

I knew the voice. I had heard it not very long ago.

"Raguel," I said. "You aren't supposed to be here."

The archangel appeared from behind a column, still wearing the same robes and cowl as before.

"Which is why this place is empty," he said. "Except for you, your friend, and me. The others have been sent away, sent to understand this threat. The real diuscrucis, with blood and gold wings."

"I already understand the threat," I said. "That's why I'm here."

"I assumed as much. If you came because you need our help, then we are already doomed."

"Are you saying you won't help me?" I asked. "Because I haven't even told you what I want yet."

"I could destroy you here and now, Diuscrucis," Raguel said. "Your power is strong, but not in this place." He waved his hand, and the runes hidden in every millimeter of the stone flared briefly.

"Awesome," Obi said.

"Do you intend to destroy me?" I asked.

He smiled like the Cheshire Cat, his face hidden under his hood. "The laws are the laws. If you don't attack me, I can't attack you."

"But you want to?"

"There have been times when I have wanted to. This isn't one of them. You came to us. It would be ill-managed for me not to hear you out."

"I need to go to Heaven."

The grin vanished, but he didn't speak.

"Is that a no?"

"Do you have any idea what you're asking for?" he said.

"Yes."

"I don't think you do, or you wouldn't ask."

"If you don't ask, the answer is always no."

"Outsiders don't go to Heaven, Diuscrucis. It has never been done."

"Does that mean it's against your laws?"

I knew it wasn't. Dante would have told me if it were.

"No, but it has never been done."

"That's a stupid reason," Obi said.

The cowl shifted slightly, the Archangel looking over. Obi's face deepened in color as he realized he called Raguel stupid.

"I mean, that's not really a reason, is it?" Obi said, trying to backtrack. "I mean, no offense, but Heaven just got pwned out there."

"And so did I," I said. "There may be a way to stop this, but the only way to make it happen is for me to go to Heaven."

"Why?"

I lifted one of the shards of Uriel's sword from my pocket. "Do you know what this is?"

His head shifted, leaning forward. Then he reached up and lowered his hood. His eyes were wide. "You have a piece of Uriel's sword?"

"No. I have the entire thing. Unfortunately, it is in pieces. I need Uriel to put it back together."

His eyes bore into me, as though that statement was the dumbest thing he had ever heard.

"Your actions have fractured a family that has been maintained for thousands of years. You caused Adam to fall and indirectly caused all of those Touched to die, not only by creating the schism between the seraphim but by allowing the true diuscrucis to live in the first place. Since your arrival, the world has seen more death and destruction at the hands of the Divine than at any other time in the history of the universe. That sword in your possession would allow you to become powerful enough to challenge God himself."

"That definitely sounded like a no," Obi said.

"I can't argue anything you just said," I said. "It's all true, and it's nothing I don't already know. It's also the exact reason why I need the blade."

"How so?" Raguel asked.

"Because if I'm gone, and Sarah is all that's left, she'll become powerful enough to challenge God. By destroying all of the Divine, she's playing God. Right now, I can almost balance her out, but she's still stronger than I am. And if I can't stop her, neither can you."

"That's not a compelling argument. If you have the sword, and you do stop her, you will be beyond our control."

"You're saying I'm not already."

"As we established, I can destroy you here and now."

"Only if I attack you."

"For now. That is one rule we intend to have changed."

"Without that rule, you become just like the demons. Can't you see what is happening here? You, of all angels?"

"I am the Archangel of Justice and Vengeance. Vengeance requires action."

"Which is why Adam fell. But you blame me for that. He took action, we both know the consequences. That won't change."

"We shall see. No angel will bring you to Heaven. Uriel will not reforge his blade. I will make sure of that."

"You're going to allow all of the Divine to be killed so that I can't become more powerful? I had all of the Beast's power, Raguel. I could have kept it. If I had, we wouldn't be here, now. I didn't, though. I didn't want to challenge God. I still don't. I don't even want the sword or the responsibility that comes with it. I don't have a choice."

"Easy words to say while you don't control the power. Things have changed. You have changed. Consorting with a demon? Visiting Hell? You are both good and evil, Landon. You will always be such, and as such you cannot be trusted."

"She'll destroy you. All of you."

"If we cannot find a way to stop her, then it will be as He wills it."

"You're making a mistake, Raguel. A big mistake."

"Go now," the Archangel replied. "Leave this Holy place, and never return to it. I will not allow you to leave it again."

I bit my tongue to keep from cursing him. That wouldn't help my cause any. I knew it was a risk to come here to make my case. I knew there was a good chance I would be rejected. This time. I wasn't going to give up that easily.

"Come on, Obi. We'll have to settle for Plan B."

18

"Plan B?" Obi asked, as soon as we were off the grounds of St. Peter's. "We have a Plan B?"

"Sort of. It's the same as Plan A, except we ask a different angel."

"You heard him, man. He said he'd make sure you don't get to Heaven."

"I also heard him say that the seraphim are fractured. He wants to change things. I'm sure not all of the angels do. They might be a little more trusting of my motives."

"And you really don't want to go up against God, right? If you took all of that power?"

"Not a chance."

"Then what would you do with it?"

"Release it back out into the universe."

"You can do that?"

I nodded.

"Why didn't you tell Raguel?"

"He wouldn't have listened, no matter what I did. He's got other reasons to cut me off."

"What do you mean?"

"Think about it. The more chaotic things get, the easier it becomes for him to push his agenda. To force change to save Heaven and humankind. He doesn't want me coming in and messing that all up. At least not until he gets his way."

"Damn. I hadn't thought about it that way. So, who do we ask next?"

"I'm not sure yet. I've got Jane back in New York. I can go see her, but I can't bring you along."

"If you need to go, you should go. Helping Sarah is the top priority."

I froze for a second. He said "helping," not "stopping." He thought my intention was to bring her back to her senses. To get her to stop. Could I make him understand that she wasn't going to stop? That the only way out would be to end her life?

I didn't think so. Not without a fight. Not without risking that he would walk away. I needed him with me, regardless of the reasons why. Regardless of the truth. I was an asshole for staying silent. I had always been an asshole.

"I need a little more time to weigh our options. Are you sure you don't need to sleep?"

He laughed. "You sound like my mom. If you want to rest we can find a hotel. Don't take too long on this, though. Maybe Sarah is going to go after the demons next, and I know neither of us has a problem with that. It's only a stay of execution for the good guys." He paused. "And for you."

"You have a cell?" I asked.

He lifted it from his pocket and began searching for a nearby hotel. We were both distracted when a figure fell from the sky, landing silently beside us.

"There you are," Alfred said, looking at Obi. "I've been searching the city for you."

"Hey man," Obi said. "What happened to you back there?"

"Kira pushed me back to Heaven," he said. "To keep the diuscrucis from killing me."

"Pushed you?"

"She was of the Heavenly Host, a higher order than a warrior like me. She has... had the power to send me back against my will. She used it." He finally looked at me. "Who is your friend?"

I looked back at him, making eye contact. His face changed as he recognized me.

"This is not the first time we have met, is it?" he asked.

"No," I replied. "You won't remember me as part of your timeline. I was there."

"At the Mass?"

"Yes."

"You saw the battle?"

"I was in it."

"You couldn't stop the death of the Touched?"

"I tried. I almost died myself."

He looked concerned. "That is not a good sign for any of us."

"Landon was just talking to Archangel Raguel," Obi said. "He asked him for a ride to Heaven."

"And he said no," Alfred said. "It has never been done. Only seraphim and ascending souls go to Heaven."

"That isn't true," I said. "What about Dante?"

"The poet? He was an ascending soul at the time."

Interesting. I hadn't known that. "Still, it isn't against the rules."

"No. He likely denied you because you're a threat to his personal motivations."

"You're aware of it?"

"All of Heaven is aware of the growing rift between us. Now that the true diuscrucis has established herself, I'm afraid they will see it as an opportunity to create further strife, not to rally around a common cause. Raguel has always been tempestuous. I feared the worst when I saw he was leading the Mass. What do you need to go there to do?"

"I have the pieces of Uriel's sword. I want him to reforge it for me so that I can collect enough Divine power to take on Sarah."

"By killing angels?" he asked.

"I hope not. I don't like killing angels. The balance is in Hell's favor right now. If we hurry, I can come back and take out a few archfiends, steal their power, and get to Sarah before she launches another assault against Heaven."

"We?" Alfred said. "You're not suggesting-"

"Why not?" I asked. "You know what's going to happen if Raguel gets his way, or if Sarah gets her way, or if Gervais gets his way. Any one of them has the power to destroy everything, even if they think they're doing the right thing, Gervais excluded."

"I'm a warrior, Landon. A fighter. I have no jurisdiction to make a decision like this."

"But you have the power?"

"To transport you? It isn't much different than recalling my blade." His sword materialized into his hand for effect. "It isn't a matter of power. Bringing you to Heaven will cause more upheaval, more fracturing between the sides."

"Leaving me here will see both sides gone. It won't matter much then, will it?"

"Admittedly, no."

"So you'll do it?"

He was still hesitant. He looked at the ground, whispering to himself. It sounded like a prayer for guidance. Then he was silent for a moment, his eyes falling closed. Maybe he said the prayer again to himself. Maybe he was listening for an answer. Either way, when he opened his eyes and lifted his head again, he nodded.

"I may be forced to Confess for this, Diuscrucis," he said. "But Josette always believed in your heart, your inert goodness. My heart is telling me to believe the same. I will take you."

I felt my body relax. I hadn't realized how tense I was about his decision until that moment.

"Thank you," I said.

"Great," Obi said. "I guess I'll meet you back here?"

"That sounds like a plan," I said. "I'll get the sword, and then-"

"No," Alfred said. "If I'm bringing one, I might as well bring two. We may need the assistance."

"We?" I asked.

"I'm not going to let you run loose in Heaven without a guide. I'm

Extinction

coming with you."

"Great," Obi said. "When do we leave?"

Alfred dismissed his sword. Then he reached out and put a hand on each of our shoulders. I felt a whoosh of cold air across my face, and then we were standing in the middle of a garden.

Because of course we were.

19

Alfred arrived a second later. He looked different. Not a complete transformation, but there was an obvious change in him that set him apart from us.

"Is this Eden?" Obi asked.

"Yes," Alfred replied.

"For real? The place where Adam and Eve-"

"Yes," Alfred said.

"Can we see the tree?"

"This isn't a sightseeing tour," I said.

"Aw, come on, man. Chance of a lifetime."

I glanced over at him. He smiled. "Right. Where to?"

"This was the safest place to bring you," Alfred said. "We have to be cautious."

"Cautious in Heaven?" Obi said. "Why?"

"This isn't the part of Heaven you're thinking of," Alfred said. "The souls don't have access to the Garden of Eden."

"Too tempting?"

"I accept that you are compensating for your nervousness with joviality, but in this case, yes. The tree remains a temptation. For many years, such temptation was permitted to weed out certain souls. Those who tasted of the fruit were cast down to Purgatory. Then it was decided that it was an unfair temptation. That those who lived completely lives in service of Him should not have to prove themselves when they arrived here. The Garden was moved to this region of Heaven, off-limits to the rank and file."

"So, we're in the Members Only section?" I said.

"Yes. Technically, you aren't permitted here at all. Technically, I am breaking the rules to bring you here."

"Why do you say technically?" I asked.

"Because you are here, and I have not yet fallen."

"So God is okay with this?"

"It would appear that way, at least for now."

I don't know why, but it made me feel more comfortable to be in Heaven knowing I had the green light from the owner. Of course, I still couldn't quite wrap my mind around the fact that I was in Heaven. Hell had been so much different. It had been obvious from the moment I stepped through the rift that I was there. The Garden of Eden was like any other botanical garden, green and lush, but otherwise normal. Even the sky was a nice shade of pale blue. It was nothing other-worldly. Maybe the clouds were a little too perfect, but otherwise, I could believe I was still on Earth.

"So what's the difference between this part of Heaven and the other?" I asked.

"Have you ever been to a zoo?" Alfred asked.

"I grew up in the Bronx. We have a zoo there."

He smiled. "From the outside, everything looks perfect. The animals look content. The grounds are neat and clean. Behind the scenes? Things may not be quite what they seem."

"You're saying the seraphim are a mess?"

"I'm saying that like all families, we have our share of discord. Nothing like murder, of course, but plenty of arguing. We hide that from the general population. This is their bright eternity, after all. My bringing you here is a can of worms I should like to remain closed."

"I'm surprised you know that idiom," I said.

"I'm not completely out of touch with the modern world, even if I am a conservative old soul. The point is, let us be careful and quiet, and perhaps we can reach Uriel without causing a scene."

"Fair enough," I said. "Lead the way."

Alfred brought us from wherever we were in the Garden, out to a worn dirt path. It meandered through the vegetation to what I felt was the east. A spotless series of glass encased skyscrapers could be seen beyond it.

"Keeping up with the times?" I asked.

"Like Purgatory, what you see will reflect your own understanding of the world," Alfred said. "For me, it is castles and villages."

"Even though you understand the modern world?"

"Yes. It is what I prefer."

"Okie Dokie."

We kept going, staying along the path. We had covered half the distance when Alfred pulled us aside, into the brush. I found myself surrounded by some large, leafy plant with big yellow flowers, peering through the cracks as an angel crossed our paths. I was surprised to see that she was naked.

"Uh," I said, once she had vanished down the path.

"Original sin is human," Alfred said. "The seraphim have no sense of indecency to the body that God has made for them. In fact, it is a matter of personal pride, regardless of shape or form."

"You're wearing clothes," Obi said.

"For your sake, as do all angels assigned to Earth. It is understandable if the sight of flesh causes you discomfort."

"What causes me discomfort is the idea of angels standing there arguing with one another in the buff," Obi said. "That is my definition of the bad naked."

"Mine too," I said.

Alfred laughed. "We don't notice one another for our bodies. It is the soul that is important. Purely physical attraction is a limitation of the human condition."

"I can believe that," I replied. "Since the world will bend to my vision of it, I suppose if I prefer the residents clothed, they'll be clothed?"

He nodded.

"What was she doing in here, anyway? Why do angels come to the Garden?"

"To pray. To meditate. To contemplate. Heaven may seem a simple place, but in reality, it is anything but. Especially if you are involved with Earth and the war."

"Are we going to have to duck into the weeds often?"

"Let us hope not."

We came out of hiding, continuing along the dirt path through the Garden. We reached the perimeter a few minutes later, crossing the dirt path to an ordinary city street. The main difference was that it was empty.

"It would seem pretty easy to be spotted out here," I said.

"Most of the seraphim are otherwise occupied at the moment," he replied. "Not loitering around the village. Recent events on Earth and up here have led to more than one emergency gathering."

We walked a couple of blocks when a thought came to me. "In Hell, time passes more slowly or more quickly, depending on how Lucifer wants it. Is it the same thing here?"

"Our sense of time here is more vague than even that, but while you are here, you will experience time as though you were still on Earth. It is easier that way."

"Hey, who works there?" Obi said. I turned to see him pointing in the distance. I followed his finger to the largest of the skyscrapers, a huge block of turning glass that looked like human DNA.

"That is the Council building," Alfred said. "It is where the Archangels reside and hold discourse."

"Archangel Michael is in there?" Obi said.

"Yes, as is Raguel if he has returned."

"What about Uriel?"

"Uriel refuses to sit on the Council. He chooses an eternity of hermitage to atone for his creation of the sword."

"Hang on," I said. "You're saying he's unhappy that he made the sword?"

"Of course. He created a very powerful and very deadly weapon. Why would he be happy about that?"

"I thought it was made during the war in Heaven when Lucifer was cast out?"

"It was. All the more reason to feel sorrow and lament its existence."

"But I need to ask him to remake what has been broken. To return its power to it. If he's that sorry he made it, why would he ever do that?"

"For the same reason he made it the first time, I suppose. To save good from evil."

20

We didn't stay on the streets for long, wandering off the beaten path to a series of back alleys and smaller crossroads. It was a part of Heaven it seemed that even the angels had mostly forgotten. It wasn't as squeaky clean as the rest, with a layer of dust or something that seemed to be resting on every sidewalk, every lamp post, every nook, and cranny.

It was weird that there were lamp posts in Heaven. It was weird that it was modern. It wasn't my first time experiencing such a thing. Purgatory was the same, and the Box had been controlled by the stronger mind. The Beast's at first, and then mine. I knew how to reshape what I saw to my will, but nothing I did removed the dust.

"What is this stuff?" I asked.

"The remains of angels who have been killed in Heaven," Alfred replied. "Most of it is from the war." He paused, shaking his head. "Most. Not all."

"What happens if an angel is killed in Heaven?" I asked. "I see they turn to dust like on Earth, but where does the soul go?"

"Nowhere. It ceases to be."

"As in nothing?" Obi asked.

"Yes. It is the worst fate imaginable. That is why God reacted so strongly to the war. That is why Hell had to be created. A crime such as ending a soul completely is unforgivable."

"What about setting it free?" I asked. "To be part of the Universe?"

"Only God can do that if He chooses."

I didn't tell him that I knew that trick, too. I was glad to hear it wasn't the worst thing.

"How much further to Uriel?" Obi asked.

"Not much," Alfred said. "We're near the edge of the city now. His home is only a mile or so past it."

"Let me guess, a light blue house with a white picket fence?" I said.

"Not quite," Alfred replied.

"I have to say; Hell was a lot more interesting than this."

"Debauchery usually is. The overload of the senses causes both mortal and seraph to give in to temptation. A life of prayerful meditation may not be as acutely exciting, but I would argue that it is infinitely more fulfilling."

I couldn't counter the point. Not when I had never experienced the meditative state he was referring to. Not that I hadn't tried. It was a hard place to get to, and a hard place to stay. The souls in Heaven probably spent their eternity trying to master it.

We finally reached the end of the city, which fell away abruptly into a series of verdant hills that undulated across the landscape. We walked a single-lane street that was lined with trees, all of them in a state of bloom that left an explosion of color everywhere I looked. Heaven was more boring than Hell, but it was also a lot more beautiful.

"Is there anything I should know about Uriel before I meet him?" I asked.

"Be strong in your conviction. Be confident in your desire. Be pure of heart and conscience. If you believe the sword is truly the only way to save us, Uriel will sense it in your heart. That will earn you his trust."

I could do that. I knew without question this was the only way. Sarah had made that painfully obvious with the wounds she had inflicted on me already.

Uriel's home didn't have a white picket fence. It did have a wrought iron fence, twelve feet high and spiked on top, each one of the bars etched with more runes that I would have believed could fit in such a small space. I could see his house behind it, a large stone building that looked dim and heavy compared to the brightness of the surrounding countryside, as if a cloud was always hanging over it, dumping rain and sadness and depression down on the angel. And maybe it was.

"Why does he need runes up here?" I asked.

"The fence was made right before the war began. It was to protect us from the usurper. From Lucifer and his army. As the legend goes, Archangel Raphael stood guard for three years while Uriel made the sword, and upon its completion he carried it to the front lines, to Michael. There, Michael began to fell his enemies with the blade, taking their power until he was strong enough to confront Lucifer directly. Only the sword became lodged in Lucifer's chest, and when God cast him down into Hell, the sword went down with him, shattering before it reached the dark plane and spreading across the Earth."

"It seems impossible that someone found all of the pieces," I said. I didn't know who had done that bit of work. Right now, I was grateful for it.

"I imagine it took thousands of years," Alfred said.

"Can we get inside?" Obi asked.

"The gate is open," Alfred replied, pointing ahead to the front of the property.

The gate was hanging open. It seemed like it had been that way for a long, long time.

"Remember, Diuscrucis," Alfred said as we reached the front door. "Be confident."

"Confident. Right."

I put up my hand to knock on the door. Then I noticed it was open a little. I glanced over at Alfred. It didn't seem to me that a self-imposed hermit would make it this easy for people to come and visit.

"Something feels wrong about this," I said.

"I agree," Alfred said. "Let me go in first. I will make sure it is safe for you."

"Okay. Holler if you need backup."

He didn't call for his blade. Instead, he stepped forward to push on the door.

Before he did, a robed figure appeared in it, small and slight. The form was immediately recognizable to me, despite the hood that covered her face.

"Landon," Josette said, lowering her cowl and looking up at me. "Uriel isn't here. Raguel has ordered him to stand with the Council. We need to get you out of sight before he knows you are here."

21

I didn't respond. How could I? I was too busy staring at her, suddenly unable to breathe. Josette. I had never thought I would see her again. Even being here, I had never imagined I would have the chance.

She wasn't the child I had known on Earth. Not anymore. She was older now, an adult, but still as naturally beautiful as she had always been. More so. The wisdom of her age was written on her flesh in a way that suited her much better than the immaturity of youth.

I moved toward her, leaning over and wrapping her in a tight hug. I felt her hands tighten around my back. I had missed her more than she would ever know.

"How?" I said, letting go. I couldn't get any of the other words out.

"We are bonded, you and I. I knew you had come the moment you arrived. In my heart, I knew I had to come to you, to warn you. It isn't safe for you here. It may not be safe for any of us."

"What do you mean?" Alfred asked.

"The Council is meeting over what they are calling the Massacre. Raguel and some of the others are arguing for immediate action, while Michael is urging peace and calm. Many of our brothers and sisters are upset that so many were killed, and we cannot retaliate. They say by attacking so many she attacked us all, and we should be permitted to fight back. Michael states only the Will of the Lord."

"Retaliate against what?" Obi said. "Sarah? By the way, it's good to see you again, Josie."

"You as well, Obi-wan." She smiled at the name, and then returned her attention to me. "Yes. They want to track down Sarah and kill her."

"They do know they don't have the power, right?"

"I don't think so. They believe they can overwhelm her. And if that fails, Raguel is willing to risk being discovered on Earth."

"And create Armageddon, all because he doesn't want me to take care of this?"

"All because this is the best chance they'll ever have to push their agenda," Obi said.

Josette shifted her gaze, looking past me, scanning the sky. "They took Uriel because Raguel knew you would keep trying to come here, and as long as you can't reach him, you can't reforge the blade. It was a mistake to tell him about it."

"Hindsight," I replied.

"Perhaps. They also took him so that if they can get the blade from you, Raguel can use it to increase his power and challenge Sarah directly."

"Like Michael did to Lucifer," I said.

"Yes. Only if Raguel gains that much power, I fear he will become like Lucifer. He is too angry. Too vengeful."

"We need Uriel if we're going to do anything with the sword," I said. "What are we supposed to do?"

"First, we must get you away from here. Follow me."

Josette ducked back into the house. We trailed behind her, following as she made her way through the structure. It was definitely the home of a hermit. The stone was dark and damp, and there were few windows to allow the light in. Only the burning embers of a forge that had been long ignored gave the space any illumination at all.

"Where are we going?" I asked.

"Back to the Convent. There is a special passage from here to there."

"What was Uriel doing with a secret passage to the Convent?" Alfred asked.

"The Sisters would meet him daily for confession," Josette replied. "Even after all these years."

I heard a thump from the front of the house. Someone pushed the door the rest of the way open.

"They must have seen you," Josette said. "Hurry."

She picked up the pace, and so did we. I could hear the footsteps behind us, moving through the house, searching for signs of our passing. I couldn't believe I was running away from angels. Then again, this wasn't Earth. The Archangels had full reign here. Even if they didn't kill me, they could still detain me, hold me until it was too late.

"In here," Josette said, leading us into a storage room. It was filled with barrels that in turn were filled with ingots of metal that looked sort of like iron, but seemed to glow despite the lack of light. I had seen the same glow on some of the blessed swords the angels carried.

Josette pushed one of the barrels aside, revealing a ladder beneath. "Climb down."

We did. She took up the rear, moving the barrel back in place behind us.

"Whoa," Obi said.

We had gone down into a small chamber filled with candles. At the rear of it was the most beautiful metal crucifix I had ever seen, plated in gold and platinum and emitting its own light. My body tingled at the sight of it.

The front of the chamber had a simple stool, and ahead of that a screen. Josette opened the screen, revealing the other side of the confessional and the tunnel leading away from the house. The angels searching for us reaching the storage room as we approached it, their feet loud over our heads.

I put my finger to my lips, and we remained still. They retreated a few heartbeats later, signaling us to resume our escape. We passed across the screen to the tunnel, and then Josette closed it all behind us once more.

She motioned for us to remain silent as we moved down the tunnel. As Alfred had already told me, the Sisters didn't speak. I wasn't sure if she was allowed to, or if these were all the words we would get to share. If they were, I would treasure them and the chance to have heard her voice and seen her face one more time.

Even so, I hoped they weren't. Seeing the crucifix had placed a sudden, immediate weight on my soul. A sense of guilt I had never experienced before. I didn't understand it. I didn't want it. I didn't seem to have a choice.

As if things couldn't get any more complicated.

22

We reached the end of the tunnel, which opened out into another dimly lit structure. Josette remained silent as she guided us out into a hallway, down to an adjacent corridor, and then across to a simple door. She opened us, motioned us in, and then closed it behind us, leaving us alone.

"It is permitted to speak in here," Alfred said, breaking the silence.

"You told me you'd been here to see Josette before," I said.

The angel nodded.

"Where did she go?"

"She must inform her superior that we are here."

"Won't that lead Raguel to us?" Obi asked.

"No. The Sisters hold everything in confidence. This is the safest place in Heaven for you to be."

"Maybe, but staying here for long is the same as being held captive," I said.

"I don't expect we will be staying. We need time to determine how to reach Uriel without drawing Raguel's attention. It will be difficult while he is being held up at the Council."

The door opened, and Josette re-entered. "Difficult, but not impossible," she said. "The Mother has agreed to see you."

"The Mother?"

She came in behind Josette. She was a large woman, with a big, solid frame and a large, jovial face. She reminded me of the Dalai Lama.

"The Diuscrucis," she said, looking at me. Her eyes traveled head to toe, and my guilt increased a hundredfold. It was as though she saw right through me. She turned her attention to Josette. "We cannot help him until he confesses. His soul is not ready."

Josette looked concerned. "Mother Hahn," she started to say.

"No. I'm sorry, child. You know our purpose."

"Yes, Mother," Josette said.

"What's going on?" I asked.

"Mercy," Mother Hahn said. "The Lord grants mercy to all who ask for it. It is this mercy which cleanses the soul. Mercy that gives us strength to carry on. Mercy that leads us down the path of the righteous and just. By confessing your sins, you will learn the healing power of His mercy."

"What if I don't want it?" I said.

"Then you cannot be helped, and you cannot be saved. If you will not confess, we have no more to discuss."

I opened my mouth to argue before stopping myself. Why was I arguing, anyway? I was in Heaven, speaking to an angel. I couldn't reason with her, and I knew it. Besides, my soul was screaming out to me to do it. Maybe I was half-evil, but that didn't mean doing bad things ever felt good in the end. What if asking for forgiveness would lighten the burden I had felt since even before I had escaped the Box?

"Can I confess to Josette?" I asked.

"You may confess to any of the Sisters," Mother Hahn replied.

"Will you?" I asked.

Josette smiled. "Of course, Landon." She bowed to the Mother and then motioned for me to follow without speaking.

We went out into the hallway, back the way we had come. She led me to a small confessional, one in a row of confessionals. I could hear muffled whispers as we passed them. There were others already inside.

"I thought confession was a punishment?" I said as we sat. She was on one side of the screen, and I was on the other.

"That is a different kind of confession," she replied. "And yes, that is a punishment. This is not."

"Do you confess?"

"At least once per week."

"What for?"

She giggled. "That's none of your business."

Right. "But I can't imagine what you would have to ask for forgiveness for. You're living in a cloistered community and spending almost all of your time in prayer."

"Thoughts still enter my mind that are unfit for such pursuits," she said. "Are you stalling?"

"Sort of," I admitted.

"Why?"

"I'm afraid if I start talking, I'm going to fall apart."

"The Mother could sense the pain in your soul, Landon. You are already falling apart."

That simple statement hit me like a hammer. I felt my eyes welling up already, and I hadn't said anything yet. Damn.

"I'm not sure what to say," I said.

"Say whatever feels natural. There is no right or wrong."

We sat in silence for a minute. Then another. This was harder than I was expecting. I didn't know what to say. I didn't know where to start.

"Landon," Josette said at last. "We have been friends since the moment we met. You saved my life. You saved Sarah's life. God had a plan for me, and I believe for you as well. Do not be afraid."

The tears started coming for real when she said that, running down my face and dripping off my chin.

"I've failed you," I said. "I've failed everyone. I put myself first. I put my lust first, my desires first, my needs first. I wasn't there for Sarah when she needed me."

I paused, trying to catch myself, trying not to say the words I didn't want to say. I felt the pressure on my soul, the weight that was threatening to crush me. Was God doing this to me? Was that even possible?

"I promised you I would protect her. I have to kill her."

I waited in silence for her judgment, the tears continuing to come. How could she forgive me for that? How could anyone forgive me for that? Thou shalt not kill. It was the most basic law in the Universe, and I had done it so many times.

"Please, forgive me," I whispered.

A few more seconds of silence passed.

"I forgive you," Josette said. "And the Lord forgives you. Your road has not been an easy one, my friend. Your journey to Him filled with struggle and pain. But He loves the least of us most of all and welcomes those who have failed and yet wish to succeed. In His mercy, may you find peace and strength and courage. When the time comes, I know you will do the right thing. In the name of the Father, and of the Son, and of the Holy Spirit, I absolve you."

I don't know what I expected to happen. I don't know if I expected anything to happen at all. I wasn't the most religious guy around, and I certainly hadn't been following the word of the Lord very much, if at all. Even so, I could sense the change in myself. The lightening of my guilt, a feeling of peace and calm, and a realization that maybe there was another choice when it came to Sarah. Maybe when the time came, I wouldn't have to end her life.

I wiped my eyes until they were dry and then stepped out of the confessional. Josette was already in the hallway, and she gave me a hug as I emerged, almost causing me to tear up again.

"All will be well, Landon," she whispered. We both knew she wasn't supposed to be talking right now. "Do not underestimate the power of your spirit."

I nodded, staying quiet. She led me back to the room where Obi, Alfred, and Mother Hahn were waiting. The Mother looked me over again as I entered, and this time, when her eyes pierced me I didn't feel such an incredible sense of shame.

"Not perfect, but it will do," she said.

23

Mother Hahn and Josette vanished from the room immediately after the Mother declared me "good enough." I still wasn't entirely sure what that meant, but I imagined that the improvement in my personal psyche was somehow visible to her, and she had decided it was acceptable. To be honest, the whole thing was still a bit of a mystery to me, though I was very glad I had been given the opportunity to confess to Josette. It was her child at the center of the storm, after all.

"Where do you think they went?" Obi asked some time later.

An hour had passed. Maybe two.

"To go talk to the Council on our behalf?" I suggested. "Alfred, do you know?"

He shook his head. "I am not invited into the affairs of the Sisterhood. Before today, I didn't allow that they ever left the Convent grounds."

"Even a thousand-year-old angel can learn something new," Obi said. "There's still hope for me."

"Whatever it is, it's taking a long time. I don't know if that's a good thing or a bad thing."

"Come on, man. This is you we're talking about. Whatever happens, it's a bad thing."

"Funny."

Obi put his hand on my shoulder. "Seriously, if they don't show up soon, I think we should head out on our own."

"I'm starting to agree."

Another ten minutes went by. I was giving heavier weight to the idea of breaking out when the door to the room opened, and Josette swept in.

"What's happening?" I asked. She looked troubled.

"Mother Hahn was trying to get an audience with Archangel Michael, to discuss Raguel's actions and call him out on them. He refused to see her."

"Why?"

"Apparently, because he's in agreement with Raguel."

I froze. "What?"

"My feelings exactly. Michael is at the top of the hierarchy within Heaven, second only to the Holy Trinity. The idea that he has begun to question God is unfathomable."

"This is worse than I thought."

"It is worse than any of us thought."

"Okay, so how do we stop it?"

"We can't stop it. Landon, Michael ordered Mother Hahn to turn you over to the Council."

"Will she?"

"She has no choice if you are still here when she arrives."

"Where is she?"

"Tied up with some other official business, I'm afraid," she said, winking.

Then she lifted her robe over her head and dropped it on the floor. She wasn't nude, at least not to my eyes. She was wearing loose fitting clothes that resembled a karate gi. A pair of wooden sticks sat on her hip.

"Mother Hahn will do her best to keep His Excellency occupied while we make our escape."

"Our escape?"

"She has ordered me to accompany you. I can't return to the mortal realm, but I can assist you here, as can my sisters. They are waiting at the southern entrance."

"I don't understand," I said. "Won't you get in trouble for this?"

"We are taking a tremendous risk, but the need is great, and Mother Hahn believes that you will do the right thing. When you shed your defenses, your soul is more good than it is evil. You can stop Sarah, and save her. I know you can."

I wasn't as confident about that as she was, but I was hopeful. I followed her as she left the room again, with Obi and Alfred behind me. There were other Sisters in the hallway, but they largely ignored our passage, looking away as we turned the corner.

"Out here," Josette said, bringing us to a final hallway.

We paused at the end of it. Josette's sisters were already sitting on the floor, their hands bound by rope. Four angels were blocking the exit.

"Sister," one of them said. "The Diuscrucis is ordered to turn over the shards and await return to the mortal realm. This directive came directly from Archangel Michael. Refusal is akin to treason."

Josette stood her ground in front of me.

"Josette, don't," I said. "You already got in trouble for me once. I don't want you to sacrifice your faith for me again."

"You speak as if my faith is something I can lose or give up," Josette said, her voice rising. "Do not be concerned. I know your cause is just. The Lord has affirmed it in his mercy." She stepped forward, locking eyes with the angels. "Be careful with your next decision, brothers. You are being led down a path that ends in treachery and a fall from grace. I would not like to see that happen."

"The decision is not ours to make, sister. It is our Master's, and he has already decided. The Lord cannot punish us for sending him back where he belongs."

"How about for stealing?" I asked. "The shards are mine."

"The shards belong to the seraphim."

"They were lost. I recovered them. Finders, keepers."

"That is absurd."

"Whatever. You still aren't getting them."

The angels started their approach. They had sticks that were similar to

Josette's, only they were metal and etched with runes. I assumed it was their version of non-lethal control.

"I won't allow you to touch him, or take the shards," Josette said.

"Then you will be disobeying our Lord and Master. You will fall."

"Will I? Let us see."

She rushed them, bringing her sticks to hand as she did. I stepped forward behind her, trying to think of something I could do or say that would stop her. I didn't want her to fall. I didn't want to cause a fight in Heaven.

She reached the angels, going for the one on the left first, attacking him with a quick series of strikes that he used his arms to block. The one on the right tried to grab her, but she slipped away from his grip, cracking one of the sticks hard on his wrist. His hand dropped numbly as she passed through to the second row.

She stood in the center of them in a ready posture, sticks out beside her, legs low and balanced. More importantly, she hadn't fallen.

"My cause is just," she said.

"Perhaps you believe it to be. That may absolve you to our Lord, but it does not make it so."

They went after her, coming at her in unison. Their metal sticks bounced off her wooden ones, her arms moving in a quick rhythm, her body held planted by her legs. She writhed and undulated around the attacks, sneaking in an occasional strike to the chest or hand that would leave the angels in limited pain. If a disabling blow was what she was after, it was going to take her a while to get it.

Or at least, I thought it was. Then she leaped out from the center of the square, getting behind one of the seraphs and hitting him solidly on the side of the head. The stick made a sharp crack against his skull, and he dropped to the floor.

The other angels moved in, eager to stop her assault. She fell back on defense, deflecting their strikes and making efforts to land her own. They were more wary of her now, and more focused on defending themselves.

"Okay, I've had enough," I said, gathering my power. I wasn't going to sit on the sidelines and let her do everything for me.

Alfred put his hand on my shoulder. "Wait," he said. "I will handle this. Using your power here and now will hurt your case."

The older angel moved forward. Unlike Josette, there was no beauty to his approach, no artistry. He grabbed the first of Raguel's cronies by the back of the neck, holding him and punching him hard enough to knock him out with one blow. He dropped the unconscious seraph and turned to the one next to him, raising an arm to block a blow from a metal stick. His wrist shattered at the force, but he didn't react, using his other hand to shove the angel against the wall. Then he reached out and took one of Josette's suddenly offered sticks, smacking his opponent hard enough to knock him out.

Suddenly outnumbered, the fourth seraph dropped his sticks and raised his hands in submission.

"The time for change is coming, Josette," the angel said. "Be a part of it, or be left behind."

"It is not for you, Raguel, or Michael to determine the pace of change. Only He may make that decision. Right now, He supports the Diuscrucis." Josette raised her stick. "I can't have you running to Raguel ahead of us."

The seraph spread his hands and exposed his temple. Josette hit him, knocking him out.

"That should keep them for a few hours," she said, leaning down beside her sister and releasing them from their bonds. "Fight with me, sisters. The Lords is on Landon's side in this matter."

"Now what?" I asked. I couldn't quite get used to the idea that God agreed with what I was doing. I wasn't going to argue the point either.

"We have no choice. We have to go to the Council building and free Uriel."

"How are we going to sneak past Raguel and Michael?" Obi asked.

"We aren't," Josette replied. "Mother Hahn will handle the diversion."

24

The Council building was the tallest skyscraper in the city, visible from almost everywhere. According to Josette, the Archangels occupied the highest floors, ostensibly to be the closest to God. In reality, the hierarchical nature was obvious, and in my opinion in direct contention with the concept of humility.

"The only one of us who is without flaw is God," Josette said in response to that observation.

According to Dante, even God had his imperfections. That may or may not have been true, and at the moment I wasn't interested in a theological argument. I just wanted to get Uriel to put the sword back together. We had already been in Heaven for three hours, which was more than enough time for Sarah to put the hurt on any number of demons.

Getting to the building was relatively easy. With Raguel's hench-angels disabled, we were able to take the backstreets right up to the building itself without being noticed. Really, the Archangel wasn't even trying to catch us on the way in. We had to come to him if we wanted Uriel, and I didn't exactly have a lot of other options.

"So, tell me more about this diversion," I said as we stood across the street from the building, staring up at its western wall of glass.

Extinction

"Mother Hahn requested an audience with Archangel Michael," Josette said. "When Michael refused, she took her case to Raphael. He and Mother Hahn have a long history of friendship, and he agreed to go to Michael at her bequest. When I signal her, she will send Raphael to Michael, while she takes up her argument with Raguel. With them both distracted, we will have an opportunity to reach Uriel."

"You know where they're keeping him?" I asked.

"The main conference room at the top of the tower," she replied. "It is the only place. They cannot keep him prisoner, they can only stall him with questions and matters of affairs. I imagine he may understand what they are doing, but then again, he might not want to help you anyway."

"So we could go and rescue him, and he'll still say no?"

"I wouldn't call it a rescue. More appropriately, we will be the ones who may be taking him against his will."

"But he's an Archangel, right? He's got power of his own."

"Yes. It is power he has sworn not to use again in conflict."

"Okay. How do we get up there?"

"Really, Landon? I am an angel."

I wondered again if her clothes were real or of my own mental design. It was probably better not to know.

"In that case, send the signal. We're-"

I stopped speaking as the silence around us was broken by the sound of shattering glass. I looked back at the tower just in time to see a body plummeting from the top. It fell halfway before turning to dust, the momentum spreading it wide and casting it down like confetti.

"Mother Hahn," Josette said, her face contorted in shock.

"Who?"

"Raguel. It must be."

"But he has to fall for that."

"Perhaps. He is an Archangel. He cannot be cast down so easily. There is no time for a diversion. If he is ready to kill for this, Uriel is not safe."

She circled behind me, her hands coming up beneath my arms. I was in the air before I could protest, being carried up toward the window.

"Oh, crap," Obi said beside me, dangling from Alfred's grip. "Did I mention I hate heights?"

We sped toward the clearly broken window at the same time a dozen seraphim appeared on the edge of the building and leaped off, swords appearing in their hands as they dove toward us.

"We're too late," Josette said. "Raguel has started the war. He is afraid of you, Landon. Give him a reason to be."

Her arms flexed, and she tossed me forward, releasing me from her grip. I didn't look back to see what happened to her or her sisters. I reached out with my power, grabbing the edge of the window and pulling myself toward it, using it like a slingshot. I launched forward in a rush, avoiding the oncoming angels. They spread their wings to slow themselves, taking ineffective cuts at me as I rocketed past, and then turning to give chase.

Then I was shooting through the window and into the building. I threw my power out again, pushing against it to slow my entrance, landing almost gracefully a few feet inside of the edge.

Archangel Raguel was standing beside a large, natural wood table. Another angel was sitting beside him, watching with resigned eyes. Uriel, I presumed.

More importantly, Raguel was still white and pure as snow. He hadn't fallen.

What the hell was going on?

A soft breeze at my back, and then Obi was beside me, dropped in the room by the passing Alfred. We stood side by side, in direct confrontation with the Archangel.

"Diuscrucis," he said, smiling. "Did you see that?"

"You killed Mother Hahn."

"I did more than that. I proved what we have long suspected but were afraid to verify."

"Which is?"

"God has abandoned Heaven."

I froze, not sure what to think of that. Was it true? How could it be? According to Josette, He hadn't abandoned me.

"I don't believe it," I said.

"The proof is clear," Raguel said. "I killed the Mother, and yet I am still clean. God did not see my betrayal. He does nothing to stop our rebellion."

"How do you possibly justify murder?" I asked. "It's a big leap from praying for change."

"You have left me no choice. One thousand followers died tonight, Diuscrucis. He allowed it to happen. He would allow all of us to perish rather than intervene, and at the same time forbid us from seeking rightful vengeance. The price of a few seraphim is a small one to pay to save the rest of Heaven and humankind."

"You're out of your mind."

"My mind is clear, as is my conscience. I am doing what needs to be done to stop the true diuscrucis, to stop the demons, and to stop you. If God is present, he agrees with what I am doing. If he isn't, it does not matter. Our seraphim will wrest control of Heaven from the traditionalists who keep our hands tied while our brothers and sisters die. What kind of Father allows that, anyway?"

I looked over at Uriel. He seemed uninterested in anything Raguel was saying. He didn't look at me either, staring into space as though his mind wasn't even there.

"Do you think he can help you, Diuscrucis?" Raguel said. "He's barely present. He can't handle violence. He can't handle conflict. The first war destroyed him, and no amount of time can fix it."

"I'm taking him anyway," I said.

"No, you are not."

I glanced over at Obi, who took a few steps away from me. He knew what came next.

Boss battle. There was no way out of it.

Damn.

25

"Obi, see if you can do something with Uriel," I said, keeping my eyes on Raguel.

"Touch him and perish mortal," Raguel said.

"I don't think so," I replied.

I threw my power out at the Archangel, catching him off-guard. My energy slammed into him, throwing him across the room. He hit the wall and bounced off, landing on his feet, a pair of massive wings spreading out behind him.

"I'm thousands of years old, Diuscrucis," Raguel said. "I am one of His first creations. I fought Lucifer in the first war."

"And now you're turning into the spitting image. Congratulations."

"You think you know. The truth is that you know nothing." A sword appeared in his hand, six feet long and glowing with angelic fire. "My heart is pure. This revolution is a long time coming. We shouldn't have to sit idle while our family dies. We shouldn't have to follow an absent Father."

I could see his eyes welling up as he spoke, and I realized I had misjudged him. He wasn't evil after all. He truly cared about the Touched who had died, and all of the other seraphim the demons had been able to kill because of God's rules. He didn't want to go against Him for power. He was only what he was made to be. He was out for justice and vengeance.

It didn't matter. It was either him or me, and it wasn't going to be me.

He charged me, using his wings to propel himself forward with greater speed. I pushed my power off the wall, throwing myself sideways and away from him, pushing off the opposite wall to send myself back. I gathered my power internally, feeding strength to my body and throwing a hard right cross that caught him in the jaw. The force sent him into the stone, cracking it with his body and leaving him stunned.

"Uriel," I heard Obi said. "Nice to meet you, sir. What do you say we get out of here?"

I glanced over at the seraph. He was ignoring Obi, still staring straight ahead.

Raguel was back in business, and he rushed me again, his sword whistling at me with impossible speed. I threw my power up ahead of it, creating a shield that it sank into, stopping only inches from my face. I used the power like hands, turning the blade, wrenching it from him and throwing it out the window.

He smiled at the maneuver, clearly impressed.

The sword reappeared in his hand.

"That's not fair," I said as he came at me a third time.

He was in close, and his sword was a blur as he struck at me, over and over again. I kept my power moving, twirling it around me like a ribbon dancer, using it to deflect blow after blow while backing away. I needed an opening to hit him again, and he wasn't going to give it to me.

I saw motion near the window, and both Josette and Alfred landed on the precipice behind Raguel. They were in good shape, slightly rumpled but otherwise unharmed. It seemed the angels defending Heaven had nothing on the ones who had been on Earth.

What about Archangels?

"Raguel," Josette said. "Stop this madness."

The Archangel didn't stop. He continued striking, pummeling my shields with his blade, his eyes streaming tears the entire time. If he hadn't been trying so hard to kill me, I might have pitied him.

"Uriel," Obi said. "Come on, sir. The angels are about to tear one another apart, and you're the only one who can stop it."

"The only one," the Archangel said softly in response. "Always the only one."

I got the opening I was looking for a moment later. I focused my power, slamming it as hard as I could into Raguel's gut. The blow sent him out and up, and he crashed into the ceiling and fell to the floor, one of his wings bent at an odd angle as he cried out.

"Stay down," Alfred said, putting his sword to the Archangel's neck.

Raguel looked up at me. I knew that look.

"Alfred," I said, trying to warn the angel.

Too late. Raguel grabbed the seraph's sword by the blade, yanking it from his hand. He spun to his feet, flipping the sword as he did, coming around and driving it through the elder angel's neck. It slid off his body and tumbled to the floor.

"No!" Raguel screamed. "No!"

He dropped the sword. His own blade vanished. His wings began to turn color, starting at the outer edges and working their way in. He had struck Alfred down in anger. There was nothing just about it.

He was falling.

"You lied to me," Raguel shouted. "You promised me I was one of your beloved. That I would always be your child."

His hands were curling into claws. He was changing in a way I had never seen before.

"That doesn't look good," I said.

"You don't know the history of the first war," Josette replied. "We have to go. Now."

"Uriel, you need to get up," Obi said. "Look what's happening to him."

"Happening?" Uriel said. His eyes flicked over to Raguel. He didn't seem impressed.

The former Archangel's bare chest heaved as he finished his fall. He had grown at least four feet, his already strong body expanding and growing stronger, his wings becoming more leathered and worn. His fingers and feet were claws, his teeth grown to fangs.

"What the heck?" I said.

"Ever since Lucifer fell, this is what happens when an Archangel falls," Josette said.

"Does it happen often?"

"No. This is only the third time. Michael and Raphael were forced to destroy Remiel."

Raguel regarded us with cold, red eyes. "This is not justice," he growled.

"God hasn't abandoned Heaven," I said. "He's still watching over you. I tried to warn you."

"This is not justice," he repeated, his lip curling in anger. "I trusted in You. I followed You. All I desired was to protect the family You created. Why have You done this to me?"

"You did it to yourself," Josette said. "Your motivations were pure, but your heart wasn't. You wanted the power of the sword more than you wanted to defend your brothers and sisters."

"That isn't true," Raguel said, growing angry. "That isn't true."

"Uh, Josette," I said.

"And now the lies begin," she said. "There is no sense in being honest, is there, Raguel? Not when you have already fallen."

"Lies?" the fallen archangel screamed. "Lies?" He looked at me. "This is your fault, Diuscrucis. Not my fault."

He pounced toward me, raking his claws at my face. He was fast. So fast. I wasn't expecting that. I couldn't get my power up in time.

His hand stopped anyway, right before it reached my cheek. I could smell the sulfur against the flesh and feel the ancient heat of it.

Uriel was standing, his hand out, holding Raguel with a power I didn't know he had.

"The taint of your sin confuses you, brother," Uriel said. "Do not force me to repeat history. There is no good end for any of us if I do."

Raguel lowered his hand and backed away from me.

"Go down to where you belong," Uriel said. "Join him in the Pit. You've been seduced by power. Overcome by temptation. It is a sad day in

Heaven, Raguel."

Raguel was still, his head bowed. He raised it a moment later, looking at Uriel. "I won't go. He betrayed me. He lied to me. To all of us. He doesn't care if we die. He doesn't care if we fall. He puts His faith in this one." He pointed at me. "He gives him His favor. He is no angel. He is half-demon. Half-evil."

"Raguel," Uriel said. "I'm warning you."

"No," Raguel screamed. Then he lunged at Uriel.

The Archangel raised his hand again, but it did no good. Raguel continued toward him, hands wide to cut him in half.

"Landon," Josette said.

I threw my power out in a taut, thin line.

Raguel tripped over it, catching it with his claw and stumbling forward.

Uriel stepped aside, and then reached out and grabbed Obi by the arm.

"We must go," the Archangel said, pulling him to the window and leaping out.

"Landon," Josette said again.

I nodded, running to the window and jumping out, letting myself begin to fall. She caught me a moment later, holding me tight to her chest. A massive shout sounded behind us, a demonic roar of anger and pain.

"What's going to happen now?" I asked.

"His followers will join him. They will fall for him if we don't stop it. Heaven will turn black as chaos consumes it."

"How do we stop it?"

Josette pointed at Uriel, carrying Obi ahead of us. We were almost clear of the city, making a beeline for his home.

"Uriel will remake the sword. You will be the Lord's champion."

26

We landed just outside the gate to Uriel's home. I looked back and could see Raguel already behind us, more angels joining him as he headed our way. There were a lot of them. Too many. I felt a pang of sadness. They had all been granted a special place in Heaven, and it wasn't good enough for them.

"Get inside," Uriel said. He looked different now. Younger and more alive.

We hurried in past the gate. Uriel swung it closed, holding his hand against it and praying. "Lord, protect me as you have in the past. Grant me your wisdom, that I may do as You will."

The gate began to glow, the millions of runes lighting up along the perimeter. The light extended from the metal upward, into the sky as far as I could see.

Raguel reached us a few seconds later, landing in front of the gate, two hundred angels behind him. They wouldn't fall just for joining him. Not until they attacked their own.

"Uriel," Raguel said. "I will kill you."

"You can't touch me," Uriel replied. "Please, my friends, come inside."

He turned his back on Raguel, entering the house.

"I will kill you," Raguel shouted, stepping forward and slamming his fist against the gate. He fell back in a blue flash, repelled by the power of the runes. "I will kill you as well, Diuscrucis. His power cannot hold forever. Even during the first war, he needed Raphael to protect him."

"Landon, let's go," Josette said, taking my hand. I followed her into the house, as Raguel threw himself against the barrier again.

"He's right, isn't he?" I said. "The barrier won't hold."

"It will hold long enough," Uriel said. "You have the shards?"

I took them from my pocket. The Archangel seemed to freeze again when he saw them, his eyes momentarily growing distant. Then he reached out and took them.

"It will take me some time to reforge the blade."

"What do we do in the meantime?" Obi asked.

"Pray."

Then he vanished, headed toward the forge.

I turned to Josette. "Where is Raphael in all of this?"

"If I had to guess, Michael is delaying him. The First Archangel will not involve himself directly and risk the same fate as Raguel. Instead, he will allow God to decide the matter."

"How can Michael be against God and with God at the same time?"

"He is not against God. He is never against God. That does not mean he agrees with all of His rules and laws and is an unquestioning follower. God does not ask us not to question. He asks us to be pure in our motives. In our hearts and in our souls. As you are. That is why you are His champion."

"Yeah, about that. I don't see how I can be his chosen one, or whatever you want to call it. I'm not a good guy. I'm not fighting for Heaven, and I don't want Him to win."

Josette smiled, looking at me like I was a child. I had always hated when she did that. I didn't realize how much I missed it until now.

"Do you think that God only cares about winning the war against the demons? Perhaps he doesn't care about winning that war at all. Perhaps, there is only one soul He is trying to save right now."

I crinkled my eyebrows. "Mine?"

She shrugged. "The point is, you are trying to guess the will of God. It is impossible to guess. All that we know, all that we can work from, is what we have in front of us. You want to save humankind, the Divine, and Sarah. You want to take in a demon, fall in love with her, and make her good."

"You know about Alyx?"

"I told you, Landon, we are bonded from our time together. Just like you were to Abaddon."

"I never felt you."

"Didn't you?"

I stopped to consider it. Maybe I had, but never realized it.

"I'm not making her good," I said. "She's making herself good. She's trying to be more than she has known. More than Satan made her to be. It isn't always easy."

"Temptations are everywhere. Once, you may have given in to them. But you have learned. So has she."

"I can't be all good. Not now. Not ever. I'm the Diuscrucis. My job is to keep the balance."

"So you say."

"What does that mean?"

She gave me the look a second time. I could feel my face flush.

"I can't tell you everything, Landon. Some things, you must learn for yourself."

"Right. Fine." I stepped toward her. "I missed you."

She stepped toward me, reaching up and putting her arms around me. We held one another for a long moment.

"I missed you, too," she said.

"Aww," Obi said beside us. "You two were always so great together."

We broke the embrace, looking at him.

"In a platonic way," he said. "Like brother and sister. Seriously." He smiled.

"How are you holding up?" I asked.

"Me? I'm just fine. I mean, I'm in Heaven, and still stuck in the middle of a war, but other than that, I'm good."

"You'll be rewarded for your loyalty," Josette said.

"Yeah." He looked up at the ceiling. "I guess I don't need to do that here." He laughed. "I better."

27

I lost track of time, sitting in Uriel's house with Obi and Josette, spending the hours talking about everything. It felt like old times, back when we were all together and things were almost right with the world. Back before the Beast seduced Sarah, and it all began to fall apart.

I told them things I had never spoken about before. I told them of my experiences in the Box, and more specifically my experiences after I got out. I told them of Charis and Clara, and how hard I tried to convince myself to stay away from the fight, to ignore the call to return as the champion of humankind only to find myself neck deep and hurting once more.

Josette was as pragmatic, devout, and wonderful as always. Obi showed a lot of empathy for my plight, even if he didn't completely understand it.

To say the experience was cathartic would be an understatement. It healed me in a way I didn't know I needed to be healed. It helped me to prepare for what I knew was going to come. There was nothing about the future that would be easy, and nothing was going to come up roses.

But at least I knew I wasn't alone.

I felt the clenching in my gut and the shift in the balance when the demons were killed, the scales tilting back towards even. It wasn't as hard to take as the death of the Touched had been, except for the fact that I knew it made Sarah a loose cannon once more, able to target either side with impunity. I realized that was how I had made the angels and demons feel. They never knew which side I was fighting for, and it drove a fear into them that nothing else could. I felt that same fear now.

I went outside to check on Raguel from time to time. He snarled at me every time he saw me, his anger at God growing to envelop an anger at everything. His words became less coherent, his thoughts a jumbled, chaotic mess. His followers seemed to be feeding off the strife, growing more restless. Some attacked the gates and wound up falling. In the beginning, their fate seemed to bother the former Archangel. Later, he seemed to be trying to entice them to attack and to join him in his darkness.

The worst part was that it was becoming more and more obvious that Uriel's protections were failing. The blue glow was less intense, the metals bars becoming bent and worn. If I had to guess, I would say two or three days had passed, and still, there was no word from the Archangel. He remained locked away in the forge, and while we could hear the clang of his hammer on the metal, we had no idea how much progress he was making, or when he would be done.

He had claimed the protections would hold long enough.

I could only hope he was right.

It bothered me that Raphael wasn't going to help us. It bothered me that none of the other angels or archangels were willing to step in. Or even Jesus for that matter, wherever that guy was hiding out. Josette told me that it wasn't safe for them and that their participation wouldn't change the will of God anyway. This was my moment, my destiny. Whatever. I still didn't believe in destiny, and as far as I was concerned, they were all selfish and useless. When I thought about it more, I came to the conclusion that I wasn't much different. All sentient things were selfish to an extent, either except for God or including Him. I couldn't convince myself which it was, and I wasn't going to push that one on Josette.

It was the fifth day, or maybe the sixth, when Uriel finally emerged from the forge into the main part of the house where we had made ourselves comfortable. There was nothing flashy or grand about his entrance. He walked out, bare-chested, dirty, and sweaty, holding the blade wrapped in an oiled cloth. We all stood as he did, and he approached me with a stoic, intense face, turning the weapon over in his hands and extending the hilt.

I was expecting something ornate. It wasn't that at all. It was a simple wooden handle, wrapped in leather to make it easier to grip. There was a single rune etched onto the pommel.

"That is my Mark," he said to me. "It connects me to the blade. I will feel the loss of every soul that you destroy with it."

The statement made me understand his guilt and his sadness. It also made the responsibility of its use crystal clear.

"I understand," I said.

"I know," he replied.

I took the grip, and he pulled the cloth away. For all the handle wasn't, the blade itself was. Perfectly formed and etched with runes, glowing softly with a power I had never felt before. It was awe-inspiring to look at, and frightening to hold.

"Use this tool in the name of the Lord, and you will never falter," he said.

"Amen," Josette added.

I lifted the blade, feeling the perfect balance. He handed me a simple sheath, and I slid the weapon into it.

Then Uriel turned to Obi.

"I have done as you asked," Uriel said, reaching into the pocket of his apron and removing a pair of metal gauntlets.

Obi's eyes grew wide at the sight of them, and he reached out and took them from the Archangel. "Wow."

"What is that?" I asked.

He showed me the gauntlets. The runes from the Fist of God's bolts were obvious on the lines of metal that rest across the knuckles.

"I told you I had an idea for what to do with them," Obi said. "My man Uriel hooked me up."

"They won't harm angels," Uriel said. He smiled. "Demons are another story."

An echoing groan from the front of the house stole the moment.

"The fortifications are breaking down," the Archangel said.

"Just like you knew they would?" I asked.

He shrugged. "You can't hide in here forever, Diuscrucis. Now, go and save the world. You can start with Raguel."

28

It was something right out of Western. The White Hats, which oddly enough included me, stepping out of the saloon and into the street just as the Black Hats, also strangely enough featuring a former Archangel, finally broke down the gates preventing them from reaching us.

They surged forward with a transformed Raguel at their head, two hundred strong. Nearly a quarter of them had already fallen, and by the din raised by the rest, they too were in danger of taking that final step over to the dark side.

"You're too late," I said, withdrawing Uriel's blade from its sheath. The glow of it bothered the fallen angels, causing them to shrink back slightly.

"I'm right on time," Raguel hissed.

He looked even less humanoid than the last time I had checked the perimeter, his legs merged into a single thick tail, his body continuing to grow. He was nearly twenty feet tall and all muscle, a frightening beast of a demon whose anger at God continued to twist and distort him.

"Give me the sword," he demanded. "And I will allow you to return to your world."

"It wasn't going to happen when you still had some good in you," I replied. "Now that you're a raving snake monster? Not a chance in

Heaven."

He hissed again in anger. It was incredible how he had changed, and how his followers continued to support him even as he devolved into something so clearly evil.

"Then I will destroy you," he said.

I lowered the sword to my side, holding it like a gunslinger would hold his piece.

"Go ahead and try," I replied.

He shot forward before I finished speaking, his body moving so quick he nearly had me before I could react. I gathered my power, pushing myself back away from him as Obi and Josette spread to either side. The fallen angels shouted and hissed in their bloodlust, while the other angels stood by.

"Good try," I said, pushing my power into my limbs, giving myself the strength and speed I would need to match the fallen Archangel. Raguel burst forward again, swiping at me with large claws, snapping at me with sharp teeth. I sidestepped his attack, countering with one of my own. He bent back, avoiding it, at the same time his tail came around to sweep my legs.

I pushed off, jumping over them and toward the demon's face. I tried to ram the sword into his head, but he ducked aside, and then lashed out with a claw. It caught me on the side, making a light cut and throwing me into the throng.

Fallen angels reached for me, trying to hold me for their Master. I swung the blade out around me, catching one of them in the chest. I could feel the power run up the blade, a tingling pain that changed into a burning sensation as it made its way into my soul. I grunted as a result, surprised that it hurt as much as it did.

Then I was launching away from the demons, rocketing back toward Raguel. I caught a glimpse of Obi and Josette as I did, wading into the melee and clearing the field of the fallen. Obi's gauntlets hit the demons in flashes of blue light, pulling them easily off their feet and leaving them steaming with sulfur.

Raguel faced me, his hands shifting to block my incoming attack. I reached out with my power, pulling myself sideways as I neared him, throwing my sword arm out and slicing across his outstretched hand. A neat line opened up beneath it, and my body writhed as some of the former Archangel's power was absorbed. I landed on the ground in a ball, struggling to deal with the input. Had Uriel messed something up, or was it supposed to feel like that?

Either way, I barely had time to recover before Raguel was on me, his tail whipping out and trying to wrap around me. I rolled away on the ground before pulling myself to my feet and facing off with him once more.

He had shrunk at least a foot after my first attack, the reduction in his power causing a reduction in size. As my pain vanished, I could feel the increase in my overall strength, and I pushed it through me, bunching myself and launching toward the demon again.

He hissed as I launched a series of quick strikes, managing to duck back from them as I moved in, keeping himself out of range. He tried to get his tail in play again to knock me down, forcing me to pause the attack to avoid it and getting himself back on the offensive as I did. I barely got the blade up in time to deflect one set of claws, and then had to throw myself aside to keep from being bitten. I rolled to my feet, taking only a moment before deciding to go for the finish.

I gathered myself and sprang at him again, launching myself into the air toward his head. He was anticipating the move, since it was the third time I had done it, and he jerked aside accordingly.

Only I was anticipating his reaction, and I had already released Uriel's blade, using my power to throw it out to the right, directly into the space he was now occupying. I could see his eyes grow as he caught sight of the sword. Then it was sticking into one of those eyes, burying itself all the way to the hilt.

I landed unarmed on the other side of Raguel, turning and facing him. His body was shrinking, the sword crackling with his power. Whoever touched the hilt next would be able to claim it as their own.

One of the fallen angels saw it and turned to reach for it. Obi grabbed him a moment later, lifting him easily with the gauntlets and throwing him aside.

"I love these things," he said.

I moved toward Raguel. His body was almost back to human size, the sword sticking absurdly from his head. It clattered to the ground a few seconds later as the body vanished into ash.

I stood over it, looking down. I knew how much it was going to hurt to lift it and claim the power. It caused me to hesitate, and maybe that was the point. It shouldn't be easy or painless to destroy other souls. It should hurt. It should force you to think before you did it.

I reached for it slowly, trying to prepare myself for the hurt to come. I didn't want this, but I needed it. There was no other way to save human or Divine from what would otherwise come. There was no other way to match Sarah, whether I took her life or somehow saved it.

I put my hand on the hilt. The sigil flared, and the pain coursed through me. So did the power. I felt it acutely like I was winding a massive ball and had just added a few more layers.

Then it was done. I stood in the center of over one hundred angels, all of whom seemed to be breaking free of a spell. They stared at me in reverent silence, as though I was their savior and not the killer of their idol.

"Well done, my friend," Josette said, coming to stand beside me.

"Well done, indeed," Uriel said, approaching from the entrance to his home.

"Does that mean the war in Heaven is over?" I asked.

"Only time will tell us that, I'm afraid," Uriel replied. "But it is a good sign, a clear signal that God supports the Diuscrucis, and continues to watch over us and uphold His laws."

"You should have told me it was going to hurt," I said.

"You should have expected it," Uriel replied.

I nodded somberly. He was right.

"We need to return to the mortal realm," I said. "We seem to have lost our ride."

I was looking at Josette when I said it. Of course, I wanted her to come back with us.

"I'm sorry, Landon," she said. "I cannot. My vow is to remain with the Sisterhood."

"I understand," I replied. "Will I ever see you again?"

"I don't know. That depends on you, I suppose."

I knew what she meant. I nodded and then embraced her.

"I love you," I said, feeling my eyes moistening once more.

"I love you, too," she replied.

"If I can save Sarah, I will."

"I know."

"I will return you to your realm," Uriel said. "Is there anywhere in particular you would like to go?"

"Mexico," I said. "Home."

"Think of it, and it will be so."

He started reaching out, one hand for me and one for Obi.

"Goodbye, Josette," I said.

"Goodbye, Landon," she replied.

Then Uriel touched me, and I was home.

29

"Landon," Alichino said as Obi and I made our way into the control room of the underground lair. "Where have you been?"

The room was filled with former slaves of Espanto, Turned men and women who had chosen to remain with Alyx when she took control of the place. They monitored different data sources, tapping into phone calls, hacking computer systems, and otherwise working almost nonstop to keep the information flowing.

That was the true currency for the Divine on Earth. The difference between being master or slave. How much more you knew than anyone else, and what you could do with that knowledge. Espanto had gained the position he did more because of his ability to capture and parse information than anything else.

Of course, having Alyx to do his dirty work hadn't hurt.

"Heaven," I replied. "Have you heard from Dante recently?"

The demon ignored the first part as if I went to Heaven every day. "Yeah, he's been stopping by every few hours to see if you're back. I forgot where you told me you went last time I talked to you, but he knew. He made me write it all down." He took a piece of paper from his pocket and scanned it. "Oh yeah, now I remember. He sent you to find a way to

Heaven. I guess you did?"

"I did."

"He'll be happy to hear that. We've got trouble, Landon. Big trouble."

I already knew that. Just because I had the sword didn't mean we were on the verge of victory. Far from it.

"Sarah?"

"Among other things."

"I felt the balance shift."

"Yeah. You need to see this."

He wandered over to one of the workstations. The Turned woman in front of it swiveled her chair to face us. She was young and attractive. All of Espanto's former servants were.

"Show him what you showed me," the demon said.

"Yes, my Lord," the woman said.

I glared at Alichino, whose leathery snout flushed. "I didn't tell her to call me that," he complained. "Did I?"

"You suggested that when Mistress Alyx is not present, we should refer to you as-"

"Well, it doesn't matter, does it?" Alichino said, interrupting nervously.

I continued staring at him. All of the Turned here had been abused by Espanto in one way or another, and subservient monikers weren't going to help them get past it. Alichino could be helpful most of the time, but he was still a demon.

"Fine," he said. "I just wanted to know what it was like for someone to call me Master."

"Now you know," I said. "If I hear someone call you that again-"

"Okay, okay. I get it. No need to get huffy about it." He pointed at the screen. "Let's stay focused, huh?"

I looked over at the screen. There were two satellite images displaying on it, side by side. The left side showed what looked like an old military bunker somewhere in the middle of a forest. The right side showed the same bunker, but the forest looked as if it had been burned away from it.

"I take it that isn't from a forest fire?"

"It's what's left of a demon army," he said. "That's why the area around the bunker is toast, and the rest of it is intact."

"Sarah?"

"Yeah. We got the report over the wire. The bunker belonged to a Fiend Warlord in Somalia. He had a whole militia of Turned soldiers hiding out there, along with a Hell rift that he could use to ferry demons up. He was about to launch an assault on a rival warlord. That never happened."

"Sarah killed them all on her own?" Obi asked.

"No, she wasn't alone. A fallen angel was with her. One with a sword for a hand."

"Adam. He's helping her kill angels and demons?"

"No," I said. "I don't think he knows what she did to the angels. I think I may have been wrong about him. Or mostly wrong. He hates me, sure, but maybe he still loves God despite his fall. Look at what happened to Raguel. His uncontrolled anger turned him into a monster. That hasn't happened to Adam. Plus, he was in contact with that blue-eyed angel from the Mass, and she saved Alfred from Sarah, and Sarah killed her. Not the kind of actions you would expect from someone who was in on it."

"True," Obi said. "So Adam is fallen, but he's helping Sarah kill demons. Do you think she told him she's fighting for the good guys? I don't see how he would buy that?"

"Help me kill demons, and maybe God will change his mind and reinstate you," I said. "If he were desperate enough, I could see how that might work."

"I just can't believe Sarah is capable of all of this," Obi said. "I never knew she was hurting so bad."

"Me neither, and that's my failure. My cross to bear. We have to take it where we are right now. The rest of it won't matter until we catch up to her." I looked at the satellite imagery again. "I felt the balance adjust. How many demons?"

"Three thousand?" Alichino guessed. "Give or take."

"What about the Turned? I don't see any bodies."

"I think they're all inside."

"Any ripple effect?"

"Of course," Alichino said. "The rival Warlord has claimed the territory. Other factions are gearing up to challenge. A lot more people are going to die because of this."

I shook my head, frustrated. "More innocent people caught up in the Divine war games. And we don't know where Sarah is, or what she's going to do next. Will she go after another group of Turned? Will she hit a seraph Sanctuary? Or will she go for more demons?"

"We need to find her before she can do either," Obi said.

"A good thought, but I don't know how we can," I replied.

"I'll see if I can dig anything else up. Maybe there's another clue on SamChan."

"Okay. Allie, can you get Obi set up with a workstation and access to everything?"

"Yeah, sure."

"What are you going to do?" Obi asked.

"Wait for Dante. I need to talk to him. After that?" I held up Uriel's sword. "Start killing Divine."

30

Not that I was eager to kill Divine.

For one thing, I didn't enjoy destroying anything. Ending Raguel was its own bitter pill. The Archangel had been a loyal servant of God for eons, and his fall had happened so fast and been so complete. In my mind, I had still killed an angel, not a demon. In my mind, his end was more directly my fault than any other. He had turned because I had failed.

Maybe that wasn't true, but it was hitting my conscience regardless. The thought of going out there and finding Divine to slaughter to increase my own power? That was like asking a nun for sex. I didn't want more power; I wanted less. Especially with the latest understanding that my very existence was part of the growing instability in our corner of the universe.

And then there was the fact that whatever I did, Sarah was going to do the opposite. If I killed demons, she would go after angels. The more power I absorbed, the more she would remove from the other end. She was still part-mortal, but she could feel the balance as well as I could. Probably better. She would know what I was doing. She would understand that part of my plan. Would she try to stop me, or was there a part of her that wanted me to win?

Whichever way it went, I needed to be ready. I couldn't rush in and start claiming power without giving real consideration to whose power I was taking. Just like wiping a fiend's zone of control away in Somalia was going to cause a wider outbreak of violence, taking out the wrong Divine could create ripples that only added to the chaos.

It was a level of finesse that I wasn't really prepared for. One that I wasn't sure I was even capable of.

Thus, Dante.

I had no idea how long I was going to have to wait for him, and to be honest the waiting sucked. I made my way down to the training area of the facility, where Espanto had taught Alyx to kill more efficiently, more like an assassin than a were. It was a grim place, filled with sharp objects, the walls bloodstained from the targets the demon had placed for his slave. It was an unnerving reminder, but it also gave me a sense of purpose. I wasn't looking to destroy Divine for my sake. I was trying to save everyone else the only way I could.

I practiced with the blade for a while, going through the motions I had learned from Josette, whipping the sword around like a badass ninja. The exertion brought minimal calm to my mind and body, but it did serve to pass the time relatively efficiently. I was in the middle of one of the more difficult seraphim forms when the door to the room opened, and Dante walked in.

I froze mid-sweep, throwing the blade down. It buried itself four inches deep into the foam mat and cement floor below it, sticking straight up like Excalibur. I had already dealt with that blade. Frankly, I was pretty sick of them all.

"Signore," Dante said, smiling. "I see your efforts in Heaven were successful."

"Mixed bag," I replied. "I got the sword, but the seraphim are a mess. There may or may not be an extended conflict continuing up there because of what Sarah is doing down here."

The smile vanished. "A war in Heaven is a problem for all of us."

"I know. I figure the best way to stop it is to take care of things here. I got to see Josette while I was there, so at least something good came out of it."

The smile didn't return. "She is well?"

"As well as can be expected. Of course, she's worried about Sarah."

"As are we all. Alichino handed me your message as soon as I arrived. I'm surprised that you wanted my advice."

"Why wouldn't I? I thought I could handle things without you. I can't. I have the sword, and I already absorbed a fallen archangel's power with it. It isn't enough. It isn't close to enough. I need to kill more Divine, and the thought of it is making me sick to my stomach. Worse, I have no idea who to target that won't cause a major backlash."

"I understand." He rubbed at his chin, considering my words. "It would make sense then that we would target the most powerful demons who aren't in control of large territories of their own."

"But then Sarah will start attacking the angels again."

"I know. The problem for you, signore, is that all angels on Earth have the same overall level of Divine power. Some may have slightly less depending on how many they have Touched, but the difference for you will be negligible. Demons, on the other hand, have a massive variability. One which you can exploit."

"Except the most powerful demons are usually in control of a large number of less powerful demons. Or they spend most of their time in Hell."

"A difficult position to work around, but not impossible. Archfiends will often summon stronger demons to fight for them when the need arises. We need to create a mapping of this information and make an attempt to predict when and where an inter-demon feud will occur. Then we can intervene."

"If I remove the strongest player, it will change the outcome of the battle. That could be a problem."

"Why should it? Does it truly matter who wins or loses if both sides are evil?"

I thought about it for a minute. "Maybe not. Still, we could be waiting days to put something like that together. I need to move on this now before Sarah forces our hand."

Dante resumed rubbing at his chin. "That is true. This is quite a bind, indeed."

He began pacing the room, not reacting to the visuals at all. He kept his head down, his hand working on his face.

"You will need to maintain the balance on your own. Attack angels and demons randomly. When Sarah sees there is no order to it, she will be unable to counter. You may also succeed in slowing her down."

I thought about it for a minute. "Or we might end up pushing things too far if we wind up attacking the same side at the same time. Is that a risk we want to take?"

"It is another option. I will continue to consider."

He paced again, up and down the space a hundred times or more. I stood beside the sword, waiting patiently for him to come up with something. Maybe I could have brainstormed it too, but I knew he would figure something out. He had hundreds of years more experience than me.

He stopped at last, looking up at me, a measure of discomfort on his aged face.

"I can think of another approach, signore, but I'm not sure if it will meet our needs."

"Which is?"

"A son of Lucifer is walking this realm, are they not?"

"You mean Zifah?" I said. I wasn't sure I liked where this was going to go. "Yeah."

"He will be quite powerful in his own right. He also double-crossed you, and his only affiliation is with Gervais." He smiled. "Who is also rather powerful, I might add."

I couldn't argue the logic or the motive. I also couldn't argue that I would love the chance to use those two the way they used me, and to put an end to both of them once and for all.

"A good reason to take them out, and under most circumstances I would agree that it's a pretty solid way to go. There's only one small problem with that."

"The Fist of God."

"Yes. I can't defeat it."

"Are you certain?"

"I'm oh-for-one so far."

"One interaction is a small sample size, signore. Besides, your power has already increased, and we should be able to improve it a little more before you have to confront the Fist or the demons or Sarah. Yes, an idea has come to me. I told you that I could be useful to you, signore. Now is my chance to prove it."

31

"It's not like it's just magic," Alichino said, shaking his head. "I mean, I don't just type 'Fist of God' into the computer and a bunch of results come up like this setup is freaking Google."

I was back in the command center with Obi, Dante, and Alichino. The poet had approached the demon with his idea, which first and foremost consisted of finding out who Gervais and Zifah might have been in contact with over the last few days. Even with the Fist of God, the pair would need allies if they were going to try to get to Sarah, if for no other reason than to distract or delay her.

"You don't need to find the Fist," Dante argued. "You need to find out who these two demons might have been in contact with."

"And how am I supposed to do that? I've been trying for weeks and haven't gotten squat."

"That was before Sarah started turning things upside down," I said. "If they're going to make a move, they're going to do it soon."

"I can help you track them down, little guy," Obi said.

Alichino shot his snout toward Obi. "Little guy? I don't need your help. This equipment is the latest and greatest, and I've optimized it with some extra data processing algorithms that increase parsing speed by thirty percent."

"So you can just type 'Zifah' into it, and a bunch of results should come up," I suggested.

He turned his stink-eye my way. "Funny, Landon. Really. You should be a comedian. I'm going to have to look through all of the meta-data we've collected from the archfiends around the world. Gervais wouldn't waste his time with anyone too far down the chain. Three, four days should be enough, don't you think?"

"Probably," I said, noticing that Obi had gone back to the workstation the demon had set up for him. "How long do you think this is going to take?"

Alichino shrugged. "Five, six hours at least. I have to cross-reference datasets, reindex the blobs, that sort of thing. I know it seems simple, but really it's-"

"Got it," Obi said. "Phone record from yesterday."

"What?" Alichino said. "How did you find it that fast?"

"Typed 'Fist of Gervais' into the search box," Obi replied.

"You're kidding," I said. That was what Zifah had called it during our little meet.

"Nope. Got a hit right away. Some archfiend in Indonesia named Srizyl had a chat with your friend Zifah about the Fist. Apparently, Gervais is claiming that they can make more of them, and offered her one in exchange for her assistance in capturing Sarah."

"And she believes him?"

"Apparently enough that they've scheduled a demo for later tonight so that they can show off the Fist."

Was this going to be easier than I had thought? "You're kidding."

"Still nope, man."

"Signore," Dante said. "You know what they say about things that appear too good to be true."

"Yeah, I know, and this fits that bill perfectly. The only thing that has me thinking that it might not be a trap is that the call was made before I got back from Heaven with the sword. How can you set someone up for a date and time you can't be sure about?"

"If anyone could do it, Gervais can," Obi said.

"If Gervais didn't want you to know about it, he would have used a messenger," Dante said. "Since he didn't, consider that he does."

"He's hoping that once I have the sword, I'll come to him with it. Maybe he already guessed either he or Zifah would be a target. We have to assume he'll be prepared, whether the meet is specifically designed to lure me in or not. If he could show off the power of the Fist against me, that would be a pretty good sell to get this Srizyl on board."

"If he even intends to make a deal with her," Obi said.

"He can't make a deal," I replied. "Nobody can recreate the Fist. The archangel who made the original scripture is dead, and there isn't another like her that can replicate it. Cain may have modified it somewhat, but he's gone, too."

"Which only makes this more obviously a trap," Dante said. "Gervais has taken advantage of you too many times for you to fall for this."

"I wouldn't call it falling for. It was your idea to take out whichever archfiends Gervais tried to ally with to build my strength, and we can still do that."

"While being attacked by the Fist?"

"If that's what it takes, yes. I can avoid it while I go after Srizyl. Once I have her power, it will even the odds a bit more."

"Enough to fight it? Enough to kill Zifah?"

I glared at Dante. I was getting frustrated with him. He wanted me to take this approach, and now he was questioning every part of it.

"I need to get a hold of Zifah if I'm going to level up enough to challenge Sarah. If they want me to come to them, then that's what I'm going to have to do. It's not like our other ideas were much better."

"Landon," Obi said.

"Signore," Dante said.

As much as I disliked their hesitation, I also understood it. Being forced to put too much faith in Gervais is what had cost me the Fist in the first place. Even so, it had to be done. Again.

The difference? Maybe this time, I could go in a little more prepared. Maybe this time, I could outthink the demon and come out ahead. Gervais would do anything he had to in order to get his hands on the sword. That was something I might be able to use.

With a little help from my friends, of course.

Extinction

32

My friends, and some other people who weren't quite my friends.

Whenever I needed something I didn't have and didn't know where to get, I went to see the Nicht Creidem. In this case, I needed two things from them, neither of which I was certain they could provide, but both of which would prove invaluable to surviving the obvious mess I was going to put myself in the middle of.

As if I wasn't already up to my neck in it.

There was no part of me that really wanted to visit Indonesia and Gervais' apparent efforts to wrap another noose around my throat. There was also no part of me that could accept the alternatives that Dante and I had already discussed. Zifah was the perfect target. I knew it. Dante knew it. Gervais knew it. When Zifah had shown up in France? That was all part of the game. I was sure of that now. They wanted me to know the score. It was a big fat hello, don't forget about me. Come and get it when you think you're ready. I was sure the demons had plenty of tricks up their sleeves.

It meant I needed to gather a few more tricks under mine.

I had Dante poof me back to New York, dropping me in the middle of a dark alley as the sun was setting across the Hudson.

"I'll meet you back here in two hours," I said to him. "Don't be late."

"Of course, signore," he replied. Then he vanished again.

I headed down the alley toward the street. I had switched my dress to include a long vinyl duster, the kind most often seen in science-fiction flicks. It was fitted where it needed to be and loose where it had to be to hide Uriel's sword in close enough proximity that I could grab it and use it should the need arise. Part of me was hoping it would. I would take any added juice I could get. Then again, I didn't want to make a scene.

There were a lot of people on the streets this time of night. It felt good to insert myself into the middle of them, to walk among them as if I were almost normal. Sometimes I really missed being mortal. Missed being ignorant about the war between Heaven and Hell. This was one of those times.

It got me thinking more about my place in the Universe, and about what Sarah had said. I didn't belong here. We didn't belong here. I already knew there was only one ending for me. One way that I could go when this was done. To the stars with Charis and Clara. It didn't frighten me. I knew it was a better end than many experienced. Still, I felt a little cheated. I had never asked to be drawn into this. I had never wanted to die and come back as humankind's champion. I was so young and had gotten so few years.

Boo hoo, lots of people died even younger. I got mad for feeling sorry for myself and stopped that train of thought dead. I was here for a reason, and apparently, God Himself had put His faith in me. That was a scary thought, and at the same time comforting. I wasn't His biggest fan. Before I had died, I had questioned His existence all the time. He was on my side regardless. Who would have thought?

I crossed a few blocks until I reached the outside of the cab terminal. A few yellows were making their way in and out of the facility, and I noticed them noticing me as I reached the front door. All of the drivers here were Nicht, and I knew some of them would recognize that I was out of place as soon as they saw me. I half-expected them to slam on the brakes and do something stupid, but something in their brains told them to stay out of it. I was grateful for that.

"Who the hell are you?" a heavyset, balding man in a greasy

Extinction

wifebeater asked as I entered the garage. He was standing next to a cab that had its hood open, a wrench in his hand.

"I'm looking for Bianca," I said.

"How do you know Bianca?"

"We're old friends. My name is-"

"Landon Hamilton," Bianca said, appearing in a doorway a dozen feet away. "We are not friends."

I looked over at her and smiled. "You remembered me?"

She held something up, turning it around so I could see it. A still from security camera footage, with my face clearly visible in it.

"I had my people grab this while you were still here the last time. I've been carrying it with me since, so I would know you in case you turned up again."

"Smart," I said. And resourceful. I was fortunate none of the angels or demons had thought of it.

"For mortals to fight this war, we have to be. But like I said, we aren't friends. Especially since you got Bradford killed."

"Bradford got himself killed," I said. "And he died saving the city from Abaddon."

"Which is the only reason I don't sick every Nicht in this place on you."

"That isn't the only reason."

She smiled. "Maybe. Maybe not. You only come by when you need something. What is it this time?"

"You've been following the news?"

"Television? Hell, no."

"The real news," I said. "Italy? Somalia?"

Her face turned dark. "Yes. I take it you know something about it?"

"I know everything about it."

"Do tell."

"Not so fast. I'm working on the cause, but you're right, I need something from you. Two things, actually."

"You can't have any more of my people. They have a knack for dying around you."

I felt a slight sting at those words. Not because of Bradford. Because of Elyse.

"Not people," I said. "Artifacts, if you have them."

"If I don't?"

"Maybe you can tell me where to find them?"

"Maybe. What's in it for me?"

"The usual. The survival of humankind."

"You don't do anything small, do you, Diuscrucis?"

"Not lately. Believe me; I'd prefer to be out chasing vampires, too."

"Yeah, well, I need a little more to go on than the survival of humankind. You're still half demon, which means you lie."

"Only by necessity."

"Whatever."

I laughed at that, and then removed Uriel's sword from my back, sliding it a few inches from its sheath. Bianca's eyes lit up at the sight of it.

"I'll give you anything you want in exchange for that."

"It isn't for trade. Where I got it is the reason I'm showing it to you. This is Uriel's sword, the one that he forged for Michael during the First War."

"Where did you get it?"

"From Uriel." I paused for effect. "In Heaven."

Her awe was mixed with her disbelief. "You went to Heaven? He gave that to you?"

"Yes, and yes. Because what we're up against is bigger than Heaven and Hell, good and evil. I know you hate the Divine, and that Joe always wanted to destroy them all. The thing is, without the Divine, humankind dies, too. My sister, Sarah, intends to kill every last one unless I stop her. I can only stop her if you help me."

Bianca was silent for a moment. She stared at the sword, and then at me. Asking the Nicht Creidem to help me stop the extinction of the Divine was a risk in itself. The whole reason they existed was to get Heaven and Hell to stop meddling in the affairs of mortals.

"Killing Divine?" she said.

"Yes."

Extinction

"If the angels and demons are gone, why does humankind go too?"

"We're too deeply enmeshed for the balance to be maintained without the opposing forces."

"Bullshit."

"Is it? What happens when you die?"

She thought about it. "So?"

"What happens if God is dead? What happens if Hell no longer exists?"

"I don't know."

"Your soul becomes trapped in your corpse," I said. "Forever."

Her face paled. "What?"

"Think about that. Your soul has a consciousness of its own. When your shell dies, it wakes up. It wants to be free, but without a Divine hand to guide it, there's nowhere for it to go. There's no way for it to escape. An eternity imprisoned."

I wasn't sure if any of that were true or not. It sounded good, and Bianca was buying it.

"Our mission is to destroy the Divine," she said. "Now you're saying we'd be screwing ourselves?"

"Your war is as endless as theirs, and you know it," I said. "The Nicht Creidem are an important part of the balance, just like everything else."

She bit her lip, thinking about it. I waited patiently. I knew she would break.

"I hate you," she said.

"I know," I replied.

"What do you need from me?"

33

"I've searched through the inventory, Landon," Bianca said. "The only one we have is in our Berlin facility."

"Can you tell them I'm coming?" I asked.

"Are you kidding? I'll be executed for treason. I'm going to get in enough trouble for helping you already."

"I'm trying to save your life."

"The Nicht Creidem are like any other group; we have people that run the gamut from right to left. Me, I lean more liberal, which is lucky for you. I'm open to the idea that we're just a cog in the machine. Berlin? They're a bunch of tight-asses over there, and they aren't going to go for the idea that we can't survive without the Divine."

"So you're telling me I can't get what I need?"

"I'm telling you that I can't help you get it. You're going to have to do some convincing of your own."

I knew what she meant by convincing. "And you're okay with that?"

"I don't love the idea, but if half of what you told me is true, then our options are pretty limited. I, for one, don't want to end up stuck in this body long after the sell-by date, if you know what I mean."

"What about the other item?"

She pushed her chair back away from her computer and stood up. "That I can help you with. Follow me."

We left her office in the garage, heading to an elevator in the back. The doors clanged shut, and she pressed the button for the bottom floor fifteen times. The elevator beeped as if she had just armed a nuclear device, and then we started to descend.

"I can give you the coordinates to the Berlin facility. Other than that, you're on your own."

"And I didn't get the intel from you?"

"That's right."

"What if your people talk?"

"They won't talk. We kill snitches. No, if they don't like it they'll challenge me directly." She smiled innocently. "And then they'll die."

I had seen her punch down a reinforced door without much effort. She had the tatts and the experience to back up her sass.

The elevator went down a good twenty floors, even though the garage was only five deep. The doors opened and fed out into a sterile white corridor. I was familiar with Nicht Creidem lairs. It seemed they had all been constructed from the same set of blueprints.

She led me through the corridors, into a small room with a guard stationed at its head. He seemed uncomfortable to see me, even if he didn't know who I was, but he opened the vault at Bianca's request without hesitation. We entered the storage area, and she ran her finger along the rows of storage safes until she found the one she wanted.

"Here it is," she said, putting her fingerprint to it to open it.

The cabinet slid open, and she lifted a flat, runed stone from it. She held it up to me.

"We got this from Reyzl's place after you took care of him for us. It was part of his private collection. Put it to the sword, and it will create a glamour of it that even Lucifer himself wouldn't be able to see through."

"You're sure?"

"We pride ourselves on knowing how all this stuff works."

"Do you have anything else I might like?"

She glared at me. "Don't push it. I'm going to have to log this thing as it is, and I don't want to put 'lent to the Diuscrucis' in the notes."

"There's a decent chance you won't get it back."

"Don't remind me."

"I appreciate your help."

"Yeah, well, I hope I don't get in too much trouble for this. I might be forgiven if you really do save the world."

"That's the plan."

She stared at me. "I don't know why I trust you, or why I'm doing this. You've changed since the last time I saw you. I can see that much."

The statement caught me by surprise. "Changed?" I didn't feel that different. "How?"

"I'm not sure. It's kind of like the difference between thinking you're doing the right thing and knowing you're doing the right thing."

"Confidence?" I asked.

"With a side of focus, yeah. That's part of it. It isn't the whole thing, but close enough."

She led me from the vault, back to the elevator and up to the garage. We returned to her office, and she pulled up the coordinates for the Berlin base on the screen.

"Take a look, commit it to memory. You didn't get this from me."

"Won't they know you accessed the file?"

"They'll know someone in this facility did. I'll make sure to send them a package, so it looks like we were just cross-checking the address. Like I said, you didn't get it from me."

"Right. Thanks again."

"You can thank me by getting things back under control. Don't take this the wrong way, but I hope I never see you again."

I nodded. "I hope you never see me again, too."

"Good luck, Landon."

She leaned up and kissed me on the cheek. Then I left the garage without another word, heading back to the alley at a fast walk. I arrived with ten minutes to spare and spent them scanning the rooftops and fire escapes. It was strange to me not to see any Divine around. No angels, no demons. At this time of night? I had been back in the city for two years. I couldn't remember the last time the place had been so deserted, or if it ever had.

I knew it was because of Sarah. Any Divine with any sense was laying low, staying out of sight and waiting for this latest storm to blow over. Both sides had likely heard what she had done in Italy and Somalia. Neither wanted to be next.

I couldn't blame them.

Part of me expected Sarah to come swooping down out of nowhere. To take me by surprise and put an end to the game right then and there. I felt edgy at the idea of it, created by the void left by the absence of other Divine. This was how the world would be if Sarah had her way, at least until it all began to crumble and die. It was cold and frightening, lonely and sad. The Sleeping might not know the Divine existed, but they would feel it too. They would know the world was ending; they just wouldn't quite know how or why.

I shivered when Dante reappeared in the alley, in the same spot he had vanished earlier. That's how off-kilter the atmosphere had left me.

"Signore, are you well?" he asked.

"I'll survive," I replied.

"How did it go?"

"I got the mimic stone."

"What about the third eye?"

"Bradford was the best they could offer last time, so I wasn't expecting much. Bianca did tell me there's a ring in the Berlin facility. I have to go and get it. I could use a lift."

"Of course. All of my life I have dreamed of being your personal teleportation device."

I eyed Dante, raising an eyebrow. "Sarcasm?"

"An attempt to create levity through humor."

"It works for Obi. For you? Not so much."

"I will leave it to him in the future then." He put his hand on my shoulder. "Shall we?"

"Let's go."

34

Dante delivered me a short distance from the facility, which turned out to be a relatively nondescript high-rise in downtown Berlin.

"Are you sure you need the eye?" he asked as we both looked at the building.

Even from the distance, I could see there were half a dozen men in suits milling around outside trying to look like they weren't part of the security detail, which consisted of another half a dozen men in uniforms. Judging by the location, this Nicht Creidem hideaway was a higher value target than the garage in New York would ever be.

"Not completely," I replied. "I'm working on the assumption that the Fist can go invisible because of Rebecca's natural ghost power. If I'm right, getting my hands on an eye will lessen the handicap quite a bit."

"It is a big assumption. Even if the Fist is using her power, it may not be manifesting the same way."

"I know, but we need an edge if we're going to have a chance, and this is the only thing I can think of."

"It is not a bad idea," Dante said. "But that is only the outside security. I imagine it is tighter on the inside."

"You don't think I can make it through? I absorbed the power of an archangel."

"One simple artifact used in a clever way can negate any amount of power."

Just like the Box had been able to hold the Beast, and Abaddon before him. Of course, there had been nothing simple about the Box.

"I know. I'll be careful."

"I'm not able to penetrate their defenses against the Divine, but I will wait for you here, signore. I will be prepared for a quick getaway if you need it."

"Thanks. Wish me luck."

"Good luck, Landon."

I headed down the street, away from the Lord of Purgatory. I glanced back over my shoulder once as I closed in on the building, just in time to see him duck into a coffee shop.

Typical.

"Excuse me," I said, reaching one of the supposed-to-be undercover security guards.

He turned to look at me, his head tilting to the side like a dog as his secondary senses registered confusion about my nature.

"My name is Landon. Also generally known as the Diuscrucis. I need to borrow something from you."

I had told Dante I would be careful. This wasn't exactly careful, but it was a lot more efficient.

He said something in German that sounded like 'red alert' or 'alarm.' Then he tried to punch me.

I stepped out of the way, grabbing his wrist and throwing him to the ground behind me. I could hear him cry out as he bounced into a passerby, and then more shouts started going up. The uniformed guards were drawing their guns while civilians did their best to clear the area.

I put my hands up. "I just want to talk. There's no need to-"

I saw the muzzle flash, heard the report, and felt the bullet enter my chest. It hurt going in, and it hurt as I pushed it back out. I pulled my power up ahead of me, catching the follow-up volley, slowing the slugs to zero velocity before they could touch me again.

"I tried to do this the easy way," I said, even as I threw the captured lead out ahead of me. It whipped back toward its origin, catching most of the shooters in their hands and causing them to drop their weapons.

I began walking toward the entrance. The guys in the suits charged toward me, producing blessed and cursed knives as they did. I gathered my power close, waiting for them to close in before pushing it out around me and into the ground. They tumbled over against the shockwave, leaving my path clear. I didn't slow as I reached the uniformed guards, who were on their knees near the entrance clutching bleeding hands.

I went inside, throwing my power up again as a second round of gunfire erupted against me. I spotted the dozen or so Nicht Creidem soldiers on the inside, outfitted in bulletproof vests and dark fatigues, carrying heavy rifles and swords on their hips.

"Hold on a minute," I shouted again, this time in German. "I didn't come here to fight."

They didn't react to my words, lowering their guns when they saw how ineffective they were and charging at me with swords. Bullets couldn't kill any Divine, but they were able to slow some down and wound them enough to make the close range stabbing easier.

I pulled my power close, running it through my veins and into my muscles, using it to toughen my skin and increase my strength. I could feel the increased energy I had captured from Raguel, and I flexed my limbs in response to the power.

The first guard reached me, his sword flashing in a quick maneuver that I had no trouble following. I batted the blade aside with a bare hand, knocking it from his grip, and then shoved him with the opposite hand. I pushed harder than I expected, sending him hurting into another guard and knocking them both down.

I felt something hit my back, and I turned to see a runed sword against my firmer flesh. I grabbed it and snapped it in half, and then threw my power out below me, pushing myself into the air and across the lobby, landing on the reception desk.

"Seriously," I said again. "Just wait a second. I want to borrow something. Nobody else has to get hurt."

Extinction

There was still no reply. The guards came at me again, trying to coordinate their movements to overwhelm me. I threw my power out again, knocking them over a second time. This was a fight they couldn't win, not unless they had a prison to catch me in or a weapon that could deflect my power.

I hopped off the desk and headed for the elevators. One of the guards charged me a third time. I slapped the sword from his hand and grabbed him, turning him easily and taking his head in my arms, positioned so it would be too easy to break.

"Why won't you listen?" I asked.

"I told them not to," Sarah said.

She swept in through the front of the building, her wings flashing as they reflected the light.

I froze, letting the captured Nicht Creidem fall to the ground in front of me.

"Uriel's blade, brother?" she said, landing between me and the exit. "Your intention is to kill me and take my power?"

She sounded hurt.

Bianca had done a good job convincing me she was playing for the right team.

Damn.

"You were going to kill me back in Italy," I said.

"Out of necessity."

"Same here."

"I'm trying to save humankind. Isn't that our job?"

"You said I was breaking the balance, not keeping it."

"Yes."

"So are you."

"Yes."

That answer stopped me in my tracks.

"Are you surprised?" she said. "I know how my story ends, Landon. I've seen it, remember? When all the others are gone, when you're gone, I will be gone, too. That is the way it must be."

"If you destroy all of the Divine, there will be nothing left for anyone."

"I don't believe that. I have seen it."

"You haven't looked far enough. Things won't fall apart in an instant, but they will over time. Everything is connected. Everything is related. You can't kill an archfiend without another taking their place. You can't destroy two realms without destroying the third."

"It will all be destroyed if I do nothing," she said. "How can I stand by and watch everything die because of me?"

"Because of you?" I asked.

"My existence caused your existence. I helped unlock the Beast. I was the reason you stayed when you could have left this world behind."

I felt my anger growing. "Is this about fate or guilt?"

"It is about what is and must be. The Nicht Creidem seek the end of the Divine, and with their help, I will achieve it."

"You aren't listening," I said.

"No. You aren't listening, brother. There are always three, remember? You cannot change what is or what will be."

She wasn't making any sense. Whatever was in her that was causing her to do this, it had stolen who she had been. The realization was as painful as if she were already dead.

I looked over her shoulder. I wasn't ready to fight her, which meant I needed to get away, the third eye be damned. The problem was that Dante couldn't pass through the entrance, his Divine power blocked by hidden runes and scripture. But if I could reach the other side, he could bamf us out.

All I had to do to reach the other side was time walk myself.

"Let us finish what we started, brother," she said, moving toward me, her wings wrapping around her, the tips pointed my way. "Dante can't intervene this time."

"You're making a mistake, Sarah," I said. "A huge mistake. I know you think you're doing the right thing, but you aren't. You're going to destroy everything. You're going to become everything your father wants you to be. Everything the Beast tried to be."

"You don't know anything about it," she screamed, so loudly it cracked the glass inside the lobby. "I am saving these people from us, and from him. I am protecting them from our chaos and destruction and death. I am sparing them from our reckless, wanton ambivalence."

"You aren't," I said calmly. "You're killing them."

"No," she replied softly. "I'm only killing you."

She swept forward, so fast I could barely follow the motion. I clutched my power tight, dropping it behind me and falling backward into the spacetime bubble. It popped open on the other side of her, and I hit the ground closer to the entrance, a little disoriented but desperate to escape.

"Stop him," she said, spinning around.

The Nicht Creidem jumped into action, rushing toward me as I stumbled to my feet. The front of the building was only a short distance away, and I could see Dante on the other side, running toward it.

A serrated feather was sticking out of his side, and blood was running from a deep gash in his neck.

Somehow, Sarah had gotten the drop on him. Damn it.

He could have gone back to Purgatory to heal. He should have, but didn't. He stayed to help me.

I spun to face Sarah again, throwing my power out like a wall. It knocked the Nicht Creidem back, but did nothing to her, as she cleaved through it with her wings once more.

"I don't know who you are," I said.

"You never did," she replied.

I pushed off with my power, sending myself hurting back, through the cracked glass and out into the street. I hit the side of a car, denting it inward and coming to rest, every one of my ribs broken. Dante reached me as Sarah took to the sky, rushing toward us.

"Dante, get us out of here," I said.

"I cannot, signore. I'm too damaged. I can only return to Purgatory."

"Why don't you?"

He looked into my eyes with his own. They bore deep into my soul, giving me an instant chill.

"Take up the sword," he said.

"What?"

"There is no time. Use Uriel's blade. Capture my power. Now." His tone was serious, furious, commanding. His eyes burned red, in a way I hadn't seen in years.

"You want me to kill you?"

"No, but you must. Do it."

He had reached under my coat and retrieved the blade. He pulled it from the sheath and held it out to me. I looked past him to Sarah, who would be on us in seconds.

"Dante," I said. "I can't."

He smiled sadly and nodded.

Then he shoved the blade into his gut.

"Take it," he said, releasing the hilt. "Take the power, or you are going to die."

I didn't have time to say anything. Not thank you. Not goodbye. Not anything. I grabbed the sword, the rune at the end flaring as I did.

The pain was intense. Excruciating. So much more so than it had been with Raguel. Dante was the Lord of Purgatory, maybe not on a level with God or Lucifer, maybe not even as powerful as Zifah, but he was no slouch. I was barely able to contain the agony, to fight against it and throw myself away from the car as Sarah came swooping down, wings stabbing at me, slicing violently through the fallen poet.

She screamed at my evasion, and I rolled over in time to see her toss Dante aside. He fell to dust as she did, scattering into the breeze.

I clenched my teeth to fight against the pain, the anger, the disappointment, and the new font of strength that was adding fuel to my fire. It still wasn't enough to beat Sarah; I could sense that much. Her power was unlike anything the Divine could muster. It was of a kind that was never meant to be.

"Now you," she said. Her eyes were cold. Cruel. She was bending the way Raguel had, her guilt and rage twisting her initial design into something more. Or was it less?

Either way, I knew there would only be one way to stop her, despite what I had told Josette.

I pushed myself to my feet. Dante's power was coursing through me, mingling with my own.

Extinction

"Not yet," I said, closing my eyes.

I felt a familiar rush of air, and when I opened them, I was far, far away.

35

"Landon?" Obi said.

I looked around the space, still a little disoriented. I was in Espanto's hideaway, standing in the center of the workspaces. Obi was off to the left, looking up from one of them.

"That really sucked," I said, falling to my knees. I felt nauseous and dizzy, and a little high on the power I had gained. It was like a massive hit of caffeine, leaving me jittery and cold.

Dante was gone. Dead. Worse than dead. Erased to nothing, just like that. And for what? To save my life?

My life wasn't worth it.

"What happened, man?" Obi asked, rushing over to me. "Where's Dante?"

"Gone," I replied. "He sacrificed himself to save me. He gave me his power through the sword. Sarah caught up with us. She has a deal with the Nicht Creidem. They're helping her kill the Divine."

"You mean a trap?"

"Yeah. Sort of. We thought Gervais was setting one for me. Sarah set her own."

"Damn."

"That's what I said." I managed to pull myself to my feet. "She's different, Obi. She's lost it. Completely lost it."

Obi looked stricken. He seemed to know what I meant without having to ask.

"Geez. I'm sorry, man."

"Me too. There are no winners here. No matter what we're all going to lose something."

We already had.

"What are we supposed to do? I take it you didn't get the third eye?"

"No. That part of the plan is shot. I got the mimic stone, though. It's better than nothing." Dante's power would be a huge help as well, though that thought was still a raw one. It was hard for the truth of what had just happened to sink in. The whole thing was surreal in the worst way possible.

"If Dante is gone, what happens to Purgatory?" Obi asked.

"I don't know. Probably nothing right away. Someone will have to take over for him, I suppose." I paused, trying to settle my stomach. "That may be the least of our concerns right now. What time is it?"

"Here or in Indo?"

"Indo."

"Nine o'clock."

Gervais' demo of the Fist was in two hours. That didn't leave us a lot of time.

"I was feeling a little better about this a few hours ago," I said.

"It's not your fault, man. I'm sure you did everything you could."

"It wasn't enough. It wasn't even close."

"You have to bounce back. There's no other choice."

"I know."

I fought against the tide of emotions that threatened to sweep over me. I railed against the upset in my gut, and in my soul. I had already known I would have to kill Sarah. The promise I had made to Josette had been made with the hope of an outcome I didn't believe in. It was like a lie, but not quite. I had told her there were no guarantees.

The door across the room opened, and Alichino wandered in. He looked at me strangely when he did, and for a moment I thought it was because he had forgotten about me again.

"Dante?" he said, his snout curling and his eyes beginning to water.

They had been friends. Close friends. Somehow, the demon could see his power in me. The truth of the last few minutes punched me in the gut again.

"I'm sorry," I said. "He sacrificed himself for me."

Alichino nodded sadly and then fled the room.

"Poor little guy," Obi said, watching him for a moment. Then he turned back to me. "So, are we going to call back your girlfriend to help us out with this?"

"No. Not that I don't want her beast-mode on our side for this, but we won't be able to surprise Gervais if her aura is blaring across the countryside."

"Do you think we're going to surprise him?"

"It's fifty-fifty, but that's what the stone is for."

"Right. When do you want to head out?"

"No better time than now," I replied. "Can you get me a location that's a little further out than we had planned? Dante was going to drop us, and I'm not that comfortable with his method of transportation just yet. I want a little breathing room in case I screw it up."

Obi laughed and returned to his workstation. "Can do."

He called me over a minute later. I had managed to quell my nausea by then, and get a better feeling for my increase in power. I hadn't been expecting to gain some of Dante's abilities along with his Divine energy. That was a surprise bonus.

"Bogor, Indonesia," Obi said, showing me the view from Google Earth. It felt like a different world compared to New York City, though it seemed equally as crowded. "It's about thirty miles outside of Srizyl's main compound. As long as we avoid the attention of any Divine, we should be able to disappear in there for a while."

"Sounds good."

"Are you sure you're up for this?"

"Not completely."

Extinction

He smiled. "But if you teleport with me, I'm not going to wind up with my head where my ass is or anything?"

"I'm not making any promises."

"I can stay here."

I looked at him. He smiled.

"Right. Let me grab my Nintendo power gloves and I'll be right back."

He headed for the door.

"You are coming back, right?" I asked.

He winked before he disappeared.

I slumped down into his abandoned chair, suddenly feeling exhausted. I didn't know how much more I could take. At least when I was fighting the Beast, I was going up against an enemy whose motivations that I maybe didn't understand but at least could villainize. Sarah was a different story. She wasn't a monster. She was a person. Powerful? Yes. Confused? Yes. Lost? It seemed like it. But still at least part human. Beyond that, she was like a sister to me, or maybe like a daughter. Either way, I loved her like family. Even her efforts to kill me hadn't changed that.

Obi returned a minute later, wearing the gloves Uriel had made for him, along with a leather jacket and jeans. He looked badass, focused and ready to bring it. I needed to be the same.

"Thanks for coming back," I said as I stood and met him halfway.

"You know I'll never abandon you when you need me."

"You're a good friend."

"Damn right."

I reached out and put my hand on his shoulder. He put his hand on mine.

"Don't get me bass-ackwards," he said.

I closed my eyes and pictured the image from Google Maps.

A moment later, we were there.

36

Bogor was as crowded as the picture had suggested, even at nine o'clock at night. The city was alive with activity, as motorcycles and scooters raced along narrow streets along with pedestrians, bicycles, and the occasional car.

Nobody took any notice of my arrival with Obi. We became an instant part of the landscape, just another flesh and bone obstacle to move past. Obi shouted with joy that his head and rear were in the right place, but otherwise we started walking along with the rest of the traffic as if we had been there all day.

The jump made me a little dizzy, but the effects were shorter-lived the second time. Maybe it was because I was more calm when I made it. Maybe it was integrating better with the rest of my energy. Maybe it was from experience. Either way, it gave me a growing sense of confidence that I could handle the power, and learn to use it to my advantage.

"What do you want to do now?" Obi asked. "We've got some time to kill."

"The teleport didn't knock me out like the last time," I replied. "We should take advantage of the extra time. Rent a couple of bikes, head for the target, and be a little more judicious with our approach."

"Agreed."

We moved through the streets. I stopped at a few street vendors, asking them where I could get a pair of motorcycles. They barked out directions, pointing and waving through the throng. It took a few tries, but we found the place before long.

It was being run by a fiend.

"We can find another place," Obi suggested.

We were standing across from the shop, out of sight. I was trying to decide if I wanted to announce myself to him or not. Odds were high that he was in Srizyl's employ, which meant if he saw me he was sure to rat me out. I didn't really need her to know I was coming before I got there.

At the same time, I knew next to nothing about the archfiend and getting a little intel from the demon had a lot of potential value. It wasn't my intent to raid her compound and go right to wholesale slaughter. If I thought I could convince her to give up Gervais, I would.

"No. Let's go talk to him," I said, making up my mind. Beating around the bushes hadn't worked for me so far.

"You sure, man?"

"Yeah. Come on."

We moved across the crowd. The shop was small, with only four bikes out in front of it that looked like they were for rent. It had an open front, and the fiend was sitting behind a rickety table that served as a counter.

He looked up at our approach. His eyes landed on Obi first, pausing on the gloves. He tried to stand.

I pushed him back down with my power, pinning him to the chair. His head didn't move, but his eyes flicked over to me.

"I've had a really shitty day," I said in Indonesian. "Don't make it worse."

"I didn't do anything," he replied.

"English," I said for Obi's sake.

"I didn't do anything," he repeated in English. "I swear."

"You work for Srizyl?"

"Yes."

"Tell me about her."

"What?"

"Information."

"She'll kill me for talking to you."

"If you don't talk to me, I'll kill you." I grabbed the sword, pulling it from its sheath. The demon flinched at the glow of it. Cliche, but effective.

"What do you want to know?"

"How hungry is she?"

"Hungry?"

"For power."

"Insatiable," the demon replied. "Unstoppable. She's only nineteen years old. Did you know that? She killed both her parents. Her brother. She made a deal with the local fiend, became his bride. He took her virginity. She killed him and took his estate the same night."

"She didn't go to Hell and come back?" I asked, surprised. I didn't think that was even possible.

"She made a deal with Satan from here. The word is that she killed herself, and he sent her right back before her corpse was even cold."

"Rosemary's baby," Obi said.

"I don't know what that is," the fiend said.

"Can she use hellfire?" I asked.

"A little. She can read people's minds. Control them. She has a whole host of mortal slaves, orphans mainly. They do whatever she wants. She controls the police, too. The judges. Everything in Bogor."

"There are no angels here?"

"Look around. You won't find any."

"If another demon offered her a deal, would she take it?"

"What kind of deal?"

"Power beyond what she can get on her own."

"Yeah, she'd take it, and turn on whoever made the offer once she had it."

"Even if the demon was more powerful than her."

He smiled. "She would find a way. Even if it took years. She doesn't like being bound to anyone. What she's accomplished already is legendary among the demons in Indo."

I looked over at Obi, considering. She wouldn't be open to a deal with me. It also didn't sound like she would be that open to a deal with Gervais either. If he was coming to show her the Fist, she would have a trap of some kind prepared for him. Then again, if he was using her to get to me, he would also be using her nature against both of us. There were too many possibilities, and I was sure Gervais had calculated all of them, manipulating everything to get it where he wanted it. That was his true gift, his real power.

It was enough to make my head hurt.

"I think we're going to do this the easy way," I said.

"Easy way?" Obi asked.

I stabbed the fiend in the chest, drawing out his power into me. It stung a little, but he didn't have much to offer.

"I'm getting kind of tired of games," I replied.

37

We took two of the motorcycles and were making our way out of the city a few minutes later. Obi didn't seem too happy that I had been so callous about killing the fiend, but seeing as how it was a demon, he wasn't too unhappy either.

Like I had told him, I was getting tired of the games. I didn't want to fall into another one of Gervais' carefully crafted traps, and I didn't want to try to figure it out ahead of time. Not anymore. The run-in with Sarah had stolen what remained of my patience, and learning about Srizyl had only solidified my change in plans.

I was done with finesse. I was done with strategy. I was going to hit Srizyl, and I was going to hit her hard. When Gervais showed up with the Fist, I was going to hit them, too.

I told Obi as much. He wasn't in love with the idea, but he wasn't going to argue either. Not now. Besides, there was a lot to be said for the power of anger and desire. Plenty of others had done more with less by sheer force of will.

We rode the bikes out into the countryside, past numerous farms and small towns and into the foothills of the local mountain. We had the coordinates for Srizyl's estate, and Obi used his phone's GPS to keep us on the right track as we finally abandoned our rides and traveled on foot. He turned off the device once we were within a couple of miles of the facility, in an effort to get close without being detected. Just because I wanted to go in guns blazing didn't mean I wanted to get taken out before we even got there.

We cut a wide angle across the landscape, through some thick vegetation and uneven ground until we reached a low stone wall that marked the beginning of Srizyl's land. Checking the time, we had about an hour before Gervais was supposed to show up with the Fist. In my mind, I was hoping to greet him with an empty compound and all of the power of the archfiend and her minions at my disposal. It might not be enough to take on Sarah yet, but it had to be sufficient to fight the Fist.

At least, I hoped it would be.

We approached cautiously, circling the estate until we came within sight of the front gates. We gained some high ground from there, looking down on the manned security stations surrounding the compound, where human slaves monitored the area while toting heavy assault rifles. A secondary security detail was spread across the spaces between the buildings, this one composed of demons. Vampires and weres for the most part, with a few succubi thrown into the mix, which seemed out of place.

The over-sexualized demons weren't normal deployed for defense. Rather, they were better suited for seduction, both of humans and other demons. It was weird to see them standing with the other guards, their over-proportioned breasts threatening to break out of their olive green t-shirts, the curve of their rears poking out from beneath matching short shorts. It was as if Hugh Hefner had designed their uniforms.

"I hadn't seen that before," Obi whispered to me, from our position in the brush on one of the hillsides near the front gates.

"I don't know what the point of it is," I agreed.

"Maybe she set them up to meet Gervais when he shows."

"Could be. I doubt they're very good in a fight."

"Especially dressed like that. How do you want to play this?"

I scanned the courtyard, pointing to the largest building. "I'm guessing Srizyl is in there, somewhere. If I carry us to the door, maybe we can sneak inside without being seen."

"Yeah, maybe. It'll make things a lot easier if we can surprise her."

"After that, just stop anything that tries to stop you. We'll secure the area, and then we'll wait for Gervais to show up. With any luck, we can take down the Fist before he knows what's happening."

"Luck isn't our strong suit, man," Obi said.

"Then we have to make our own." I put my hand on his shoulder. He flexed his hands beneath the gloves Uriel had made him.

I was only moments away from teleporting us when I saw a beam of light appear some distance away. My hand slid from Obi's shoulder as I turned toward it, squinting my eyes to make out the source. Headlights.

A limo was headed toward the facility, its lights cutting through the darkness. I didn't need to see the occupant to know who it was.

"Damn it, he's early," I said, annoyed with Gervais for showing up ahead of schedule. Of course, I didn't believe he was early. He was there at exactly the time he wanted to be.

"You're sure it's him?" Obi asked.

"As sure as I can be," I replied.

"Does he have the Fist with him?"

"I don't think so."

"A double-cross?"

"I doubt it. He's probably got some grand entrance planned for his prize."

"Look," Obi said, pointing back to the compound. A light had gone on in an upstairs window of the main building. A moment later, a head of long, dark hair leaned out of it, locking onto the oncoming lights.

Srizyl. I knew her as soon as my eyes landed on her. I could sense her power, feel her aura. I ducked as her head swept up our way as though she had felt me at the same time. That was impossible. I didn't have an aura of my own. Neither did Obi. Still, something had attracted her attention.

Her eyes passed over our position, and then she vanished back into her room. A moment later the guards on both sides of the walls were in motion, organizing into ranks. The succubi lined up at the front of the defenses, standing crisply at attention ahead of the compound gates, their appearance within the ranks of soldiers almost comical.

There was more to them than met the eye. I was sure of it. Part of Srizyl's ruse to try to steal the Fist from Gervais? He would assume they were, but then again, maybe that was the goal. It took a lot of layers of misdirection and mistruth for one demon to get the best of another.

The door to the main building opened as the limo was slowing in front of the gates. Srizyl slipped out into the night in a brightly-colored but sheer robe, the lines of her body suggestive beneath it. She was flanked on either side by two more succubi. They resembled the others, though their clothing was composed of more modest business attire.

Two dozen mortals spilled out behind them, carrying trays of food and drink in their mistress' wake.

"You have a new plan?" Obi asked me as the gates opened to let the limo inside. It moved forward about a dozen feet before coming to a stop again.

The door opened.

Gervais slid smoothly from the limo. Zifah was standing contentedly on his shoulder, leaning against the side of his head.

I glanced over at Obi, confused.

First, was the diminutive demon the one calling the shots?

Second, where the hell was the Fist?

Srizyl met the two demons at the front of the car, bowing her head to both of them, or maybe just to Zifah, before motioning her mortal slaves forward bearing their trays of food. Zifah moved back and forth across Gervais' shoulders as he examined each tray, waving it all past until he was presented with a large bowl of popcorn. The demon smacked his lips and pointed to it. One of the succubi reached into the bowl and recovered a kernel, bringing it to Zifah's face. The demon flicked it from her fingers with his tongue, and then licked her fingers for good measure.

"This is disgusting," Obi said.

"Tell me about it," I replied.

Srizyl's lips moved, and Gervais nodded in response. Then she pointed back at her demon soldiers, singling out the succubi. She said something else and they came forward. Zifah looked at them, his eyes lighting up.

He always had been a perv.

"Okay, now what?" Obi whispered.

"I've got an idea," I replied. "Wait here. Back me up if I look like I'm in trouble."

"Wait? Back you up? What?"

I fixed my eyes on the spot between the three demons and teleported myself to it.

38

I came back into existence right in the middle of things, appearing from nowhere between Srizyl and Gervais. I didn't hesitate, certain of what I needed to do, pulling in my power and strengthening my body.

Then I punched Gervais as hard as I could, my fist blasting into his nose and teeth.

Pain lanced through my hand as the impact reverberated through my entire arm, rattling me and pushing back in a way I hadn't expected, while a shower of blue energy exploded from the archfiend's head.

What the?

The deflection shoved me back into the still shocked Srizyl, throwing me backward and down on top of her in a heap. I kept my eyes forward, locked on Gervais, as the glamour fell away and the Fist of God was revealed.

"Oh, wow," Zifah said. "Landon. I wasn't expecting that. Holy moly. Where'd you learn that trick?"

I threw out my power, getting myself up and off the demon and ready to defend myself. Gervais wasn't Gervais? Where the hell was he?

"I mean, we figured you were going to show up, even if you didn't want to. But that? That was awesome. I mean it."

"You didn't glamour the Fist for me?" I asked.

Zifah was standing on the things shoulder. It had its hands up, ready to fight back if I attacked it, but otherwise wasn't making any aggressive moves.

"Nah. Why would we bother with that? That part of the ruse was for Srizyl here."

"What?" Srizyl said behind me.

The Fist's left hand moved, spreading away from me. Three bolts fired, launching through the succubi beside me. They vanished in a heap of dust.

"They're sexy, don't get me wrong," Zifah said. "But I know what you did to them. Poison? Really, Srizyl? I'm the son of Lucifer. Do you think I'm that stupid?"

"My Lord Zifah," Srizyl said. I looked back to see her drop to her knees. "My apologies. I couldn't be sure that you were not using me."

"Blah, blah, blah. I am using you," Zifah replied. He looked over at me. "You have something we want."

"You knew about the sword?"

"We guessed after we heard Sarah went cuckoo on you. If anyone was going to be able to talk Uriel into putting it back together, it was you."

"You keep saying we," I said. "Where is that asshole, anyway?"

The Fist pointed up the hill, back the way I had come.

Damn.

I turned my head slowly. Gervais was coming down the slope, a knife to Obi's neck.

"We had eyes watching out for you and your friend in Bogor," Zifah said. "I thought you would have guessed that."

"I didn't see any demons."

"You don't always need to use demons," Zifah replied. "Cash works just as well. Hey! I just had a thought. You got the sword from Uriel, and you dropped in on me like Dante." He stared at me, his eyes narrowing to slits. "You sneaky devil. You're more evil than I thought."

"He did it to himself," I said.

"Sure he did. Come on, Landon. If you're going to be bad, be bad. Don't make excuses."

Extinction

I didn't respond to him a second time. He was probably trying to get under my skin.

Gervais marched Obi through the gates and around the car, stopping beside the Fist.

"Hello, mon ami," he said. "I'd shake your hand, but as you can see, I'm a little tied up at the moment holding a knife to your best friend's throat."

"I still can't believe you and Zifah are working together."

"It is a marriage of convenience, I admit. I would prefer to do this on my own, but we do what we must. Now, I will need the sword, s'il vous plaît."

"Landon, don't," Obi said, his breath short from the choke hold.

"Be quiet," Gervais said. "He isn't going to listen to you, anyway."

"If I give you the sword, you'll kill all of us, and take enough power that you can use it on Sarah." I looked at Zifah. "He'll use it on you, too."

"Landon, what kind of monster do you think I am?" Gervais said. "I wouldn't hurt my own daughter, even though she killed me and sent me back to Hell. No, I want her to rule at my side, as always."

"Nobody believes that," I said.

"But it is true. I am capable of telling the truth once in a while." He tightened the knife against Obi's neck, enough that a line of blood formed along the edge. "Come now. We already know what you are going to do. You will give me the sword because in your heart you believe that you will still succeed. You always have been stupid that way."

"I've always succeeded," I said.

"No, others have succeeded for you. There is no one, mon ami. No friends left to come to your aid. Elyse, Rose, even Rebecca and apparently Dante. They are all gone. Obi is all you have left, and if you don't save him, he will be gone, too."

I looked Obi in the eye. He wasn't afraid to die. He had seen Heaven already, and I had no doubt he would go there.

"Fine," I said, reaching a hand behind my back.

"Slowly," Zifah said.

I did as he asked, keeping my movements deliberate as I reached under my coat and found the mimic stone. I tapped it against the sword as I brought it back, feeling the form change in my hand. I was just like the real thing.

I brought it out and up. It was an identical replica, a perfect glamour. It weighed the same, balanced the same, glowed the same. I shoved it point-first into the ground and took a step back.

"There it is. Let him go."

Gervais smiled, and actually did as I asked, shoving Obi to me as he stepped forward and picked up the blade.

"You really are stupid, man," Obi said.

Gervais hefted the sword, clearly fooled by the glamour.

"Step aside, Landon," he said. "You're free to go. I don't need your power when there are so many other Divine to kill, and you can't hurt me anyway."

I moved out of his way, and he thrust the sword forward, into Srizyl's chest. Her eyes widened as she expected to be stabbed, only to find the attack ineffective.

"What?" Gervais said, caught by surprise. If I could have framed the look on his face and held it in my soul forever, I would have.

"It's showtime," I said.

39

I reached behind my back for the real sword, at the same time Gervais tried to stab Srizyl again, not quite believing what was happening.

"Attack," Srizyl shouted, putting out her hand toward the demon.

He barely escaped a short burst of hellfire from her, even as I got Uriel's blade free and chased after him with it.

Srizyl's demons didn't seem to know who to attack right away. They headed for me instead of the Fist, while dozens of her mortal slaves began pouring from the buildings, armed with standard issue guns.

Obi intercepted the demons, slamming into them with the power gloves, flinging them aside. The bullets started coming a moment later, digging up divots of the ground around us as their wielders tried to find their aim.

"Zifah," Gervais said, doing his best to get away from me. "Don't just stand there."

The Fist started to move, lurching toward me, a massive arm swinging out to him me in the chest. I ducked beneath it, bringing the sword up in a quick test of the armor's ability to withstand the special blade. It skidded off the scriptured metal without leaving a mark.

I had figured it would be impervious.

I stopped chasing Gervais, using my power to stop myself and reverse course, shooting up in a spray of earth and reaching for Zifah. The Fist vanished a moment later, and my hand wrapped around empty air.

"Landon," Obi said, his voice tense.

I rolled on the ground to my feet, throwing up my power and creating a wall between him and the shooters, watching as a dozen bullets froze in mid-air before they could slice him in half. I closed my eyes for an instant, reappearing beside him, grabbing him and teleporting again. I dropped him on the wall beside one of the shooters, and he took hold of the mortal and wrenched the gun from his hand.

"I don't want to kill these people," he said.

"We don't have a choice right now."

"Kill her, lose the mind control."

"I'll do my best."

He didn't look happy, but he turned on the other slaves and returned fire, bullets knocking them from their perches.

I teleported again, to where Gervais was desperately trying to defend himself from Srizyl. I was getting more used to the power with every use, finding it easier and quicker every time I jumped.

The archfiend sent another blast of hellfire at Gervais. He stepped aside, his form changing, his hands elongating into claws. He had already used his own gift to claim power from Randolph Heart's goons and make himself an uber-vampire, and now he used it, leaping at Srizyl and catching her off-guard.

I used my power to push him away from her, sending him sprawling. I wanted the Divine energy she could provide for myself.

I threw myself at her, bringing the blade up to strike.

The Fist appeared beside me. It's arm launched out, hitting me square in the side and sending me tumbling away. I hit the ground and rolled to a stop, pushing myself back to my feet. The Fist vanished again.

Uriel's blade rested a few feet away. I pulled it back to me and made a quick survey of the battle.

Gervais was going after Srizyl again, while Obi had managed to clear half of the shooters from the wall, and was pinned down in a firefight with

Extinction

the other half. Where was Zifah?

I closed my eyes, teleporting across the field, reappearing and looking back to see him materialize where I had just been standing. I had figured as much. I blinked out again, coming back to the world a few feet from Srizyl. She saw me and stopped. I grabbed her by the arm, throwing her aside, bringing the sword around as Gervais pounced. His eyes became saucers, and he rolled his body, landing awkwardly beside me and scrambling to get away. I turned to reach for him, only to sense the Fist as it appeared behind me.

I kicked backward, feeling my foot connect with the Fist's chest and knock it back. I used the momentum to throw myself forward, wrapping my arms around Srizyl and teleporting again, bringing us up to the top of the hill outside the compound.

"Diuscrucis," Srizyl said, her expression fearful.

"Let go of your slaves," I said.

"What?"

"Release them. Help me fight the Fist, and I'll let you live."

She nodded. The shooting stopped a moment later. "Very well."

I teleported her back to the fray, dropping her in front of Gervais. She put her hand out, hitting him with a blast of hellfire that singed the side of his face. He screamed and rolled away, calling out for Zifah.

The Fist appeared again, closing in on us. Srizyl turned toward it, sending a gout of hellfire from her hands, which bounced harmlessly off the scriptured metal. Zifah aimed the armor toward her, while I tried to circle around. He broke off the engagement, facing me instead, not worried about the archfiend.

"She can't hurt me, Landon," the demon said.

"No," I heard Obi say behind him. "But I can."

A gloved fist appeared behind the Fist's back, smashing hard into the diminutive hellspawn. The force sent him flying from the weapon's shoulder, screaming as he tumbled through the air, landing on the ground fifty feet away and steaming from the scripture on the blessed gloves. He got to his feet, shaking himself off, his aura growing around him as he reversed the damage. He was the son of Lucifer. He wouldn't be that easy to kill.

The important part was that we had knocked him away from the Fist, and broken the connection that allowed him to control it.

"Score one for the home... oof!"

Obi was thrown backward as the Fist continued to move, spinning and hitting him hard in the gut. He landed with a thud and didn't move again.

"Son of a bitch," I whispered, seeing him laying there. The Fist readjusted, coming about and marching toward me. I could hear Zifah's laughter at my back.

"Nice try, Landon," he said. "You almost got me. Riding the Fist is fun, not a necessity."

The Fist vanished.

I felt my teeth lock together in anger, and I threw myself at the small demon, desperate to stick him to the end of Uriel's sword. He jumped back in fear at my approach, pulling one of his needles and throwing it at me. I batted it aside easily, closing the gap between us in seconds.

The Fist reappeared in front of me. I slammed headlong into it with enough force to lift it up and back, knocking it over Zifah and landing on the other side. It grabbed me by the shoulders, the swords on its wrists extending and sticking into both sides of my chest, leaving me hanging from it.

Zifah climbed up beneath me, sticking his face in mine. "Sorry about your friend. Thanks for the sword."

He reached for my hand, dangling at my side and holding the blade.

I didn't say anything. I closed my eyes and teleported away, coming to rest on my hands and knees beside Obi.

"Diuscrucis," Srizyl said, rushing to us. "You can't leave me here with them."

"You're right," I said, looking up at her and raising Uriel's sword. "You have something I need."

She shrunk back in fear, her hands coming up to shoot hellfire at me. I threw my power out, pushing her hands aside, spreading her open so I could plant the blade in her gut. In my anger, I barely noticed the pain.

She turned to ash as I put my hand on Obi's shoulder and willed us

Extinction

both away.

40

I didn't go back to Mexico. That would have been stupid. Obi was hurt, and there was nothing I could do to save him. My power to heal didn't extend to others. Not anymore.

Instead, I came into existence at New York Presbyterian Hospital, right in the middle of the lobby. I quickly hid Uriel's blade back beneath my coat, and then called out for help at the same time I removed Obi's gloves from his hands. A nurse rushed over a moment later, oblivious to the fact that I had just appeared out of nowhere.

"What happened?" she asked, at the same time she motioned for help.

"He got hit by a car," I said. It was close enough to the truth. The Fist had a similar amount of force.

She looked back at him. "Detective Sampson?" she said, recognizing him. She looked at me again. "You found him like this?"

"No. I was with him. I'm a friend of his. Must have been a drunk or something, came around the corner and slammed right into him. He didn't even slow down."

"Did you get a plate?"

"Yeah, right. I carried him here as fast as I could. We were only a couple of blocks away."

Extinction

"You shouldn't have moved him."

The orderlies brought a gurney. A doctor knelt next to him and checked him from the ground. "Let's get him loaded up and stabilized. He's alive but unconscious."

I felt a bit of relief at the fact that he was still alive. A seraph could heal him once he was stable.

"We'll take it from here," the nurse said. "Can you fill out some paperwork for us?"

"I can't. I have to run."

She moved to protest, but I closed my eyes and teleported away, coming to rest on the steps of St. Patrick's. I paused there for a moment, leaning over, my body exhausted. Increased power or not, I was using a lot of it in a hurry. I needed to slow down. I stumbled on the steps, coming to rest and putting my hands up to my face.

"Damn it," I shouted into them, muffling my scream.

Not only had Obi gotten hurt, but Zifah had shown his control of the Fist to be greater than I had realized. Worse, I still couldn't hurt the damn thing, and I needed to at least slow it down in order to reach the little asshole. The failed attempt left me angry and frustrated and more than a little overwhelmed. Sarah had beaten me. Zifah had beaten me. I was getting tired of losing.

I rubbed at my face, feeling weary. Maybe Sarah was right. Maybe things had already gone so far that they were beyond my ability to stop. Maybe I was more problem than solution.

I turned back to look at the Cathedral. Josette said God was on my side. I certainly hadn't been feeling it while I got my ass kicked. Unless that was what she meant? I laughed at the thought. Was the Man Upstairs enjoying watching me make a fool of myself?

I got to my feet and headed up the steps and into the building. I felt a chill as soon as I entered, a reaction I had never experienced before. A moment later, my entire body began to tingle, every nerve ending reacting to something I couldn't see or sense. As I walked down the aisle, it seemed as if my steps were growing lighter and more energetic, my tired body and soul lifted and held by an unseen hand.

Was this God's work? Uriel's? Josette's?

Jane appeared from the transept, intercepting me in front of the altar.

"Landon," she said.

"I need help," I said. "My friend, Obi."

"New York Presbyterian?" she replied.

"How did you know?"

She looked up in answer. I got the point.

"Is he going to be okay?"

"He will be well. A novice has already been dispatched to treat him."

I let myself relax. At least something was going right.

"What happened?" she asked.

"The Fist. I thought Zifah needed to be touching it to control it. I was wrong."

"How, then?"

"Your guess is as good as mine. Adam was controlling it with some kind of cybernetic interface. It was part technology, part Divine. But I destroyed it, and I didn't see any kind of control interface on Zifah. He's too small to hide anything like that."

"How did you break the control the last time?"

"I cut Adam's arm off. That won't work here. I can't even get close to Zifah without the Fist blocking me, and after Obi managed to slap him, I don't think he'll risk putting himself in the open again." I lowered my head, feeling the weight returning. "I'm losing this one, and I don't see any way not to."

"How can I help you?"

"If you sent someone to help Obi, you already have." I looked back at the pews. "If you don't mind, I'm just going to hang out for a little while."

"To pray?" she asked hopefully.

"To think," I replied. "I need to figure out what to do next, and everyone I used to lean on for support is gone."

"Not everyone, Diuscrucis," Jane said, pointing to the crucifix behind the altar. "If you need me, whisper my name. I will hear you."

"Thank you, Jane," I said.

"You're welcome."

Extinction

She headed off again, leaving me alone. I retreated to the front row of pews, taking a seat on the corner. I glanced up at the crucifix for a moment before leaning back and closing my eyes. Jesus had been absent while I was in Heaven. Why would he do anything for me here?

No. I was on my own. I couldn't count on Dante for advice. I couldn't look to Obi to monitor SamChan or scour the Darknet for clues. Alyx was still out there, but I was more convinced than ever that getting her involved would be the same thing as getting her killed.

I needed to solve this one myself.

I tried to relax, to breathe deep and even, to let my mind go. I needed to forget about the chaos swirling around me and find some measure of focus within the maelstrom. I couldn't do everything at once. I was one person, and could only do one thing at one time.

Right now, I needed to figure out how to stop the Fist cold so that I could get a solid shot at Zifah and his power. If I could accomplish that, I could move on to dealing with Sarah.

The hours passed as I retread my memories, from my first encounter with the Fist to the present, searching them for clues. As far as I knew, there was only one way to control the armors remotely. While it was possible Zifah had come up with an interface that was either smaller or completely different than the one Adam had used, the odds that he had altered the Fist itself were slim. The scripture on the armor shielded it from manipulation and making the wrong changes anywhere created the risk of making the entire system brittle. Assuming that was a risk that neither Zifah or Gervais was willing to take, it meant that there had to be a way to send signals of my own to the armor.

The trick was to figure out how.

The Fist's creator was dead and gone, but there was one person involved in the project that could potentially shed a little more light on how it worked.

I got to my feet, abandoning the pew and heading for the exit. Jane met me there.

"Your friend Obi-wan is on the mend," she said.

"I'm happy to hear it," I said, making a note to visit him as soon as time allowed. "Thank you for your intervention."

"Don't thank me," she replied. "Thank the Lord."

"You'll have to do for now," I said. "I've got work to do."

Extinction

41

The problem, as I saw it, was that getting my hands on Zifah was currently a catch-22. I couldn't stop the Fist without grabbing the demon, and I couldn't grab the demon without stopping the Fist. Rock, meet hard place.

The good news, if you could call it that, was that there was once small chance for me to get my hands on a pick and start chiseling away. The bad news was that the pick's name was Adam, and he wasn't exactly my biggest fan at the moment.

Adam had a direct hand in the creation of the Fist. He had been the one to hire Matthias and set him to work on the design; more specifically, the technical design of the interface between angel and machine. If there was anyone who knew how to disable it or knew someone who knew how to disable it, it was him.

Of course, I didn't know where to find Adam, and even once I did, I had no idea how I was going to get him to help me. My understanding was that he and Sarah were currently a thing, and it had been Sarah who instigated the whole relationship. She had convinced the fallen seraph to help her. Through lies? His own volition? That was what I needed to find out. If he was on her side, contacting or otherwise capturing him was going to be a huge risk. If he told her where I was, that was going to be a problem.

Then again, her killing of Dante was a blessing in disguise for me, and a gross miscalculation on her part. As long as I could use his teleportation skills, I would be a much more difficult catch.

As if that would help me while the rest of the world burned.

All of that aside, the bottom line was that I was out of other options. Dante was gone, and Obi had landed in that hospital in payment for his solid friendship. I didn't take that fact lightly, and it was motivation that I needed.

I left St. Patrick's and started walking along 5th Avenue, absorbing the sights and sounds of the city, my city, as I crossed town. I knew from Alichino that Adam and Sarah had been staying in contact through Yuli, the little messenger demon who had once been Reyzl's pet. I remained surprised he was still kicking around the mortal realm, but in this case, I figured it could work out in my favor. I wasn't on bad terms with the little demon, and once I was able to locate him, I might be able to get him to hook me up with Adam. Considering the nature of a messenger's work, it would probably take a bit of torture or other coercion, but I could be a lot more persuasive than most demons or angels, especially since I wasn't bound by any of their rules or concerns.

I was almost down to the New York Public Library by the time I had finalized my plan of action in my head. I glanced over at the structure for a moment, doing a quick scan for Divine, noting that the area was uncommonly clear. Sarah had both sides on edge, and they were laying low and waiting to see what was going to happen next. Thanks to the fact that Sarah was one of the few people who would never forget about me, they had probably caught wind through the Nicht Creidem that we weren't on the best of terms at the moment. When two diuscrucis squared off, it was better just to get out of the way.

I closed my eyes, blinking out of existence there and back into existence on the flight deck of the U.S.S. Intrepid. It was another landmark that held memories for me, most of them not that great. The damage we had caused there had been long repaired, but I could still see it in my head.

Extinction

I had to push the rising tide of sadness aside and refocus myself. I wasn't here for a walk down trauma lane.

I made my way from the flight deck to the interior, sweeping the area visually. Yuli could be anywhere in the world right now. He could be sitting on Sarah's lap or meeting with Adam on the other side of the world at the very same time I was moving through his home base. My odds of finding him here were somewhere between slim and none.

That was okay because I didn't need to find him. I'd learned a lot about messenger demons since I had become Divine. One of the more important things I'd learned was that demons became familiars to a fiend or archfiend by using their true name, some energy, and some runes, and using all of these things to create a token that bound them. I knew that Reyzl had once had control over Yuli's token. Then Rebecca had taken it after she betrayed me and literally stabbed me in the back. I didn't know what happened to it after that, but my assumption was that unless Sarah had found the small bit of the demon's flesh, it was still under Yuli's control and tucked away somewhere.

Why the Intrepid? I knew for a fact this was where an entire pool of messenger demons were living. I hadn't cared enough at the time to know if Yuli was part of their community.

I cared now.

I moved away from the public exhibits, and through an access door marked 'Employees only.' I remained on that track as I navigated the interior of the ship, checking the cracks and crevices for signs of the demons. Pretty soon I was coming across clumps of cat hair, and soon after that larger bunches of fur still attached to flesh. Demons like Yuli were too small and too weak to take on much else.

I caught sight of the first demon trying to stay hidden between a pair of pipes that ran along the ceiling. He was pressed in pretty tight, holding to the shadows and hoping I would go past. I looked up at him; he looked back at me. When I held his gaze, and he realized who I was, he squeaked softly and tried to back up into the wall even more.

"Don't make me drag you out," I said.

The demon hissed.

"Really?"

He cursed under his breath, and then pushed himself out between the pipes, his body cracking as his skeletal structure returned to form. A small pair of wings held him up over my head.

"Whatsss do you wantsss, Diuscrucisss?" he asked.

"I'm looking for Yuli."

"Who?"

I reached out with my power, throwing the demon against the wall and holding him.

"You know who," I said.

He smiled. Messenger demons weren't known for their backbone. "Yuli isssn't here."

"Where is he?"

"What do I looksss like? Hisss mother?"

"You're way too ugly to be his mother, which says a lot. I need to talk to him."

"I haven't ssseen him in two monthsss or ssso. He left one day. He sssaid he had a job that would paysss very, very wellsss."

Two months? Had Sarah been planning this for that long? That was a little before the day that Adam had fallen. Had she really seen everything unfolding the way she claimed?

"Is his token here?"

"I'm not telling you thatsss," the demon said.

I pressed against him with my power again, flattening him to the wall. "I know there's one thing that demons like you value more than secrets."

His snout opened in a wicked smile, his tongue flicking between his teeth. "I can'tsss. Pleassse, Diuscrucisss. If you needsss messenger, I cansss do it for you."

"Sorry, pal. I need Yuli."

"He can'tsss tell you anythingsss."

"I don't need information from him. I just need him to take me to someone. Bring me to his token. I'll use it to get him here, and that's it."

"You liesss."

I let him go. He slapped his wings furiously and rubbed at his neck.

Extinction

"I'm not a demon. I don't need to lie. I promise. Take me to the token, let me summon him, and I'll be gone. Nobody will even remember I was ever here."

"Hmmm. You setsss many of usss free, Diuscrucisss. For thatsss, I will bring you."

He swooped down into the corridor, flying ahead of me. I walked behind him, keeping his pace as he navigated easily through the decommissioned aircraft carrier. Within minutes we were in one of the larger open spaces. There were at least two dozen of the small demons living here, each of them perched in dark corners behind pipes and equipment, their eyes barely visible through the cracks. They didn't protest my arrival. In fact, they all tried to shrink further away, just as my guide had. I left them alone.

"Here isss Yuli'sss space," the demon said, bringing me to a small opening between two metal boxes.

He ducked inside it, and I could hear him moving things aside beyond my view. He emerged a moment later, holding a small strip of worn flesh with runes etched into it. All of the demons in this room would have a similar token tucked away into their spaces, declaring them as free. My guide was showing a lot of faith in me to turn Yuli's over so easily, and to have led me here. I could easily gain control of every demon in the room if I decided to break my promise.

Not that I had any intention of doing that. I didn't want to be down here, and I had no need for two dozen nearly powerless demons. I reached out and took the token from the demon, running my fingers over the runes. The I pushed some of my power into it, feeling the change as I made the connection with the demon. If he were with Sarah, she was going to know something was up as soon as he disappeared, which meant that the second he showed up here the clock accelerated that much more.

"Yuli'grk'ishcalizi," I said, using his full name. "I summon you."

The runes on the token flared for a moment. Then the demon was hovering in front of my face.

"Diuscrucissss," he said, his eyes growing wide. He looked around in a panic. "You gavesss him my tokensss? Whysss?"

"Yuli, relax," I said. "I need you to tell me where Adam is. That's all."

"She'll killsss me. She'll killsss usss all."

"She's going to anyway if we don't stop it. Adam. That's it. Where is he?"

He dropped onto my hand, grabbing at his token. I let him take it. I didn't need it anymore. He seemed calmer once he had it. He looked up at me.

"He won't be happy to see yousss, Landonsss."

"I know. I can't worry about that right now. Where is he?"

"You can'tsss reach himsss. No onesss can."

"If he's in the mortal realm, I can reach him," I said, getting impatient. "Where is he?"

"No, you can'tssss. Isss impossible."

"Can you show me? If I can see it in my mind, I can go there."

He nodded. "I cansss show you." He held out a clawed hand. "Takesss it."

I took his hand. I could feel the power pass between us, and then I saw an almost ethereal view of Adam layered over reality. The fallen angel was sitting in a small room. A cell of some kind, with dark hewn walls and little light. He didn't look happy.

I didn't know where in the world the cell was. I didn't need to. All I had to do was picture it, and as long as it wasn't protected with runes or scripture, I could travel there.

I pulled my hand away from Yuli's. "I have what I need," I said. "Thank you."

"Be carefulsss, Landonsss," Yuli said, surprising me. "Isss dangerousss."

"Thanks for the warning," I replied.

I closed my eyes and transported myself once more.

42

Adam looked up at me the moment I appeared in his cell, his face twisting into an angry, expectant smile.

"Of course," he said. "My hero."

"What are you talking about?" I said, glancing around the room.

It was a cell for sure, the bars of which were loaded with writing that looked too familiar, and made my stomach drop.

Djinn runes.

Damn.

"I see you figured that out for yourself," he said. "I'm a prisoner here, courtesy of my stupidity."

"Sarah?" I asked.

He nodded.

"Tell me everything."

He shook his head. "Screw you, Landon. I don't owe you anything."

"You're going to owe me your freedom in a minute. Maybe you can pay me in advance."

He laughed. "Freedom? What the hell is that worth? I was making a real difference before. Then I tried to do something good. I tried to do the right thing. I almost had you. I almost solved the equation. Then God does this to me?" He motioned to himself. His dark hair, his black eyes, his sooty wings.

"We already had this discussion," I said.

"Yeah, because you're perspective means anything to me. I knew something that apparently was more correct than I realized."

"Which was?"

"That you're a stain. A dark spot on the Divine. The problem, not the solution."

"Which is why Sarah reached out to you?"

"Yes. She came to me soon after I fell. She told me that I was right and that we could help one another. She had a plan to help me make amends with God, and to take care of you at the same time. I would get my revenge on you, and be able to return to Heaven. Who wouldn't jump at the chance?"

Nevermind the fact that God wouldn't be too accepting of an angel who was acting out in the name of revenge. "Except it didn't go the way you were hoping."

"Brilliant deduction. We started organizing other angels, trying to get a number of other seraphim and Touched on board, so we could petition God through prayer."

"You made quite an impression on Raguel," I said. "And quite a few other Touched."

"I know. I thought everything was going perfectly when Sarah told me how many would be at the Mass. She told me you might be there, too."

"And you told blue-eyes to expect me."

"Sarah wanted to make sure you would stay for the proceedings. She didn't want you disappearing."

"She wanted to kill me."

"I know. I was hopeful she would succeed." He looked away from me, at the wall to his prison. "She didn't say anything about slaughtering the rest of the Touched. I didn't know she planned to do that."

"You were there when she killed the changelings. You didn't have a clue that she was off-center?"

"A bunch of demonlings? Why would I care about that?"

"Brian was an angel."

"He wasn't a real angel. He was a twisted distortion, the worst kind of changeling if you ask me."

Half his words were in line with his formally good soul. The rest were dark enough to match his outward complexion.

"When did you find out she killed them?" I asked.

"After I helped her kill the demons in Somalia. The Warlord we killed mocked me about it before he died. I confronted Sarah about the Mass, and she brushed it off as inevitable. Like the whole thing was just a thread that needed to wind its way around history. Then she admitted her full plan to me. Her desire to kill you notwithstanding, she's out of her mind. I told her as much. I thought she was going to kill me, but she brought me here instead."

"A djinn prison. Why?"

He smiled. "To capture you. Why else?"

"She knew I was going to come for you?"

"She can see into the future. I thought you knew that?"

"Her visions aren't always clear, and they aren't always correct."

"Maybe not before. She seems pretty accurate lately."

I reached out and put my hand on his bare shoulder. "Time to go," I said, closing my eyes. I pictured the steps of St. Patrick's again.

I opened my eyes. We were still in the prison.

"Shit," I said.

"She told me you're going to die in here, Landon. She told me if I kill you, she'll set me free. She'll let me remain when the others are gone."

He shifted, drawing a blade from behind him.

"You can't kill me," I said.

He stared at me, the anger obvious. "As much as I hate you, I know that's true. What choice do I have? There's no way out of here for either of us. She's seen what happens."

"She's seen a possibility. I told you, she isn't always right."

"Can I take that chance?"

"I can't decide that for you. We've got better odds if we work together, especially if it goes against what she's seen. If you attack me, I will end you."

I pulled Uriel's blade, holding it up ahead of him. How would the sword react to the power of djinn? The creatures weren't truly Divine, which explained how Sarah had been able to bring them over to her side. Would the sword be totally ineffective against them?

"Uriel's sword," Adam said, mesmerized by it. "He remade it for you?"

I nodded.

I could see his jaw working, clenching and loosening as he tried to deal with how much he hated me.

"You have God on your side," he said at last. "Killing you isn't going to help me much, is it?"

"No, but mending fences might."

He slid to his feet, his eyes flaring. "Can you get us through those bars?"

I gathered my power, pushing it against the cell door. It broke free of its moorings, slamming into the opposite wall.

"I've only got one arm," Adam said, lifting his dagger. "How many djinn do you think I can kill with it?"

43

We moved out into the hallway. The corridor was similar to the cell, cut directly into dark stone, buried somewhere on the planet Earth. I tried to teleport again once we were beyond the bars. I had as much luck as the first time.

"Do you know where we are?" I asked.

"Deep underground," Adam said. "Somewhere in the Congo. I could feel the moisture and the humidity when they brought me here."

"Is Sarah here?"

I expected she would be. If she had known I was coming, she probably baked me a cake.

"She wasn't before. She might be now. She can travel faster than an angel with those wings of hers. Not as fast as instant. That was a good trick, by the way. Where did you learn it?"

"Dante died to give it to me," I said.

He nodded slightly. He wasn't sorry. He didn't really care that much. He was trying to do the right thing, but every thought he had was tinged with evil.

We moved through the corridor, finding a stairwell leading up. We took it, coming to a second magicked doorway. I blew this one from its hinges as well, surprising the djinn who were standing guard on the other side. They drew swords to fight us, their bodies remaining just material enough to swing the blades.

I blocked with Uriel's sword, slashing back, slipping the sword from the parry and getting it around to block again. Adam circled the other djinn cautiously, his single arm nearly a blur as he sought an opening. The blade whisked through the air toward the djinn's eye, and would have removed it if the creature hadn't dematerialized completely. It reformed a moment later, slashing down at Adam, who fell back cursing as a few more of the creatures appeared at the end of the hallway.

"Can't you do something a little more forceful?" he said as he slipped away from an incoming strike.

I gathered my power, lifting it up ahead of the incoming djinn. They ran into it as though it were a force shield, bouncing off the power. One of them put his hand to it and began summoning his magic, pushing against the barrier. It wouldn't last for long.

I ducked beneath a sword blow, planting my feet and shifting, hitting the djinn's sword with my first strike, reversing and getting the backhand through. I was surprised when I felt the blade sink into the phantasmal flesh of the creature, registering its existence.

I tried to draw its power out, preparing myself for the pain to follow.

Nothing happened.

The djinn cried out, stuck on the blade, unable to pull himself free. I cursed as well, struggling to pull the blade loose. It held fast to the creature, as though it wanted to steal its Divine energy but couldn't find any.

"Damn," I said.

Adam was struggling with his opponent, barely able to keep the pace with his one good arm. The reinforcements were almost through my shield, the power of it falling to their magic.

I didn't have much time to react. I had to get the blade out so I could keep fighting. I had to get rid of this djinn so he wouldn't be able to keep fighting.

I had an idea.

Extinction

I pulled a piece of my power from the quickly crumbling barrier, pushing it gently into Uriel's blade. I felt a bit of resistance at the maneuver, as though I was trying to shove the energy through mud. It flowed through the blade, changing the blue glow to a strange green as I calmly willed the djinn's energy to relax, to release itself back into the universe where it was first formed. If I couldn't take the creature's power, maybe I could at least disperse it.

The djinn seemed confused at first, unsure of what I was doing. He tried to materialize his sword arm, to bring his blade around and into me. I flinched as it passed through my face, unable to gain purchase in the mortal realm.

Then he began to scream.

I almost screamed with him. The power started to flow back into me, the djinn's energy escaping in every direction at once, blowing out from his spirit wherever it could. A portion of that power returned to me, not much, but something, as the djinn's form became complete.

I pulled the blade from his chest, ready to move on to the rest. Then I froze in surprise. The djinn was still alive and unharmed, standing in front of me whole and healthy. He lowered his hand to the point of entry, feeling for a wound. I watched as his fully white eyes changed, the pupils becoming a very human brown.

"What have you done?" he said to me, moving his mouth in confusion after the words came out, uncertain of the feel.

I stared back at him, the rest of the escape forgotten. What had I done, indeed? At first, I wasn't sure. I couldn't quite put a finger on it. The djinn was different; I could tell that much. How?

"A little help here," Adam said, noticing me standing limply beside my attacker.

I watched as his blade came up, biting into the side of the djinn's neck. He cried out in shock and pain as the blood began to flow.

Normal, human blood.

"What have you done to me?" he said again, reaching up to touch the wound, his life force leaking through his fingers.

Human, I realized.

I had dispersed the energy that made him different and returned him to his original mortality.

My mind was ready to spin with the sudden implications of the discovery. If I could do the same to non-djinn, it would change everything.

There was no time to give it any more thought. My defenses fell beneath the magic assailing it, and the additional enemy forces moved in to join the fray.

44

They approached us with swords drawn, ready to join the fight. Then the djinn who had been tangling with Adam noticed his companion slumped against the wall and bleeding to death. The entire complexion of the fight changed in an instant, the first djinn breaking off his attack and backing up toward the others.

"Sorcery," he said, the fear tangible. "Dark magic."

He spread his arms out, causing the rest of the group to come to a stop behind him.

"She didn't tell us we would be killed," he said out loud, to no one in particular.

"No," the others said together. Then one of them moved next to the first.

"This is no longer fun, brother," he said.

Djinn were powerful, immortal, and also immature. They existed to partake in vice. Drinking, gambling, sex. It was one thing to kill for sport when you didn't think you could be killed back. It was another to watch one of your comrades die.

"What did she promise you?" I asked.

"Angels," the djinn replied. "Beautiful young golden angels for our harem."

I laughed. "She lied to you twice then." I moved around Adam, approaching them with the blade. Now that my power was not coursing through it, the glow had returned to a soft blue.

"We have no wish to die," the lead djinn said. "Not now. Please, leave our home."

"Is she here?" I asked.

"No. She said we would destroy you and escape unharmed. That she had seen it happen."

I looked back at Adam. My point was proven. Sarah believed too strongly in her visions. She had never learned to take them for the potential that they represented.

He shrugged, a dark, sheepish smile spreading across his face. I looked back to the djinn. I had been preparing for the worst. I had fought my way through their kind before, but it hadn't been easy, and I wasn't thrilled with the idea of doing it again. I was glad I wouldn't have to.

"Show me the way out," I said. "I have what I came for."

The lead djinn bowed to me and waved his hand. They all turned back the way they had come and led Adam and me up a steep, narrow stairwell and into their house proper. It was as would be expected. An abundance of colored rugs, statues, artwork, gold, gems and other finery decorated every inch of the place, along with silk beds, pillows, and brightly colored, translucent cloth, all of it stolen or won or captured over thousands of years. I paused when we passed by the current harem, tempted to free the girls I knew would be inside, most of whom would be slaves to the creatures. My hand tightened on the sword, which I didn't trust the djinn enough to risk putting away or letting leave my grip. I said nothing and did nothing in the end. If I failed in the rest of my tasks, I would be leaving them to an even worse fate.

We finally reached the entrance to the home. The djinn had thinned out as we walked, leaving only the one who had attacked Adam by the time we got there.

"Bar your doors as best you can," I said to him as he put his hand to the side of the wall. It shimmered and faded, opening us up to the outside world. We were in the rainforest for sure. I could hear the calls of parrots, see the thick vegetation, and feel the humidity as it began to pour in. "When she finds out you let me go, she won't be happy."

"We can protect ourselves, sorcerer," the djinn replied.

I didn't respond to his attitude. I moved out into the open air, turning as I cleared the entrance. It had already vanished back into the trunk of a large tree.

"That was interesting," Adam said, standing beside me. "How did you do what you did to that djinn?"

"I can disperse energy," I said. "Release it back into the universe. When the sword got stuck on him, I figured that might get it free. The side effect was unexpected." I felt my heart begin to beat a little more rapidly. Unexpected, and potentially valuable. If I could do the same to Sarah, I could save her from herself without having to take her life.

Of course, I didn't know if it would work on true Divine. There was only one way to find out.

"So, now what?" he said. "You came to rescue me for a reason. I'd love to know what it is."

"I got you out of there, and away from Sarah. You owe me. If you want back in His good graces, you'll do your best to help me out, no tricks."

He scowled a little but nodded. "No tricks."

"For what it's worth, I'm sorry about your girlfriend."

"Don't ever talk about her, Landon," he snapped. "You have no idea."

I didn't press the issue. "I need you to tell me everything you know about the Fist of God."

"Why?"

"Gervais and a son of Lucifer have control of one of them. They want to use it against Sarah, and then to begin waging war against everything until they've satisfied their hunger for power."

"They're demons," Adam said. "They can never satisfy their hunger for power."

"Exactly. The son of Satan, Zifah, is able to control the Fist remotely without any obvious electronics. I need a way to either take control of the

Fist myself or to interrupt his signal."

"I'm not well-versed in things of such a technical nature."

"You helped design the Fist."

"Matthias did all of the engineering, but thanks to you Matthias is dead."

Ouch. "You didn't keep records anywhere? Schematics? Anything?"

Adam considered. "In the beginning, Matthias didn't know what he was working on. The entire project was skunkworks, top secret and classified. Yeah, I'm sure he had a backup, but it could be that Gervais already got his hands on it. That may be how they figured out the means to control it."

It was possible. Likely, even. The demon could kill anyone, and become anyone in the process, with all of their thoughts, memories, and knowledge. It would be easy for him to get in somewhere and get the intel he needed. The bigger question was if he would be able to destroy it?

"Where would the most likely location for a backup be?"

"I know the communication tech was earmarked for use in American military combat drones," Adam said. "There were other engineers from DoD-funded companies working on that portion of the project. The U.S. has a number of data centers throughout the country." He paused. "But if you want to be able to access all of it, I would say hacking the Pentagon would be your safest bet."

The Pentagon. Right.

I guess it was a good thing I knew someone who not only used to be in the military but also knew his way around a network.

45

I was nervous, standing outside Obi's room in the hospital. I wasn't in love with the idea of dragging him back into this thing, especially this soon, but what choice did I have?

"Time's wasting," Adam said beside me.

I had bamfed from the Congo back to Mexico, grabbed the fallen angel some new clothes, and then transported us here, where I had stood and hesitated going in to ask for my friend's help once more.

Mainly because I knew he would give it.

I was about to open the door and make my way in when the door opened from the other side. Obi was in front of me a moment later, a look of surprise taking over his face.

"Landon?" he said. "What are you doing here, man?"

He wouldn't remember fighting the Fist, or taking the hit. He likely woke up in the hospital, already healed by the seraphim.

His eyes fell on Adam, narrowing immediately. "You son of a-"

"Obi, wait," I said, getting between them. "Don't."

"What the heck do you mean, don't? What is he doing here, man? After what he helped Sarah do."

"I helped Sarah kill demons," Adam said. "That's what angels do. We kill demons."

"Brian wasn't a demon, you asshole."

"He was close enough."

Obi lunged toward Adam. To the orderlies in the hall, it looked like a muscular black guy going after a one-armed man. In other words, it didn't look good.

"Obi," I said, pushing him back with my power. "Use your head."

He paused, scowling. "Why is he here?"

"The Fist. He's the only link we've got."

"Damn. I should have guessed."

"You should know, Sarah turned on him, too. He was being held by a group of djinn."

"She's got djinn helping her?"

"Not so much, anymore."

"I didn't know about the Mass," Adam said. "She used me."

"Why would I believe that?"

"I don't care if you believe me, but it's true."

"Whatever."

"Can we focus?" I said.

"Okay," Obi said, standing down somewhat. "Do I have you to thank for this stay? I can't remember anything since Mexico."

"You got hit by the Fist. He broke a bunch of your ribs. The seraphim took care of you."

He smiled. "I remember one of them coming to me when I was half out of it. She was a dream." He snapped out of it. "So you were watching over me while I healed? That's sweet, man."

"Not exactly," I admitted. "I was bailing Adam out. I learned a new trick in the meantime. I may be able to stop Sarah without killing her."

"That's great news."

"It's still a pretty big maybe. Right now, we need to try to get our hands on the documentation for the communication system Matthias built for the Fist. If we can figure out how Zifah's controlling it, maybe we can break his control."

"I thought he was using his power to boss it around?"

"He probably is, but it has to be receiving the commands somehow. Rebecca is a prisoner inside the thing, not a willing participant."

"And there is only one way for it to receive commands, regardless of how the source is generated," Adam said. "I know that much."

"What do you know about military datacenters?" I asked.

He raised an eyebrow and stared at me. "Say what?"

"Department of Defense security protocols, black hat hacking, you know, that sort of thing?"

"No way, man," he said, shaking his head. "Can't you get Alichino to hack the Pentagon for you?"

He had before, but there was a limit to what he could accomplish. "What level of clearance was the FOG program?" I asked Adam.

"Top Secret. We didn't want the tech falling into the wrong hands."

Obi laughed at that. "Nice work, then."

Adam glared.

"The point is that kind of clearance is going to require a little more finesse than Alichino can provide," I said. "Social engineering from someone who knows people."

He bit his lip, considering. "If I can get into an account with high enough clearance, I might be able to find a way through. But man, if I get caught, it's going to be that soldier's life that gets completely messed up. Someone who trusted me, or at least in the ideals of the system."

"That's easy enough to solve," I replied. "Don't get caught."

He looked like he wanted to hit me, and I didn't blame him. I was asking a lot. Just coming back to him after the Fist had nearly killed him was asking a lot.

"What do you say?" I asked.

He sighed, clearly resigned to his fate as my sidekick.

"Let's do it."

46

I brought us back to Mexico, leaving Obi with Alichino to work out the details of their planned electronic break-in. For as much power as I had gained from Raguel, Dante, Srizyl, and the djinn, all of the globe-hopping was starting to leave me feeling the drain. We didn't have any time to waste, and I wouldn't have considered trying to rest if it weren't for the fact that when it came to hacking government systems, I was a miserable failure.

Then again, my hacking days had been limited to pre-written scripts and fast-talking. Obi's skills were far more advanced and far less likely to be detected. I winced at the thought of the days I had spent in prison, all of those years ago when I was still a mortal. If I had only known what my afterlife would become back then.

I fell onto my bed, the one I had intended to share with Alyx. I stared up at the ceiling. It was mirrored so that Espanto could see every part of whatever happened in here from whatever position he was in. The idea of watching yourself was nauseating to me, and I reached out with my power, putting pressure on the glass until it cracked into a thousand pieces. Then I looked over each of the slivers, catching my reflection there. Some people theorized there was a new dimension for every decision every person made, an infinite number of timelines that stretched infinitely across time and space. It was a mind-boggling concept, and as I stared up at the hundreds of me, I wondered if I was looking into those other places, getting a glimpse of who I would be if I had done things differently at any one of a thousand points in my life.

The funny thing was, every one of them looked the same.

I closed my eyes. In theory, I didn't need to sleep. In truth, I had always found it helped restore me, if only because I didn't have to worry for a while. I drifted off in a hurry.

I woke to someone shaking my arm. I opened my eyes, looked over, and saw Alichino standing there.

"Hey boss, we're ready."

I slid off the bed and trailed behind Alichino, back to the control center where I found Obi and Adam standing over a workstation. Obi was wearing a headset.

"What's the play?" I asked.

"Okay, so Allie got me hooked up with a line onto the Pentagon intranet," Obi said, pointing at his monitor. "He's got a login, too, but the clearance isn't high enough to get to the goods. So, I'm planning on giving Ms. Cecilia Jackson a call. She's the secretary for Colonel James Lamont. I served under him in the middle east fifteen years ago, and the guys always told me I did a spot-on impression of him."

"You're going to try to get her to give up his credentials?" I asked.

"Yeah. I already tried his birthday and all that crap, but he's too smart for that."

"Why would she know them?"

"Because that's how Colonel Lamont is. He wouldn't trust writing something like that down. He would give it to a second source he felt he could trust."

"Even though it leaves them open to this sort of thing?"

"Anyone working under Lamont is going to be a tough nut to crack. That's where the impression comes in. Either she believes she's talking to the Colonel, or we get nowhere."

"And you're sure Lamont's not the guy Gervais used to get himself in?" I asked.

"Yes," Adam replied. "I already had Alichino check it out. You probably won't be surprised to hear that a General Weston was found murdered in his home a few months back?"

"The murder, no. A few months? That would predate Matthias' death."

"I know," Adam said. "It seems like Gervais had been watching me for a while. He knew quite a bit about the program."

"That asshole. He led me into thinking he didn't know what the Fist was."

"Playing both sides, waiting for his moment," Obi said. "Sounds just like him."

"And you're sure he isn't in the office today?"

"I called him already. I asked him if he were in New York because I was thinking about him and wanted to see if we could meet. He said he's in Los Angeles for a speaking engagement." Obi smiled. "He remembered me like he had seen me yesterday."

"Okay. It sounds like we're ready. Do what you're going to do. Let's see what we can get."

Obi nodded and then tapped a key on his workstation.

"We're spoofing Lamont's caller id," Alichino said. "That was my idea."

Obi put a finger to his lips. He looked completely relaxed, but I knew he was feeling the pressure internally. The last thing he would want would be for his former XO to take any heat over this.

"Hi Cecilia," Obi said, adding a couple of octaves to his voice and gaining a southern drawl. "How are you today?" He paused while she spoke. "Good to hear. How are the kids?" He paused again. "Great, great, great. Oh, Maggie? She's fine. Just fine. Thanks for asking. Hey, listen, Cecilia, I was just firing up my laptop so I could grab a copy of the slide deck I've been working on for this here gig, and I'll be damned if I can remember my password. Yeah, yeah, I know. Losing my head in my old age."

He laughed raucously. I tried to imagine what the Colonel was like in real life. Probably a real ass-kicker.

Extinction

"I know, I know, the channel's not secure. I'll tell you what, can you text it over to me? End-to-end encryption. No spies except maybe our own boys in the NSA." He laughed again. "You have the number right?" He paused. "Yeah, that's it. I appreciate it, Cecelia. Okay. I'll call you back if I have any trouble. Have a great day."

He pressed a button on the workstation and the phone hung up.

"Text you the password?" I asked.

Alichino smiled. "The pièce de résistance, Landon."

A bubble popped up on the workstation, with only the password in it.

"How?" I said.

"Espanto has some very cool toys," Obi said. "Including a back door into every major utility in the country. We hijacked his cell number for a few minutes."

"What if he were on the phone?" I asked.

Obi shrugged. "There's always some risk."

"Well, you've got the password. Now what?"

"Now we try to get the files. We've already routed our traffic through a VPN in LA that should be close enough to trick any auditors into thinking we really are Lamont's laptop. Unfortunately, we don't know his MAC address to fake that, too, or I'd feel even more comfortable."

He returned to the portal and typed in the password from the text. Then he was into the main Department of Defense index. There was a search field in the top-right corner, and he typed in 'Project Fog.'

Nothing came up.

"Hmm," Obi said, looking over. "Maybe Gervais was able to delete it? That doesn't make sense, though. This kind of thing should be read-only once it's submitted."

I thought about it. "Project Fog was the codename at Taylor Heavy Industry. But you said the Pentagon didn't have the entire project under their wing."

Adam nodded. "That's right. Only specific portions."

"What was the command module called?"

Adam shook his head. "I don't remember."

"You have to remember."

He considered, tapping his fingers on the side of the cubicle.

"The longer I sit here, the more suspicious it looks," Obi said.

"Oh, I know," Adam said. "Amplified Neural Gateway for External Logistics."

"Angel?" Obi said. "You couldn't remember that?"

"Falling from Heaven takes a lot out of you," Adam said in defense.

"That's your own damn fault," Obi replied.

Adam looked like he wanted to start with the former Marine again. A glare from me got him to step away.

"Here we are," Obi said, getting a single result on the hit. He clicked on it, opening up a document that was over a thousand pages in length. "I'm going to download it so we can get offline. I just hope the security team doesn't ask Lamont what he needed it for."

The PDF downloaded quickly. As soon as it was done, Obi signed out of the account, passed the document to Espanto's internal network, and shut off the workstation completely. Then he leaned back in his chair as though he had just finished a marathon.

"That was easy," I said.

He turned his head to glare at me with his shut-the-hell-up face.

"I'm printing it now," Alichino said. "Give me a few hours with it and I'll figure something out."

"Thanks, Allie," I said. "I'm going to head out for some reinforcements."

"Reinforcements?" Obi asked, leaning forward.

"Yup."

It was time to bring Alyx back into the game.

47

Once Alichino found a way to stop the signal to the Fist, or to otherwise disable the link between Zifah and the armor, we would need a means to bring them to us so we could actually use it. Since I had sent Alyx off with her sister to keep her bright red, Great Were aura from giving my position away, it made sense that I would take her back to do the opposite.

Sure, there was a risk that Sarah would latch onto the signal and go on the offensive, but she knew that thanks to Dante I could get away any time I wanted to. She also knew that eventually, one way or another, I wouldn't want to. The idea of it created a number of subsequent thoughts and questions that swirled around my head. Mainly, I wondered how her visions had reacted to my escape from the djinn? If she had truly believed I was supposed to end there, how would her farseeing abilities spin what had really happened?

I didn't have too much time to consider it. Within a few minutes of leaving Obi, I was standing on the front porch of Onyx's house on the French countryside. It was early morning. I could hear roosters crowing in the distance. I could smell waffles and eggs and bacon cooking inside the house, and for a moment I thought I had gone to the wrong place.

Alyx was at the door a moment later, her entire face lighting up when she saw me. She opened the door and rushed to me, taking me in her arms.

"You're back," she said.

I accepted her embrace, leaning down to kiss her. She returned the affection with a chastity that surprised me.

"We were just having breakfast. Do you want to come in?"

I nodded, a little dumbstruck. Alyx was wearing a long black dress with long sleeves that covered ninety percent of her body. It was a massive shift from her formerly provocative dress.

She headed back for the door.

"Alyx, wait," I said.

She paused and turned back to me.

"Yes?"

"I didn't come for breakfast. I need you to come back with me. It isn't over yet."

"What do you mean?"

"Gervais and Zifah are still out there with the Fist. Sarah is still out there. I have a plan to remove Gervais from the equation, but I can't do it without you."

She stared at me for a long moment. I could sense a change in her, one that confused me, and sent a wave of anxiety up my gut.

"No," she said.

"What?" I replied, not sure what else to say.

"I can't help you, Mast.... Landon. I don't want to fight anymore."

"You're a Great Were."

Her eyes narrowed. "So what? I am a demon, and so I have to fight? Is that what you're saying?"

Yes. Sort of.

"Uh, no," I replied. "Alyx, I really need you."

"I don't want to fight anymore. I won't fight anymore."

"Al-"

"Do you not understand no, Landon?" she snapped. "Or do I only have the right to decide as long as it's in line with what you want?"

I closed my mouth and didn't speak. It was like she was a completely different person.

"What happened to you?" I asked a moment later.

"You ask me that like not wanting to fight is a bad thing. Like all I should be is a monstrous killing machine."

That was what I needed right now. It was clear I wasn't going to get that.

"No. It's definitely not a bad thing. It's just, you've changed so much, so quickly. I'm trying to understand you because at this moment I feel like I don't know you at all."

She softened a little. "You were the one who started me on this path. You were the one who told me that I could change. That I could be different than what my background made me or said I was. When I took Onyx home, I saw how much pain she was in. How much the death of her mate was hurting her. They didn't go out looking for a fight. They were trying to help you. Now she is devastated. After I got her settled and resting, I came outside, and do you know what I did?"

"No."

"I prayed. For hours, I prayed. To understand what she was feeling. To understand what I was feeling, and who I am supposed to be." She smiled. "And He answered me. God answered me. I would never have believed it. He told me I was whatever I wanted to be, and that a creature of Satan could be a daughter of God if only they live His word in their heart. That is what I am trying to do. That is what I want to do. Nothing you can say will change my mind on that."

"The angels fight demons," I said. "It isn't wrong for you to fight evil. God is supporting me in this." I drew Uriel's sword from my back to show it to her. "The archangel Uriel gave me this sword in Heaven, to help make things right."

She stared at the blade, and I could tell she was thinking about it. I didn't care if she wanted to fight for Heaven. I just needed her to fight.

"No," she said at last, crushing that hope again. "I can't. The idea of it makes me feel sick. It makes me feel guilty and wrong. If you love me, you won't keep asking."

I stared at her blankly, a part of me feeling betrayed. She had promised to be my ally. To protect me. Now that I was asking her to make good, she was balking. For all the right reasons, sure, but right reasons wouldn't mean anything if Sarah destroyed all of the Divine.

I had another idea.

"Alyx, I understand. There is another way you can help me."

She seemed pleased with my acquiescence. "What is it?" she asked.

"The sword can draw the energy from any Divine and transfer it to me. Normally, it destroys the target in the process, but I've discovered that I can use my power to change the outcome, and instead of killing, change them back to mortal instead." I swallowed hard, knowing that I was about to ask a lot of her, and also knowing that I wasn't even sure if the trick would work on non-djinn. "If you don't plan on fighting anymore, I could really use your power."

She looked at me as if I had just slapped her in the face.

"What?" she said, giving me an opportunity to change my stance.

I froze. I wasn't expecting things to go this way. "You don't need it anymore," I said. "Not if you're going to spend the rest of your life as a pacifist."

She shook her head sadly as if she felt sorry for me. "I can't believe you would even ask me this."

"I'm only asking because I'm desperate," I said. "Please?"

"My power is part of who I am. It is the only reason I exist in the first place."

"Right now it is. But Alyx, your power makes you immortal. If you never die, you can never go to Heaven. If I make you human, fully human, you'll age. You'll die. And then you'll have a chance."

It was the one card I had to play that might sway her, and by her expression, I knew that I had played it well. She stood in front of me, her face flat, her eyes thoughtful.

Finally, she let me down again.

"No. This is who I am."

I felt my heart clench along with my teeth. My hand tightened on the hilt of Uriel's sword. She was close enough; I could stab her with it before she could defend herself, take her power and render her mortal. In the end, it would be the best thing for her. She could live a normal life as one of God's children, instead of the life of a demon.

I raised my arm slightly. She noticed the motion, and her eyes widened slightly. Still, she didn't move.

"I don't know if I'm going to succeed," I said, lowering the blade. I wouldn't take it from her against her will, like Espanto did.

"I'm sorry," she replied.

I believed her. She was trying to find herself, the same way I had always been. I couldn't fault her for that. If the world burned because of her decision, at least she would know it was because she had used her free will.

We would both know that.

"If I don't see you again, take care of yourself," I said, putting the sword back in its sheath.

"You, too, Landon," she replied.

I stepped forward and embraced her again. I held her for a few heartbeats. Then she leaned up and kissed my cheek. Her eyes were moist. So were mine.

There was no reason for me to stay. Not now.

So I didn't.

48

"Where's Alyx?" Obi asked as I made my way back into the control center.

I had been gone for a while, having made my way back to the beach where I had spent the better part of two years pining for Charis and Clara, and steeling myself for the next chapter of my journey, a chapter that I had a feeling was nearing its end. Alyx's rebuttal was the most unexpected thing I could have encountered, and it not only hurt me emotionally, but it also left me feeling less than positive about, well, about everything. I felt like a boxer who had gone ten rounds and was hanging from the ropes on the verge of being KO'ed.

"She found God," I said.

What else could I say? I had thought the Big Guy was on my side, but then He had stolen one of my best weapons right out from under me. Was I supposed to do this alone? I had heard the expression that God never gives people more than they can handle.

I was ready to call bullshit on that one.

"Found God?" Obi asked.

"She won't fight. That's the bottom line. We have to do this without her."

His face fell. "I'm sorry, man."

"That's the hand we've been dealt. We need to work around it. Is Alichino making progress?"

"Why don't you ask Alichino?" the demon said, appearing beside me. Adam was a few steps behind. "And yes, the demon has been making very good progress." He pointed back at the fallen angel, who was sporting a new arm.

I shivered at the sight of it, my memory of our first encounter still fresh. His new arm wasn't as advanced as the first had been; it was more of a metal frame with some exposed wires and circuits poking into the stump of his flesh. That didn't mean it was incapable.

"A remote device would have been better," I said.

"The design requires Divine energy to function," Adam said. "And a direct interface to the nervous system."

"No offense, but how do I know I can trust you?"

"I want to go back to Heaven, Landon," he said. "More than I want to kill you, which you should be thankful for. Making right what I did wrong is my best chance of doing so."

"Fair enough," I said. "Are we sure this thing will work?"

"Not at all," Alichino said. "There's no way to test it ahead of time."

"But it will give us control of the Fist?"

"Complete control? I doubt it. It will interfere with Zifah's signal, and compete with it. That kind of confusion should be enough for you to take demon by surprise and put him out of commission."

"How long will it keep it confused for?"

"There are a lot of factors at play. Too many to guess."

"Ballpark?"

"Five seconds."

"That's it?"

"It could be longer," Alichino said. "I wouldn't put my life on any more than that."

"Wonderful. Okay, well, we're down one Great Were. I'm open to ideas on how to attract Gervais' attention without bringing Sarah down on us at the same time."

"Already done," Obi said. "You didn't need your girlfriend to bring him in. He's making plenty of noise on his own."

He turned his monitor so I could see it. He had a few windows open to different news feeds, all of which were reporting incidents of non-minimal proportions occurring around the center of London, all of them vague on causes and ranging from terrorist attacks to general accidents. It was classic Divine intervention, in the worst sense of the term, the general chaos and destruction fitting the profile of the Fist. With so many other Divine in hiding, it was a clear signal to anyone who cared to hear it.

"How long has this been going on?" I asked.

"A couple of hours," Obi replied.

"Sarah's bound to see that, too."

"Maybe Gervais is hoping as much."

"He's not ready to fight her," I said.

"Even with the Fist?" Adam asked.

"He wanted the sword for a reason."

"To level up," Obi said. "But what if he's decided to be satisfied to try and talk her into joining him. At least in the short term."

"No. He must have decided that the Fist can take her. If it does, Gervais has another way of stealing her power." It was too disgusting to think about, but it was still possible.

"We can't stop her from getting involved," Obi said.

"Do we have any idea where she is right now?" I said.

"Negative," Alichino replied. "Not in London, or we would."

"She could get there any second," Adam said.

"We can get there faster." I turned to Obi. "I understand if you want to sit this one out."

He shook his head forcefully. "No. No way, man. You know there's not a chance I'm stepping out of this action. It takes more than a few broken ribs to keep me down." He smiled. "Besides, if I get beat up again you can send that angel to come and fix me. She was like a... well, like an angel." He laughed.

"I know better than to argue," I said. I turned to Adam. "We need to get the timing right on this. Stay up and out of sight, and keep a close eye on me. Don't trigger the system until I'm close. Five seconds isn't a long time, and I expect Zifah will put up a fight of his own."

"A reasonable expectation," Adam said. "I'll monitor the situation from the air, and be ready."

"Don't double-cross me, Adam," I said. "If you try, I swear you'll regret it."

"I wouldn't expect anything less from you."

"Good. Put your hands in."

I put my hand out. Obi slapped his down on top of mine, followed by Adam and Alichino.

"On three. Keep your hand in," I said.

"Wait," Alichino said. "Landon, I'm not a fighter."

"Then you're a distraction," I said. "We need all the bodies we have."

He used his free hand to wave to the command center crew. "What about them?"

I ignored him, grabbing his hand when he tried to pull it away.

"On three," I repeated. "One."

"Two," Adam said.

"Three," Obi said.

I blinked.

49

The news reports would say that the damage done to London was the result of a natural gas explosion or a similar horrible accident.

I knew as soon as we arrived that it was the work of demons. Not only Gervais and Zifah but also some other recruits they must have gathered from somewhere. Fiends with control over hellfire who had used it to turn the bottom of a skyscraper to slag.

We didn't get assaulted as soon as we arrived. Maybe if Alyx had been there. Instead, we moved as a group away from the first building, where mortal emergency crews were trying to clean up the mess, crossing a few streets in search of the demons.

"I'll see if I can spot them," Adam said before launching into the sky.

"Adam, wait," I tried to say. Too late. His dark wings lifted him like a bullet. I silently cursed him as he vanished. That wasn't the way to earn back my trust.

"I think I'm going to go look over there," Alichino said, pointing back the way we had come, where a crowd of mortal onlookers proved there were no Divine nearby.

"I don't think so," I said, grabbing him. "If anything comes after you, lead them toward me, and I'll finish them off."

Extinction

He looked terrified at the idea of being chased but nodded.

We covered a few more blocks. Obi pulled out his cell, checked the BBC, and then pointed us toward the river.

"Report of a malfunction with the Eye," he said.

We headed that way, getting in view of the Eye a minute later. At first, I didn't see anything wrong with the massive Ferris wheel.

Then I saw the Fist of God standing on top of it.

"That's a problem," Obi said.

A big problem. The people on the ride had nowhere to go, and so they couldn't escape the battle that was to come. A quick scan of the ground told me that they had all been abandoned to that fate.

"At least we found them," I said, reaching under my coat and bringing out Uriel's sword. I looked skyward in search of Adam, not finding him.

Had that son of a bitch abandoned us?

I didn't try to do anything subtle. That wasn't going to help here. Instead, I made a straight line toward the massive structure. I had seen the Eye get destroyed in movies before. I hoped not to make that a reality.

I heard the parting of air before I saw the vampires that jumped us, dropping down from the building to our right and falling into our midst. It was almost a joke for Gervais to start with the creatures. I was pretty solid against them before, and unstoppable against them now.

I danced among them, their scratching claws and biting teeth a blur as I used all of the moves I had gained from Josette's memories, letting my muscles take over as I fed my power to them. I swept in low, bringing the blade up and slicing one of the vamps nearly in half, sucking the power from it as I did. It barely registered a prick on the pain scale its overall Divine energy was so weak. I did a neat pirouette-style maneuver from that one, using the back of a second vamp for balance as I came about, stabbing another of the creatures and taking its power as well.

I broke free for a moment, my eyes landing on Obi. He was in the midst of a pair of the demons, a smile on his face. One came in at him, and he caught its arm in his glove, causing a satisfying hiss of steam and sulfur as he pulled it to him and punched it in the face, knocking it down and out. The second pounced, and Obi recovered, bringing his arm up, grabbing it by the neck, and throwing it easily aside.

"Landon," Alichino said, doing as I had asked, running from the vampire that chased him. He slipped between my legs, and the demon wound up impaled on my blade.

I felt a wash of heat, as a gout of hellfire caught me by surprise, searing my flesh on the left side. I grunted in pain, pushing myself back and away and taking the opportunity to heal. Hellfire had always been more challenging to recover from, but now I swept it aside easily as if it were no more than regular fire. I had always been afraid of having too much power, and it was easy for me to recognize why.

I felt invincible.

I came back down, throwing my power out at the fiend, grabbing him with it and pulling him toward me. He was still in the air when I cut through him with the blade, capturing his power as he fell to the ground behind me. That time there was more of a sting, but nothing I could manage.

"Bravo," I heard Gervais say, followed my sarcastic clapping. "Bravo, mon frere."

I scanned the field. The demons were all gone, save for the French fop. He was standing alone ahead of the Eye, looking very pleased with himself.

I glanced up at the sky again, looking for Adam. Judging by Gervais' reaction, I had a bad feeling the fallen angel was working with him. Was his line about getting back in God's good graces all a bunch of bullshit? It wouldn't surprise me.

"Why are you getting mortals involved?" I asked, pointing back at the Eye. I glanced at the scared faces of the passengers. They likely didn't see Divine. What did they see?

"Why not?" he asked. "I figured upping the stakes would keep you from running. You see, if you leave, they die."

It made sense in a typically demonic way.

"I'm not going anywhere," I said, noticing he still had a scar on his face where Srizyl had burned him.

"Good. I owe you for this, Landon. Among many other things."

Extinction

If he knew about Adam, he wasn't showing it. But then, why play his hand too early?

"I'm right here. Where's Zifah?"

"Doing what he does best, I'm afraid," Gervais said. "Hiding."

The Fist appeared beside me, its wrist blades extended. I brought Uriel's sword up in time to block the first series of strikes, stepping back as I maneuvered.

Game on.

50

It came at me in a blur, twin blades hacking and slashing toward me as I moved away, frantically angling my own blade to block the attack. I saw Obi move in behind it and make to punch it in the back, only to have Gervais change into his super-vampire mode and tackle him. They rolled on the ground together until Obi managed to throw him off, getting to his feet and squaring up against the demon.

"Alichino, see if you can find Zifah,' I shouted to the harlequin demon. He looked at me like I was crazy and then ran off toward the shadows.

Demons. Sigh.

I threw my power out at the Fist. Its scripture flared, reducing the power. It was still enough to drive it back, to buy me a little more breathing room. I teleported as it closed the gap again, moving a couple dozen feet behind it. It turned, raising its arm to fire its bolts.

They launched at me, the Fist vanishing the moment the rounds cleared it.

I dove to the side, rolling to my feet as the bolts hit the wall behind me. The Fist appeared right ahead of me, an armored hand slamming into my face and sending me airborne, ten feet back and onto the street.

It appeared right above me, swords ready to come down. I tried to look

Extinction

past it for Adam. If there was ever a time for him to do his thing, it was now.

I felt a hand grab my collar and pull me along the ground, bringing me clear of the blades as they dug into the cement where I had just been.

"Close call," Obi said, turning and slapping one of Gervais' claws aside. I threw myself to my feet, hitting the demon with my power as I did and sending him tumbling back.

The Fist vanished.

"Where the hell is Adam?" I said, getting more pissed at him with each passing second.

"He must have left, man. There's no other way to explain it. First chance he got to get away from you, he took it."

"No matter what happens here, I'm going to find that asshole, and I'm going to cut his damn throat."

"One thing at a time."

The Fist materialized behind Obi, its sword arm already moving forward to stab him in the back. My reaction was instant, tugging at my friend with my power while pushing against the Fist. I managed to create just enough distance to keep him from being skewered.

The Fist disappeared once more.

Gervais was close by, and he came at Obi again. I grabbed him with my power before he could, lifting him and throwing him like a ragdoll, sending him hurtling through the air. He went through the wall of the Eye's ticketing booth and landed with a crash.

The distraction worked, the Fist appearing beside me, wrapping massive arms around me and lifting me in a tight bear hug. I strained against it, pushing power to my muscles and fighting back, trying to break the hold. Its scripture flared, fighting against my power, meeting it with imbued Divine energy of its own. Obi moved in, hitting the Fist with his gloves. They were useless against it, and it ignored him.

I felt a rush of cold air as the Fist vanished, bringing me with it to wherever it was going.

I stopped struggling for a moment, my heart feeling as though it had stopped.

We were somewhere between realms. Somewhere that time seemed to slow. I felt the stillness of it. The loneliness of it. The silence.

The armor had turned translucent, like bright sigils on a pane of frosted glass. Through it, I could see a face.

Rebecca's face.

It was twisted in pain, the eyes sadder than anything I had ever seen.

The Fist continued to apply the pressure, to crush me in the place outside of time where it could destroy me before anyone could intervene. I pushed my power against it, harder and harder, to no avail. Gervais had done what he had intended to do all along. To catch me with the Fist. To trap me here where he knew I couldn't escape. To end me, and perhaps to leave my body here for eternity.

The eyes shifted, looking at me. They changed slightly then. She could see me here. I knew she could.

"Rebecca," I mouthed, my lungs too compressed to put any air behind it. Was there even any air here to begin with?

She didn't respond. She only continued to look. She was in pain. So much pain. It hurt me to see her like this. Even after all that she had done, it was hard to know she was hurting this bad.

I gathered my power, pushing back even harder than before. I felt some of the pressure against me ease for a moment, letting go as though I were finally shifting the balance of power. A few heartbeats later it was gone, and I heard and felt one of my ribs crack.

I cried out. In pain. In anger. In frustration. In hurt and loss. To have fought so hard and have it end like this? It hardly seemed fair.

Nothing was fair.

I pushed even harder, the strain of the power making my body feel as though it were on fire. Again, the pressure eased, and I managed to grab a single breath before it returned. It was enough to delay the inevitable, that was all.

Except, the Fist was moving, running through the landscape between time and space, crossing the mortal realm in an instant. It went right through a solid wall and into a small clothes boutique where Zifah was standing.

Alichino had a single sharp finger to the demon's throat.

Somehow, he had not only found Satan's son, but he had managed to sneak completely up on him and take him by surprise, causing the demon to summon his protector.

It paused in front of the scene, squeezing even harder. Zifah knew he could kill me and then save himself as long as he was ready. And he was ready. I could feel my body weakening, and my vision was beginning to fade. I was going to die here unless I did something about it.

I looked at Rebecca again.

"Help me," I mouthed, hoping she could understand but expecting nothing.

Her eyes narrowed, shifting enough that I thought for a moment that maybe she had heard, and maybe she would react.

"Yes," she mouthed back.

The Fist fell from the interim realm, back into mortal time. Zifah screeched a little in surprise at the momentary loss of control, recovering in an instant, the Fist hitting Alichino so hard he went through the boutique window steaming, crushed by the scriptured gauntlets.

It had to release me to do so, and I tumbled to the floor, desperately trying to recover from the episode. Uriel's blade fell beside me, out of my hand. The Fist stepped on it before I could pull it back, holding it in place.

Zifah jumped onto my chest, one of his poisoned needles in his grip.

"You almost had me, Landon," he said. "Almost."

Something large and dark hit the window and barreled through in a flash of hair and feathers, slamming into the small demon and knocking him from me. It smashed into the chest of the Fist a moment later, hitting it like a steel wall. I heard Adam's bones crunch beneath the impact, and he slumped to the floor at its feet, halfway between it and me.

"What the hell was that?" Zifah said, reappearing on the boutique's counter a moment later, and then putting his eyes on Adam. "You? What happened to your arm?"

Adam glanced up at the demon. His face was bloody and broken, his wings bent at odd angles behind him. He looked like he was in agony, but he smiled anyway.

"This," he said.

The Fist stood straight up and froze.

"What?" Zifah said, immediately recognizing his loss of control.

Five seconds. That was all the time I had.

I only needed two.

With one motion, one massive push and pull, I yanked the sword from beneath the Fist, lifted myself, and blasted toward Zifah. He tried to get his arms up. He tried to run away.

He failed at both.

I grabbed him by the neck, carrying him as momentum brought us into the rear wall of the boutique and through, out into the alley behind it.

"Landon, please, don't," Zifah said. "We can still be friends."

"I don't think so," I replied, stabbing Uriel's blade into his chest.

51

I fell back, screaming, as the power of a son of Satan began pouring into me. I could feel my body convulse, every limb superheating in an instant. I writhed on my feet, holding the blade inside the demon's gut, drawing in every last bit of power.

I stumbled as Zifah turned to dust, reaching out and grabbing the wall to brace myself.

I took a few heaving breaths and then made my way back into the boutique. The Fist was moving again, bending to lift Adam in its arms and turning toward me.

He didn't look good. His body was steaming, the scripture on the Fist causing him to burn. He stared at me, his eyes dim.

"I thought you left," I said.

"It wouldn't have done me any good to stop the Fist until you were close to Zifah," he replied. "I thought taking them by surprise would be best."

"Turns out it was. You didn't have to take me by surprise."

"I had to get back at you somehow."

He smiled. His body was burning away slowly. "Do you believe in second chances, Landon?" he asked, eyeing Uriel's sword.

I nodded. A long time ago, I had needed a second chance as much as anyone.

"Would you?"

"You might die."

"Whatever happens, it has to be better than the alternative."

"Okay."

He closed his eyes as I drove the tip of Uriel's sword into his chest. I pushed my power into it, feeling his Divine energy gathering, and replacing it with something else. I still didn't know if the transfer would work on a real Divine.

As the process was completed, his body healed. Even the metal arm that had been affixed to him fell off, as a replacement limb sprouted from the stump. Finally, his red eyes turned blue once more. He shifted himself, falling from the Fist's cradling posture and standing in front of me.

"Did it work?" I asked.

"Yeah, I think it did," he replied, looking at his new arm. "Amazing."

"You wanted another shot to get back to Heaven," I said.

"You had better stop Sarah then, so I get to take it."

My attention was diverted by cursing outside the storefront. I slipped past Adam and the Fist, leaving the shop and finding Obi holding Gervais by the neck.

"You beat him?" I said.

"Don't sound so surprised, man," he replied. "I'm feeling pretty damn motivated right now." He looked past me. "Since that hunk of metal isn't moving, I assume you got Zifah?"

I could feel the demon's power rippling through me with the rest. I was quickly approaching god-mode if I hadn't reached it already.

"Yup."

I approached Gervais.

"All that planning. All that scheming. You lost again."

He glared up at me without speaking.

"You have ten seconds of existence left, and you have nothing to say?"

"I'll be back, Landon. I always come back."

"Not this time."

Extinction

I shoved Uriel's sword into him, feeling the sharp bite as his power transferred to me. I had never felt more satisfied with anything as I did watching him turn to ash in front of me.

"It seems a little anti-climactic," Obi said. "After all the shit he put you through."

"I don't need drama," I replied.

"You ready to take on Sarah?"

"Almost. Not quite."

He was surprised. "You need more power than that?"

"No, I don't think so."

"Then what is it?"

I turned back to where the Fist was standing with no one to control it. I approached it, gathering my power as I did. The scripture would protect it, but not enough. Not now. I reached out, wrapping my power around it and pulling. It came apart at the seams, ripping open in a bright flash of light as the sigils tried to protect it and failed.

The power allowed me to see her then, her form barely visible against the backdrop of the mortal realm.

"Rebecca, don't go," I said.

She looked at me, frightened.

"You've done a lot of bad things, but you've done a lot of good things, too," I said.

"I only wanted God to love me," she replied.

"You can't force it. You have to earn it."

"I tried."

"Over years. Over the course of a lifetime."

"It's too late. I've done too many things wrong."

"It isn't too late," I said, holding up Uriel's sword. "I can give you another chance. Do you want it?"

Her eyes welled with tears. "Yes," she said.

I jabbed the blade into her. I felt it gain purchase on her otherwise invisible form, my increased power allowing it to cross the space between this realm and that one. I fed my energy through it, changing hers, removing it and replacing it with a new form to house her soul. She materialized back into the real world, as naked as the day she was born.

"Oh, man," Obi said. "You look like Bruce Valanch. Good thing we're in a clothing store." He grabbed the nearest thing from one of the racks and handed it over.

Rebecca took it, clutching it in front of her, her face flushed with embarrassment. The fact that she was embarrassed was a good sign.

"Thank you, Landon," she said. "I know I don't deserve this." Her eyes were wet, the tears rolling down her face.

"Make the most of it," I said. "You won't get any more chances."

"I know."

I turned to Obi. "Do you want me to leave you here with them, or drop you somewhere?"

"What do you mean?"

"I know where Sarah is," I said. "I know where every Divine on the planet is. I can feel them all. Sense them all."

"You're going to go to her?"

"No. She's going to come to me. But not here."

Obi looked at Adam and Rebecca. "I'll stay," he said. "These two will need a little help getting settled."

"Okay. In that case, wish me luck."

"Good luck, man," Obi said, stepping forward and man-hugging me.

I clapped him on the back, and then stepped away, looking over the three of them one last time.

Then I went somewhere else.

52

The where was a split-second decision. I needed a place where there wouldn't be too many people, and where a battle between two powerful entities wouldn't cause a lot of collateral damage. At the same time, Sarah was still part mortal. She couldn't withstand the extreme temperatures of a place like Death Valley or the North Pole.

Instead, I ended up standing in the middle of the Bonneville Salt Flats in Utah. It was as good a place as any, and a better place because it was wide, open, and flat. I would be able to see Sarah coming from miles away, long before she arrived.

Not that it mattered. With my increase in power, I could already see Sarah coming. I could feel the power of every Divine in the mortal realm, and she was easy to spot. Her signature was different from all of the others. Instead of running hot or cold, she was even and plain, a white light instead of a colored one. Could she sense my power in return? Would she have continued approaching if she could?

She had said I was the problem, that my existence was throwing the balance out of balance for as much as I attempted to steady it. So much of my experience over the last few months had proven it to be true. It was something I knew in my soul. Something I could feel. At the same time, I also knew now that my return to the fight had been necessary. I also had a niggling feeling that there was a higher power behind it. That God wasn't just on my side now, but that He had been on my side all along, even as the angels had sought to get rid of me with the Fist.

It was all conjecture, but standing out on the salted plains watching Sarah swoop in on wings of red and gold, I had the feeling He wanted me to fix what Gervais had broken.

He wanted me to stop Sarah, to return her to what she was always supposed to be, and in turn, make right all that had been wrong since Dante's decision first to send back Charis, and then me.

At least, that's what I was coming to believe.

"Brother," Sarah said, as she fell from the sky, landing smoothly a dozen feet away.

"Sarah," I replied. "Thanks for coming."

"You didn't leave me any choice."

"You had a choice. You could have come to London. You could have interfered there."

I didn't know why she hadn't. A vision, I assumed.

"Too many innocents," she replied. "Too many mortals in harm's way."

It wasn't the answer I was expecting, but I appreciated it. She wasn't a monster, not by mortal standards. She wasn't looking to kill regular men and women.

Only Divine.

"I don't want to fight you," I said.

"I don't want to fight you, either," she replied. "If you submit to me, if you allow me to do what I need to do, we don't have to."

"You know I can't do that. You'll destroy the mortal world. People need Heaven and Hell, even if they don't know it."

Her wings spread out wide behind her, the razor edges gleaming in the sunlight.

"Then let us-"

I hit her with my power. All of it with one blow. It pummelled into her, enough to knock her over, to send her sliding backward across the salt nearly a quarter of a mile. It wasn't meant to hurt her, not yet. It was meant to send a message.

She wasn't immune to my power anymore.

She returned to her feet, taking to the air and launching toward me like a bullet. I could feel the onrush of displacing air as she charged, and I gathered my power again, throwing it out like a net. I wrapped her up in it, turning and throwing her away from me. She shot aside again, tumbling end over end before regaining herself.

I drew Uriel's blade, holding it in front of me, waiting for her to strike again.

I didn't wait long. She swooped in, the speed of it breaking the sound barrier and causing a thunderous clap as she arrived. I pushed myself up and back, reaching the sky, closing the distance with her.

We were both airborne, locked in melee. Her wings served to both hold her aloft and make rapid strikes against me, while I held tight with my power, bringing it to bear to keep my skyward while parrying her attacks and looking for an opening.

Her left wing came in at my neck, and I slapped it aside while her right targeted my gut. I blocked that one too, caught by surprise as her fist came in, nearly hitting me in the nose. I faded from this realm to avoid it, becoming vapor just long enough to avoid the blow. She crinkled her eyebrows in surprise anger, flipping backward and coming to rest on the plains once more.

I followed behind, landing a few feet away.

"You put yourself at a severe disadvantage, letting me reach Gervais. I took Rebecca's power." I blinked from the mortal realm to that one for a moment. I didn't seem to be able to remain there to take advantage of the time difference, but it was still useful enough.

"Did I?" she asked.

I heard the rumble in the distance and realized my mistake.

I pushed out my power, circling it around me as a dozen missiles honed in on me, fired by the Nicht Creidem forces she had rallied. I had been so busy watching the Divine, I had neglected her allies in the fight, as well as the firepower they had to bear. Explosions rocked off my Divine shield, the force of it threatening my concentration. I found the beacon attached to my arm, planted there during the skyward duel and threw it to the ground. Then I teleported, crossing to the other side of the Flats in an instant.

I saw the helicopters in the distance, an entire squadron of them approaching with Nicht Creidem on board.

The missiles had been little more than a distraction, what could they do?

I turned as Sarah swooped down on me, taking advantage of that distraction, barely getting my blade up in time to knock aside an approaching wing. She stepped up her assault, coming in faster and more furious than I could believe. I used my power to leap backward, keeping time with her offensive as the choppers continued closing in.

There was no respite from her assault. No time to do anything but defend. I ducked and jerked, blocked and dodged, in awe of her Divine energy while at the same time fearing that for all I had collected, it still wasn't enough. She continued coming, relentless in her pursuit, even as I began teleporting across the field.

She was fast, so fast, her wings carrying her to my new location within seconds, forcing me back into defense without a break. Her demonic side made her a natural born killer, a predator, a huntress.

The Nicht Creidem drew nearer, the choppers circling us. I could see the pilots watching us fight, ready to move at a moment's notice. What were they doing here? They couldn't shoot at me again without risking Sarah.

At least, that was what I thought before the bullet hit me.

It came as a single crack from one of the choppers. I saw the muzzle flash, and a moment later something big and heavy hit me in the chest, blasting right through me and causing flesh and bone to explode away. I cried out, falling back, losing my balance at the sniper's ambush. I fell to the ground as Sarah landed on top of me, her wings sweeping forward for the kill.

No. I wasn't going to go like that. I pushed just hard enough to slide away from her wings, rolling through the air to my feet and facing her again, throwing out my power in a massive shield that put the Nicht

Creidem outside of the fight. I pushed more of the power to my wound, knitting my shell back together in an instant.

I raised my blade in front of me and looked at Sarah. Her eyes were red. Evil. Whatever she had seen, whatever logic she thought she was following, it had fallen by the wayside. Her desire to destroy had overcome all of it. It had turned her into the creature that Gervais had always wanted her to be. The one that he knew could cause the entire world to burn.

And that's what she would do if I fell to her. She would destroy the Divine, and in her fury she would destroy humankind as well. It didn't matter if I knew how to stop her without killing her. I knew by her face that I had to stop her any way I could.

"Do you even know who you are anymore?" I asked, feeling nothing but sorry for her. She hadn't chosen any of this.

"A monster," she replied. "We are both monsters."

She came at me again, a blur of wings and hands and feet, integrating her other appendages into the assault. I did the same, using every move Josette had ever known, circling her within the globe of protection I had created, doing everything I could to keep that shield up and prevent another unwelcome surprise.

We moved back and forth, around and around in our deadly dance, so quickly that the salt at our feet began to swirl around behind us, pressing up against my barrier and leaving us like a scene in a massive snowglobe. We twirled and lunged, pounced and retreated, in a ritual too fast for human eyes to follow, releasing so much Divine power it seemed to me that the world would break.

And then, finally, came that singular instance where everything came together, the point where the most balanced battle in the universe reached its final, almost predictable end.

I don't know how long we had been at it for. I know the sun was up when we started, and down when it was finished. I know the Nicht Creidem had long since landed their choppers before they ran out of fuel and crashed. I know that it happened when I stepped an inch too far to the right in blocking one of her attacks, leaving a micro-millisecond opening on my left side. Her wing slashed into my gut, piercing through and holding. I cried out in pain, and at the same time used the situation to drop the energy shield, sending a cascade of salt around us that distracted her just long enough. I drove Uriel's blade into her stomach, even as she caught my arm with her other wing, impaling me and holding me, joining us together in a distorted lover's dance.

I know the Nicht Creidem started shooting then, no longer concerned with who they hit once they saw the position we were in.

I know that I closed my eyes, and in one of my last throes of power carried us across the country, to the middle of Central Park, where a light snow was falling.

I know we stood there together, looking into one another's eyes as I began pulling her power away from her, and pushing what remained back. The blade began to glow green, and I howled in agony, biting, searing, endless agony, as I took away the stain that had covered her since the day she had been conceived, the Divine power of a union that was never meant to be, and never should have been.

I don't know how long that lasted either. For me, it felt like a millennia or more. It was infinite, endless, painful and at the same time exhilarating. It was as if all I had ever done was suddenly given purpose, and at the same time, my purpose was completely erased.

And then it was over.

Sarah's wings vanished, shrinking to nothing as her Divine power was removed. The redness of her eyes faded as well, leaving them a very plain, very human brown.

I fell to my knees in front of her, hardly able to contain the power I had absorbed. It was almost as much as I had held in the Box. Almost as much as the Beast had controlled. It left me feeling drunk and angry and joyful and sad.

I don't know if there was a better or worse feeling in existence.

53

I stared up at her, and she stared back at me. Like Rebecca, her eyes ran with tears. Were they were joyful or sad?

"You're going to destroy it," she said, her voice meek. "You're going to destroy the world. Why do so many have to die? Why do the Divine get to decide?"

"Because that is the way He wants it," I replied. "That is the way He designed it. Right, wrong, it doesn't matter. If we want to continue, if we want to go on, we have to play by those rules."

"It isn't fair."

"Maybe. Maybe not. I guess we'll see."

"I'm cold," she said, shivering in her light tank top, low cut in the back to leave the wings she no longer had room to move.

I took off my coat, passing it to her. "Here."

She smiled. "Thank you. What happens now?"

"I thought you were the one with the visions."

"In the dreams, I always defeated you."

"Then why didn't you now?"

She shrugged. "I guess you wanted it more than I did."

Or maybe on a subconscious level, she hadn't wanted to win.

I got to my feet. "I'm going to take you home."

"To France?"

"No, to my apartment. Things are different now, Sarah. You're different. Do you believe in second chances?"

She nodded. "And third. I have to, or I'll fall apart."

I knew what she meant. I put my hand on her shoulder and transported us there.

"I'm sorry I killed Dante," she said, still crying.

"I know," I replied.

I brought her over to my couch. I could still smell Alyx in the room, and the thought of her made me both happy and sad. She had found what she was looking for, at least.

"Here, sit."

She did, grabbing one of the pillows and holding it close to her.

"I killed Brian, too," she said, the tears really starting to come.

I kneeled down in front of her and wiped a strand of hair from her face. "It's okay. Just sit back and relax."

"How am I supposed to live with this?" she asked, sounding as weak and pitiful as I had ever seen anything.

"You aren't," I replied.

I put my hand to her forehead.

I always had the power to make people forget and it was stronger now. So much stronger.

"Go to sleep for a while," I said to her, once it was done.

She closed her eyes, and I shifted her with the power, laying her out on the couch and putting a blanket over her.

I left her there, returning to the park. I needed time to absorb everything. The power, the implications. I needed time to think.

I found a bench facing the lake, now lightly frozen over. I took a seat, staring out at it. I let my mind wander. I knew what I had to do. I knew that it was almost time.

Almost.

Something was missing.

I could feel it in my soul. An emptiness that I hadn't noticed before. A black hole that no amount of power could fill.

I leaned my head back, looking to the sky for answers. Not that I expected any to come from there.

Two hours passed. I didn't move. I didn't breathe. I just sat, letting the power settle, letting myself come to terms with all that I already knew. My journey had come to an end. My story was nearly written. It would be over soon. On one hand, I was ready. On the other, I didn't want it to happen.

No man was ever meant to hold the power I was holding. It was true when I had taken it from the Beast, and it was true now. Only this time, there was no keeping some. There was no going back. There was only me, the universe, and God.

I felt her presence even as she descended, coming down from the Heavens in a flash of light. I wasn't surprised they had sent someone to urge me along. I was surprised they had sent her.

"Landon," Josette said, appearing in front of the bench. She was still in her older form, beautiful in her simplicity.

"Josette," I replied.

"Can I sit?"

"Of course."

She came and sat beside me.

"I did it," I said.

"I know. Thank you."

"You don't have to thank me."

"Even so."

"I'm glad you came."

"So am I."

I turned to face her, looking into her eyes. There was a light there. A peacefulness. In an instant, I felt the black hole in my soul begin to resolve into something wonderful.

"How are things going in Heaven?"

"Settled, now. You proved He still cares."

"I did?"

"Yes. Does that surprise you?"

"Shouldn't it? He went through a lot of trouble to save humanity."

"Exactly."

I smiled. She smiled back. We sat together in silence for a little while, enjoying one another's company.

"I know I can't keep it," I said at last.

"What do you mean?"

"Isn't that why they sent you? To make sure I do what I have to do?"

"Not exactly."

"Why then?" I asked, confused.

"Landon, I. I prayed to Him. I asked Him to allow me to come."

"You did? Why?"

"Do you still have the sword?"

It was resting against the bench beside me. I looked at her. "You aren't suggesting?"

"I prayed to Him. I asked for time to spend with my daughter. With my family. He granted my request." She stared hard into my eyes. "Use the sword on me, Landon."

"Josette," I started to say in protest.

"The answer to my prayers, Landon. Please."

I nodded solemnly. We both stood, and I sank only the very tip of the blade into her. She smiled as I pulled the Divine energy out and replaced it, her smile only growing bigger as she became mortal once more.

"Thank you," she said.

I nodded. "You're welcome."

"Now, Landon, break the sword. Shatter it into dust and spread it to the stars. Let it carry the power you have claimed with it. Set it all free to the universe."

I didn't question. I simply did as she asked, using my power to pulverize the blade, and turn it into glowing, silvery dust. I held it with my power, gathering it close, swirling it around me and pushing the power out into it with finality. It turned around me, glowing brighter and brighter as more of the energy joined with it and it began floating toward the sky.

I don't know how long it took. An hour? Two? As the power fled I began to feel colder and colder, my energy fleeing with it.

I was shivering as the last of the dust began to drift into the air, vanishing into the night. I looked at Josette. She was shivering too.

"I didn't die," I said, surprised but not surprised.

"No," she replied.

"I'm mortal again, aren't I?"

"Yes."

"So are you."

"Yes."

I felt a lump in my throat. I pushed it down. There was no reason to be nervous.

"Josette," I said.

She smiled as if she already knew what I was going to say.

"Yes?"

"I know this is going to sound strange, considering everything that just happened but... will you marry me?"

"Yes."

I moved to her, taking her in a solid, loving embrace. We kissed once, a simple kiss.

"I love you," she said.

"I love you, too."

How many people ever got to spend the rest of their life with someone whose soul had literally been one with theirs?

"It's cold," she said.

"Yeah, I'm cold, too. Let's go home." She looked at me sideways, and I smiled. We weren't married yet, and she was still a former angel. "I have two apartments."

She smiled in return, blushing beautifully. "Then yes, let us go home."

We started walking through the park, holding hands. It was cold, but we would live.

"So, what happens now?" I asked.

"Life goes on," she replied. "As it always has."

"Not as it always has," I said, gripping her hand a little tighter. "Better than that."

Let Heaven and Hell have their war. The world would keep turning, and the balance would always turn with it. Maybe one day a long, long time in the future, humankind would need someone to fight for them again. But not now, and definitely not me.

I was going home.

THE END.

Extinction

54

M.R. Forbes

Author's Note

Balance was the first novel I wrote and self-published, and so I have a special place in my heart for the book and the series. Like with many things, it means ending Landon's adventures it is a bittersweet occasion. I am incredibly grateful for the experience I have had writing these books. Balance was the novel that launched my career.

Of course, a book can't be a success without the readers. I don't know what percentage of you have been following me and the series since Balance was my sole entry on Amazon, and who have stuck it out over the three years it's taken me to write the seven novels in this series. I can't thank you enough for taking this journey both with Landon and with me. You're the foundation on which a lifelong passion was expressed and a career was born and raised.

As are all of you who have reached this page, who are reading this note, and who are having your own reaction to the end of Landon's adventures. I couldn't have done it without you.

Thank you. Thank you. Thank you.

Cheers,

Michael

Extinction

More Books By M.R. Forbes:

http://www.amazon.com/author/mrforbes

Man of War (Rebellion)

http://amzn.to/1KWlyrW

In the year 2280, an alien fleet attacked the Earth.
Their weapons were unstoppable, their defenses unbreakable.
Our technology was inferior, our militaries overwhelmed.
Only one starship escaped before civilization fell.

Earth was lost.
It was never forgotten.

Fifty-two years have passed.
A message from home has been received.
The time to fight for what is ours has come.

Welcome to the rebellion.

Starship Eternal (War Eternal, Book One)

http://amzn.to/1xSYZeY

A lost starship...

A dire warning from futures past...
A desperate search for salvation...

Captain Mitchell "Ares" Williams is a Space Marine and the hero of the Battle for Liberty, whose Shot Heard 'Round the Universe saved the planet from a nearly unstoppable war machine. He's handsome, charismatic, and the perfect poster boy to help the military drive enlistment. Pulled from the war and thrown into the spotlight, he's as efficient at charming the media and bedding beautiful celebrities as he was at shooting down enemy starfighters.

After an assassination attempt leaves Mitchell critically wounded, he begins to suffer from strange hallucinations that carry a chilling and oddly familiar warning:

They are coming. Find the Goliath or humankind will be destroyed.

Convinced that the visions are a side-effect of his injuries, he tries to ignore them, only to learn that he may not be as crazy as he thinks. The enemy is real and closer than he imagined, and they'll do whatever it takes to prevent him from rediscovering the centuries lost starship.

Narrowly escaping capture, out of time and out of air, Mitchell lands at the mercy of the Riggers - a ragtag crew of former commandos who patrol the lawless outer reaches of the galaxy. Guided by a captain with a reputation for cold-blooded murder, they're dangerous, immoral, and possibly insane.

They may also be humanity's last hope for survival in a war that has raged beyond eternity.

Dead of Night (Ghosts & Magic, Book One)

http://amzn.to/1kfpqnS

For Conor Night, the world's only surviving necromancer, staying alive is an expensive proposition. So when the promise of a big payout for a small bit of thievery presents itself, Conor is all in. But nothing comes easy in the world of ghosts and magic, and it isn't long before Conor is caught up in the machinations of the most powerful wizards on Earth and left with only two ways out:

Finish the job, or be finished himself.

His Dark Empire (Tears of Blood, Book One)

http://amzn.to/1e0T0tz

They told Eryn that he was a cruel and unfair man, that he hunted the magically gifted, and that he named them Cursed for the tears of blood they shed. They told her she needed to keep her power secret, or he would be coming for her next.

No one could say why he took the ones who stayed, or why he killed the ones who ran. No one knew why he forced innocent people into hard labor, or why he kept such a massive standing army. Nor did they know who he was, where he had come from, or where to find him. The only thing they were sure of was that he had been there when they had been born, and he would be there when they died.

Eryn didn't know why she ran, but she swore she would survive.

She didn't know the dangers of his roads, or of the monsters that lurked in every shadow. And she would never, ever have guessed that she would find the greatest of allies in the form of a fugitive and murderer.

It could not have been foretold how his actions would change their lives, or how their lives would change the fate of the world.

For nothing was as it seemed in his dark empire.

About the Author

M.R. Forbes is the creator of a growing catalog of speculative fiction titles, including the epic fantasy Tears of Blood series, the contemporary fantasy Divine series, and the world of Ghosts & Magic. He lives in the pacific northwest with his wife, a cat who thinks she's a dog, and a dog who thinks she's a cat. He eats too many donuts, and he's always happy to hear from readers.

Mailing List: http://bit.ly/XRbZ5n

Website: http://www.mrforbes.com/site/writing

Goodreads: http://www.goodreads.com/author/show/6912725.M_R_Forbes

Facebook: http://www.facebook.com/mrforbes.author

Twitter: http://www.twitter.com/mrforbes

M.R. Forbes

<<<◇>>>

Printed in Great Britain
by Amazon